Tumbling in Bethnal Green

Tony Dickenson is an English teacher working in an international education. He attended Georgia State University in Atlanta, graduating with degrees in English Literature and Applied Linguistics.

His interests include the study of Latin languages and discovering new parts of London, the city in which he lives.

Tony Dickenson

Tumbling in Bethnal Green

Olympia Publishers
London

www.olympiapublishers.com
OLYMPIA PAPERBACK EDITION

A CIP catalogue record for this title is
available from the British Library.

ISBN: 978-1-84897-464-7

(Olympia Publishers is part of Ashwell Publishing Ltd)

This is a work of fiction.
Names, characters, places and incidents originate from the writer's
imagination. Any resemblance to actual persons, living or dead, is purely
coincidental.

First Published in 2015

Olympia Publishers
60 Cannon Street
London
EC4N 6NP

Printed in Great Britain

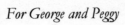
For George and Peggy

Acknowledgements

The Navigators

Dr B Bergeron

I Waters

Dr A Segura

and

To those who had to leave the party early

1

Home

When I was fifteen my bed played an instrumental part in my life. Dreading that first waking moment each school-day morning, I wanted nothing more than to stay curled up, warm and happy within its magnetic grip. But as the clock struck seven, the horrifying shrill of the alarm jerked me awake for the start of yet another tedious day in school, a dreary institution where forty minute lessons felt more like a couple of hours, and where, by legal obligation, I was forced to go five gruelling days a week. On these mornings, as my eyelids cracked open to reveal the grey light of the room, I always felt that blunt pang of disappointment that seemed to have lodged permanently inside me during my teenage years. Wrenching myself from my beautiful bed was, in fact, the most difficult challenge I faced most days, and I doubt I would have ever made it to school if it weren't for Mum making herself hoarse as she rattled off reasons from the bottom of the stairs for why I should already be up.

However, on the morning this account begins, I was awake well before the alarm rang, yet this odd variation from the norm did little to forewarn me of events about to unfold on a day I consider a turning point in my life, a day my life finally started, a day I now know changed me forever.

From about the age of ten I'd been hearing from a number of sources the difficulties that came with being a teenager, and so I expected the worst. At around thirteen puberty kicked in and I started becoming a man, sprouting hair on various parts of my body, and sure enough, just as I'd heard, the difficult years of adolescence descended upon me and I gradually felt my life sliding into a slow and cheerless grind.

But there was one particularly pleasing aspect at this stage of my life, and it required my being in bed. Some months prior to the day on which this account begins, I'd started to have the most wonderful dreams, and, probably like most fifteen-year old boys, I fell asleep each night hoping to dream of beautiful girls who required lots and lots of sex. In this regard I was incredibly lucky, as each night my dreams were full of exclusively beautiful girls providing me with lusty episodes of wild erotic wonderment, all in beautiful Technicolor, so real, so splendidly vivid. And that's how that day began, with me coiled within the covers staring blankly into the darkness of my room, thinking of the girls in the dream I'd just had.

However, before providing you with more detail here, I pause to inform you that over the months and years that I considered penning these accounts of that period of my teenage life, I decided that if I were indeed to do it, then I shouldn't hold back, that I must abandon all reservation and reveal to you exactly my innermost thoughts and feelings about the tumultuous impact that meeting that girl, that day, had on me. And so for some time, as I'm sure you can imagine, the decision to share such deeply personal details has racked me with a certain sense of ongoing anxiety. What I experienced that summer is certainly not typical of the average fifteen-year-old Londoner, but I have come to the conclusion that, to some degree, the preoccupations I had in dealing with love, with girls, are not unlike what every fifteen-year-old boy experiences who falls in love for the first time. But as you'll see, it was a period when, without doubt, I can only describe myself as a "horny little bugger," and so I suppose I should *warn* you at this point, that delivered here are my thoughts and feelings just as I remember them then, as a fifteen-year-old boy.

And so back to that morning and to waking up from another perfect dream where, as the central player, as usual, I was surrounded by a harem of pretty and willing co-stars. The girls had excelled in their duties that night, whipping me into a state of such frenzied erotic excitement that I woke to feel my heart thumping in my chest. If you're older than fourteen or fifteen and happen to be male, you know exactly how the plot unfolds, but for those outside of this demographic, and to cover all bases, it goes something like this. I'm in the middle of a meadow surrounded by five to six beautiful girls, all naked, all virgins, and they're seductively dancing in circles around me, each with one simple ambition: to have me. I'm well-armed for such duties, faithfully accompanied by my *constant companion* during adolescence, such a willing ambassador for the cause, my unrelenting erection. But, in that particular dream, when the girls had finished their naked swirling and had fixed me with *that* gaze, the one indicating it was time for me to fulfil my duties, even in a dream I was so overwhelmed by the prospect of successfully fulfilling such obligations, I was reduced to the most pathetic, nervous, bumbling wreck, clearly ill-equipped to satisfy demand with supply, and I suddenly awoke to hear the beating of my heart thumping loudly in my ears.

The alarming prospect of having to deal with the nitty-gritty of *real* sex in the not-too-distant future was a world I imagined fraught with impossible complications, so much so that I'd ruled out any possibility of connecting with a girl on any level, even an ugly one. When these dark but sensuous thoughts surfaced, I found a certain degree of solace knowing that I was more than happy for these night-time fantasies to continue sustaining a sexual appetite I saw little point in complicating by considering real sex with real girls.

And so, lying in my bed wide awake, the glowing faces of these sexy girls lingered in my mind, and as I reached down towards my erection I thought I heard a creak on the stairs and the girls immediately fled. Though I made every effort to resurrect them, my thoughts had already turned to the day ahead, to school, the bane of my life.

With the exception of visits to the bathroom, I'd spent the previous two days in my room left to my own devices, the result of a grand deception I'd orchestrated on the Wednesday of that week when, after a restless night, I woke up unable to face the drudgery of school that day. So, on Mum's first call, I slipped into the bathroom and applied a steaming hot flannel to my forehead, keeping it there until her second call. Then, with my skin hot and red, I dashed back to bed and called her to my room. Moments later she was at my side, inspecting me, listening to me whine as she held the back of her hand to my forehead. Then, just as I hoped, with a worried look appearing in her eyes, she diagnosed a possible fever, ruling out any chance of my leaving the house that day. The following day, Thursday, required another stellar performance, my distress that morning emanating from my throat, an awkward place to inspect, but a successful strategy that guaranteed me another day off. However, late in the afternoon I didn't hear her coming up the stairs to check on me, and catching me unawares laughing along to a comedy show on the radio, she stomped angrily in, then quickly out of my room, declaring, quite adamantly, that the following day, Friday, I would be returning to school.

I could hear her downstairs, busy in the kitchen making my breakfast just as she did every morning. I looked at the clock, five past seven, five more glorious uninterrupted minutes in bed before her first call. My thoughts drifted back to Wednesday when alone in my room, I whiled away the day engaged with unabated enthusiasm in activities that consumed most of my free time at fifteen: sleeping, looking through porn magazines I had hidden discreetly amongst my Beanos, masturbating and drawing.

I can't remember a time when I haven't enjoyed drawing. The moment I have pencil in hand I slip into an impenetrable world where time feels insignificant, a vacuum into which I can escape the tedium of my daily routine. This was certainly the case for me then when few things, except drawing, sincerely interested me. Once school reports began arriving with teachers praising my talent, after she had read the glowing report aloud, Mum would speculate as to where my ability had its origins, suspecting my talent had miraculously trickled genetically via her side of the family, skipping a generation when she was born, and almost certainly coming from her father, a man she claimed was artistic in a whole number of ways.

Drawing was a suspension from the drab reality that was my daily life, a solitary activity that suited me perfectly. On Saturdays I would often hop on the tube to the Embankment and walk along the river searching for interesting things to draw. In the early stages of sketching Hungerford Bridge on one such trip, an American tourist stopped to admire my work, complimenting me on how well I'd captured the metalwork on the underside of the bridge spanning the river. Before leaving, he quipped I should consider being an artist, and, as he walked away, I stopped drawing, and though only briefly, for the first time considered the possibility of becoming an artist as a genuine career option. But I knew such ambition was foolish, a fleeting moment of madness really, and quickly dismissed the idea as pure nonsense.

But these trips into London moved something in me, and not just because of the occasional flattering words of strangers, but because I had something to look forward to outside of school, a hobby that forced me to seek beauty in a city that, to many, was worn-out and crumbling, which of course it was. It also offered me a meaningful opportunity to develop my drawing skills while providing temporary refuge from the humdrum of my day to day life. But that was all about to change, and in the traumatic weeks that followed, my skills as an artist would prove both pragmatic and functional, providing me with a permanent reminder in later life of moments when I felt most alive.

Besides drawing however, for a year or so, I'd been honing my skills in another activity relatively new to me, and, like drawing, was solitary in nature and required a certain degree of dexterity with my fingers. When I first discovered that rubbing my dick was pleasurable, I felt like the luckiest boy alive. Rather innocently, I also believed it was a physical thrill unique to me, and not until the third year of senior school did I realise this hobby was commonplace among all boys. Though my early attempts at masturbation were over in seconds, in time, and with lots of practice, this wonderful distraction opened up an exciting new world for me, and each day I looked forward to that beautiful moment when I heard its mysterious call, immediately submitting to its devilish temptation, and rushing off to find a quiet place to knock one out.

However, I digress, so back to that morning, to ten past seven and to the depressingly familiar pounding of Mum scaling the stairs, thirteen determined thuds, each one its own dull reveille, until she stopped outside my door. Then, after a quick knock, she stomped into the room mumbling something under her breath, stopping at the foot of my bed where she sighed heavily and informed me that I *would* be up for school, that my father *would* be having words with me when he got in that evening, and that the school *would* be knocking at *her* door regarding *my* absences. Then, muttering warnings of a similar nature, she rushed around the room snatching up clothes strewn about the floor.

Despite her early-morning tantrums, Mum could never really pull off the angry parent, and that morning, probably because she knew I'd conned her into keeping me at home, she had reason to be impatient with me. As my eyes followed her around the room, ever alert to the possibility of her snatching it from me, my hand gripped tightly to the quilt – even though the virgins had long disappeared, pinned hidden strategically between my legs, my erection, ever vigilant, awaited their return. Her inspection complete, she stood in the doorway with her arms full of my clothes, her patience frayed. Shaking her head, one word, sternly delivered, ruled out any possibility of a third day off.

"Out!"

From experience I knew that when Mum was reduced to imperatives, resistance of any description – theatrical protestations, pleading, begging – all were futile, there was simply no battle to be fought. I swung my legs over the side of the bed, and through the window she'd opened I felt a current of cool air sweep into the room and rush across my thighs.

"Your uniform is down here. Get a move on. Do you want toast?" she shouted as she descended the stairs.

Crossing the landing on my way to the bathroom, I cleared my throat, and stretching out over the banister, grunted a yes back down the stairs.

In the bathroom I splashed my face with cold water, then leaning into the sink, scooped some water across my head and ran my fingers through my hair. As I straightened up, my head struck the sharp rim of the tap and I felt a sudden burning sensation across my scalp.

"Fuck!" I shouted, splashing cold water across what felt like a deep gash on the top of my head.

"Did you call, love?" Mum shouted moments later from the bottom of the stairs.

"I'll be down in a minute," I replied.

I looked into the mirror to see, set in a perfectly ordinary and sullen face, the same vacant eyes of youthful despair I saw every morning, opaque windows through which I saw little that pleased me. However, later that evening, after the events of that day, I'd be back in the bathroom looking in the mirror, into eyes that possessed an unfamiliar sprightly glint.

On Friday mornings Mum was always a little frantic, worrying that she'd be late for the cleaning job she had at an estate agents on the High Street. Running in and out of the kitchen reciting to herself chores to be done before she left, she paused to place on the table in front of me a steaming mug of tea and two slices of toast. I licked the two rich golden puddles of melted butter from the toast and waited for the words I heard each morning, adapted only slightly for days she didn't leave before me.

"I've left a note for your teacher on the stand in the hall, and a pound for your tube fare. I've made you some sandwiches and they're with the pound. Don't forget them like you did last week. And don't forget your key. I'm off to work. Don't be late for tea tonight. And get a move on," she said, gliding from the kitchen into the sitting room then down the hall and out the front door.

I sat at the table thinking of the depressing day ahead, my mood lightened temporarily by the poppy sounds of music coming from an old wooden radio on a small table next to Dad's chair. The dial was fixed permanently to Radio Two, the station which played songs that reminded Mum and Dad of their youth which, inadvertently, became the soundtrack for much of my youth. A song I liked came on, but its dulcet melody was suddenly interrupted when the front door clattered open and Mum reappeared in the living room.

"I forgot. Here's another pound for the passport photos. Don't forget them or your father'll kill you. You know how keen he is to get abroad. If I had my way, Clacton, Butlin's, would do just fine. But you know your father – once he's set on something. So, don't forget, you've got to get those passport pictures. Today!"

And then, for a moment, she stood staring at me, shaking her head, etched into her face and hard to decipher, a look of either bewilderment or disappointment.

"Come on, finish your breakfast and get moving, you'll be late," she said, still shaking her head. "Bethnal, I simply have no idea why you are so, so…" and, not quite able to find the right words, she sighed. "Come on, get a move on. And I think there's one of those passport machine things in the tube station. I'm late, and don't forget the photos," she said as she flew down the hall and out the door.

Though I'm sure it didn't appear that way to them, even at the complicated age of fifteen, I appreciated everything Mum and Dad did for me. Of course I never told them this, and with the notable exception of making me attend school, they rarely put pressure on me to do things I didn't want. I never purposely set out to upset them, but on the rare occasion they found me disagreeable, their most severe of punishments was a brief but frosty period of silence making the house a strange place where I felt like an interloper among them. There was seldom friction between them, and though they rarely displayed overt forms of emotion, they were always so gentle with each other. I secretly hoped the girl I eventually landed was someone with whom I could share that same sense of easiness that they had so successfully managed to find.

They made sure my childhood was idyllic, and as an only child I was well loved and I knew it, spending a good deal of time either in Mum's arms or on Dad's lap, bouncing around the house returning their hugs and kisses in abundance. But like most teenage boys dealing with the complexities of adolescence, this all changed in my mid-teens when all I wanted was to be left alone to deal privately with my many emerging insecurities. It was a period in my life when I felt completely inept, useless, worthless – qualities I genuinely believed would mark me for life, and which I suspect had something to do with the arrival of those wonderful dreams, dormant fantasies where I was worthy, super confident, super popular, constantly in demand, and so desirable. I felt I lacked everything a boy my age was expected to have and, quite possibly, if it wasn't for those lusty beauties visiting me at night, I might not have survived my teenage years.

It didn't help that I was the only remaining virgin in my year, a truly painful status I was made aware of most mornings before registration as I sat quietly in the corner at the back of the room listening in on other boys' graphic accounts of sexual conquests, explicit step-by-step recounts of how effortlessly they charmed their way into girls' knickers. Though they summarily dismissed their conquests as mere *sluts* and *scrubbers*, reputations that would remain with these girls for the rest of their schooldays, I was intrigued by even the most minor details of their exploits, and no matter how extraordinary or dubious their narratives became, I believed every lie they uttered because I knew, that, literally, only in my dreams could I pursue a girl as they claimed they did. And so, with these daily updates of my peers' successes, I knew exactly how far I lagged behind them in connecting with a girl, I was light years away from my first kiss, let alone my first penetrative encounter. Even with a slut.

But again I must pause to clarify, remind you perhaps, of my pledge to uphold an honest and faithful recount here, and so reluctantly preamble onto a topic I'm embarrassed to comment on. I refer once again to what was for me the thorny topic of 'girls' in order to mention Lucy and Wendy, girls who *were* regular features in my life. But of course these girls appeared only in my dreams, and their names, though amusing and ingenious at the time, now make me want to skip this commentary completely, but these names, based solely on their areas of expertise, excited the fifteen year-old me. Lucy Licker wore long leather boots, liked to talk dirty, and as her name suggests, liked to lick. She normally visited with Wendy who had a forearm like Popeye's which, in a nutshell, highlighted her skill set. I mention these girls as I have often thought that my dependency on them may have directly hindered my progress with real girls. In reality, this mattered little at the time as the only girls I came into *real* contact with were those sneering moody things at school who looked nothing like Lucy and Wendy, stunning sexy starlets no doubt inspired by the glossy pages of porn magazines stashed under the wardrobe. Lucy and Wendy looked good, didn't say much, but they knew exactly what to do, and with them as benchmarks for what I felt constituted sexy, girls at school were ordinary, unappealing, dull, a different species to the raunchy girls of my dreams.

Male friends were thin on the ground too. I never really had a best friend, perhaps Billy Brown in primary school, but he mysteriously left secondary school one day and never returned. In fact, I preferred being alone, perhaps why Mum often refers to my mid-teens as my *solitary years,* a period where she claims I spent a lot of time alone in my room reading. However, when I think back, I can't recall developing a passion for reading novels during this time, but what certainly remains crystal-clear in my mind are those beauties from within the pages of my porn magazines.

The stories I do remember from my childhood however, are those Dad read to me as I lay in his lap as an infant. He had a real skill for telling a story, introducing me to many a strange world, magically making stories come to life, captivating me with each tale. He rarely talked of his childhood, but from the scant details Mum revealed to me after his death, it sounded bleakly

Dickensian. Raised in a small northern mining town, he grew up in a poverty shared by the entire community, and during the few years he attended school, stories read to him there were his only happy memories of a miserable childhood. He managed to escape at fifteen by moving south to London looking for work, arriving in the capital with a couple of mates and "without a penny to my name," as he often told me.

A determined young man, he worked hard, and when Mum appeared, quickly followed by me, his life felt complete. He often told me stories of his epic journey south, using animated expansive gestures to deliver a slightly new version of the same narrative, fascinating accounts of Quixote-like adventures on his way to London. Cradled in his arms, I would look up at him wide-eyed, listening to the changing intonation in his voice, hanging on to his every word. On the occasional Sunday afternoon when he returned from a rare, but clearly fruitful afternoon trip to the pub, I often ran to him knowing he'd toss me into the air and I'd somehow land on his knee from where I'd hear more of those wonderful, magical adventures he'd had on his way to London. Mum, dishing up dinner in the kitchen, would be listening, correcting him in moments of forgetfulness. I always got so excited waiting for the part where he met her, at which point he leant back in his chair, lifted me into the air, and, making sure she could hear us in the kitchen, asked me "and then what happened?" to which we both responded at the top of our voices, that "everything got better."

Another story he often told us with such pride is how he met Mum on the platform of an East End tube station, a tale of love at first sight. He'd seen her a number of times but, as he put it, was waiting for "the right time to strike." And then one day, during an unusually long delay in normal service, the right time arrived. As the platform began to fill, he went and stood next to her, and, though desperately nervous, he made his move. To his surprise, Mum was immediately receptive to his advances, drawn to his "stony good looks" and his cheeky northern accent, and on their first date they arranged to meet at the tube station. The moment Dad saw Mum looking so beautiful, it was a "moment of magic" for him, an epiphany, and he simply knew that one day he'd marry her. Though not superstitious, he was certainly sentimental, and considered their meeting place, the tube station, as special, almost sacred, and he promised himself that memories of their first encounter would be with them both for the rest of their lives.

He proved everything he professed to be, an old-style romantic who didn't break his word, and shortly after a successful courtship, they married and moved out of the East End, to a leafy part of north London where I grew up and Mum still lives. Before long, they were making plans for my arrival, and when I did, and Dad saw me in Mum's arms for the first time, he held her hand, and with tears streaming from his eyes, thanked her over and over again for bringing me into the world in fine working order. Then he whispered to her the name he'd chosen for me, and, in the whirling emotional rush of the moment, she fell back into her pillow, and through delirious tears of her own, thought the name not only beautiful, but one which had a familiar ring.

Almost without exception, when I meet English people for the first time and they hear my full name, I see a chink of recognition in their eyes, often quickly followed by a flicker of disbelief. For those of you familiar with London, you'll have heard of the vibrant and popular neighbourhood of Bethnal Green about four miles east of central London, famous for being heavily bombed during the war. But in our house this name was a constant reminder of the time and place where Dad met Mum, a moment Dad made sure would be central to our lives, especially mine, always. I suppose there was an element of luck that his surname was Green, and so in keeping with his pledge to keep the place where he met Mum in our lives forever, he named me Bethnal, thus forever connecting us all with the place he met her, Bethnal Green tube station. Though long gone, I think of Dad often, and feel very proud of being his son; he was and is my role model, a simple man who had a beautiful heart.

And my parents were the perfect match, Mum keeping the house spotless and Dad keeping it in good working order, able to turn his hand to any job around the house that needed doing. One evening over a fish and chip dinner, shortly before the upheaval in my life that summer, he revealed plans for a summer project which involved the three of us. Swiftly allaying Mum's fears of more alterations to the house, he informed us that as far as he knew, no-one from any part of our extended family had ever been abroad, and so we, the Greens, would lead the way, the first of our clan to leave the tiny island of Britain and step onto foreign soil that summer, to a destination yet to be decided. Despite her initial reluctance to sample anything remotely foreign, the moment Mum heard passports were required, she flipped into a mild state of hysteria, swiftly claiming we were being "very posh," before rushing out to the hairdresser's to bring forward her appointment.

Our forthcoming expedition made for lively dinner-time conversation over the next few evenings. A range of possible exotic destinations was discussed; my spirited recommendation was Yugoslavia, a country which held a certain mystery for me, hearing of it for the first time in primary school many years earlier. We'd just returned from the summer break and the teacher asked the class where we'd been on holiday. Having spent a few days on the south coast that summer, as one does in those tender years of primary education, I avidly set about my innocent soliloquy on the beauty of Weymouth beach. Barely two sentences into my delivery however, I was cut short in favour of the girl next to me who, without interruption, elaborated on the delights of Yugoslavia from where she'd just returned the previous day, looking incredibly healthy, very tanned and very pretty. But neither Mum nor Dad knew or cared to know of Yugoslavia, quickly dismissing it and plumping for the new hotspot for Brits in Spain, Lloret de Mar.

Like many of the events that followed shortly thereafter, I could never have imagined that I would be taking my first trip abroad in only a matter of weeks, not only without them, but without them knowing. As far as I know, they knew little of what I got up to in the next month, and it all started with me *not* making it to school that day, the day my life changed forever.

2

School

"School. The best years of your life." Absolute utter tosh!

Rain-clouds hung heavily in a low sky as I turned the corner onto the High Street. As on every morning, gathered in small groups, kids from rival schools waited for buses, smoking and spitting on the pavement as they eyed each other up. These little pockets of horseplay were rough and tumble on short fuses, and when they clashed, the mini-riots that followed often brought traffic to a stop. Even pretty girls that time of the morning were quickly snubbed by rapid fire of crude and stinging insults if they strayed too close, and so people on their way to work gave them a wide berth.

I was greeted by the rowdy shouts of noisy schoolkids as I entered the tube station, and was soon skipping with them past commuters on the escalator to the northbound platform below. The southbound platform across the tracks was packed with businessmen waiting for tubes into central London, the only sounds rising from among them, the occasional stifled cough and scraping of shoes on the platform as they jostled for position. Many had their heads buried in newspapers as if hiding from one another, while others maintained a constant vigil, craning their necks as they squinted into the darkness of the tunnel for the lights of the oncoming tube.

I was always struck by their lifeless, jaded faces, especially those of the younger men who I occasionally caught staring blankly back across the tracks at us, haunting gazes I'd begun trying to avoid. Their weary grimaces made me anxious, and I worried that perhaps, in a year or so, with my own schooldays fast coming to an end, I'd be standing on that platform with them, wishing I was back at school.

But just the thought of me in a job was ridiculous, yet I knew having to find one would soon be a reality. I still felt very much a child, and despite the frequent, nostalgia-laden lectures I often heard from adults on the glory of their schooldays, I reasoned that whatever tedious tasks filled the days of those young men on the other platform, any mediocre occupation would be preferable to what I had to endure at school each day, a place, simply put, I detested.

There was a time however, when I didn't feel this way about school. In fact, memories of my first year of secondary school are mildly agreeable, especially the day I arrived to discover its endless corridors on five different floors, easily the biggest building I'd ever been in, making the primary school I'd recently abandoned appear Lilliputian.

As new arrivals, we were exceptionally keen to make an immediate impression, the lucky recipients of our unabated exuberance, our teachers, who shot us puzzled looks at our endless displays of enthusiasm for what they had on offer. Our eyes followed them around the room as if they were deities, our eager hands launching into the air to answer even the most simple of questions. All work they set we quickly finished, then with our little hearts pounding nervously, we scuffled one by one to form an orderly queue stretching from the teacher's desk, along the aisle, then down the middle of the classroom where we waited for the big red ticks about to land in our immaculately-kept exercise books.

However, over the course of that first academic year, the fire burning in our eager little bellies slowly faded, and by September of our second year, the sparkle we'd seen on that first day in our new school had long expired, and as a new set of arrivals skipped among us, we watched on, bemused by the gleeful optimism radiating from each and every one of them.

There was a brief flurry of excitement at the start of that second year though. On the first day back, rumour spread quickly that a new cohort of pretty girls had joined our year which sent us boys into a spin. But our delight was short-lived when, on closer inspection, we were mortified to discover that these pretty new things were, in fact, the same creatures who had already shared our classroom the previous year, the ones who had spent every lunch hour during the summer term sitting together on the grass in their frilly summer dresses making daisy chains. But they had returned transformed. No longer were they the harmless little things who had proved, for the most part, easy to avoid. They had undergone a bewildering metamorphosis, the innocent twinkle in their eyes replaced by icy stares, the catalyst for this change in them clearly visible as they passed by sneering at us, parading dazzling new attributes they'd acquired in the few short weeks during the summer break: breasts. Though each of us secretly marvelled at these magical transformations in them, we observed the girls with suspicion, speaking in hushed tones whenever they came near. And we learned very quickly that the changes in girls with whom we'd merrily shared seven years of primary school had terrible consequences for us boys, our very presence riling them, turning them into moody tormentors, resulting in a deep division, an enduring split so acrimonious, it lasted for the remainder of our schooldays.

From that point forward lessons began each day simmering with hostile tension hovering in the room, conflict normally kicking off without warning when a girl suddenly started screaming at a boy who had deliberately annoyed her with provocative or untoward gestures. This flash of rage was quickly followed by a rapid meltdown with boys and girls at each other's throats resulting in any form of meaningful learning swiftly dwindling as teachers, employing all and any technique to keep us from killing each other, became little more than agents of crowd control.

In the third year nothing improved. If anything, the conflict escalated to the point where the headmaster, the most feared man on the planet, spent a good deal of his day removing roughnecks from classrooms. So this broken institution is what I had to look forward to each day, and with no choice but to be present amid such mayhem, school was a cruel obligation, taking up most of my life and making it so very dull.

The irony was not lost on me that a place which, in theory, should have been liberating, was in fact one of entrapment. This was a truth I finally accepted a week or so after discovering a book in the library on conspiracy theories. I spent many a lunch hour poring over it, absorbing facts on how faceless monolithic powers colluded to keep us all downtrodden, which ultimately led me to question why we were forced to go daily to a place which we clearly all hated. After a week or two of studying the ins and outs of social control, I concluded that we were simply being prepared for long monotonous lives of no fundamental value, confirmed to me one day in a Religious Education lesson when, for the first time, I heard from a "reliable" source what life had in store for me.

Like most lessons, it got off to the most uninspiring start, a familiar, lengthy diatribe of biblical anecdotes about miracles and the like we'd heard so many times and that we all knew were nonsense. But we perked up when the tone of the teacher's voice suddenly changed, dipping deep into subject matter which he clearly considered of the most grave importance. As he spoke, we saw in his eyes a curious plea, urging us to listen to a message swerving slowly towards the apocalyptic, all hell, fire and brimstone, an inescapable destination for those of us who refused to suffer silently here on earth. As his bleakly depressing homily continued, he reassured us that this condition was fixed, that true happiness could only be found once we entered the kingdom of heaven. Though I didn't believe in heaven, I thought he might be on to something. His warped sermon on the inevitability of suffering described my existence perfectly, and, though deeply depressing, it provided a logical revelation for why my life was constantly dull. The faces of those weary looking souls I saw each morning across the tracks sprang to mind, and I thought, quite possibly, there were shades of truth in what he said. Perhaps somewhere, somehow, in this brief and bitter life of mine, I'd already had the best life could offer, and that the long stretch before me would continue on this current, dreary trajectory. And so from the tender age of thirteen I resigned myself to the infinite pointlessness that lay before me, knowing this condition, like the weather, was out of my hands, and would remain so for the rest of my days.

A group of noisy boys bundled onto the platform and formed a line along its edge. Impervious to the baleful looks they received from commuters on the platform across the tracks, they began wrenching up bullets of phlegm from within their chests before ejecting provocative arching flobs across the tracks, landing just short of the commuters' shiny brogues.

I made my way to the far end of the platform where I checked my timetable to discover the most uninspiring day ahead: double Physics, double French and then, after lunch, cross-country, an afternoon of squelching through the cold and sticky mud of suburban fields. I rarely exerted myself physically and saw no possible benefit to cross-country running, and though I also hated team sports like football, at least I could see in them a semblance of logic in trying to win. But cross-country was excruciatingly pointless, certainly not an activity for a boy like me. And almost without fail, our runs were always made worse each Friday afternoon by the arrival of the most hideous weather. Even in spring and summer, relentless rain and howling gales descended upon our little patch of north London just as we set out, making these runs the most physically enduring challenges of my life. Once we were off, I had little choice but to plough on knowing that each sticky footfall carried me one step nearer the sanctuary of the school gates, the finish line. In the changing rooms afterwards, our bodies caked from head to toe in splatters of cold wet mud, we would sit in silence waiting for our pulses to slow, each of us harbouring bitter thoughts of deep hatred for the PE teacher, many of which would be found purged shortly after in permanent marker across the walls of the cubicles in the boys' toilets.

The cheeky sounds of schoolboy laughter filled the air as more kids shuffled onto the platform. I thought back to the solitary pleasures I'd enjoyed over the last few days, and of how super it would be to contract a rare medical condition which would keep me absent from school until I was sixteen. I sat on a bench and searched my pockets for the sick note Mum had written, smiling as I read of the fictitious physician who'd attended to me.

Dear Mr Russell

Bethnal has been absent from school due to a severe stomach complaint which the doctor says should clear up on its own as long as he drinks lots of water. Could you please remind him to do this?

Sincerely,

Mrs M. Green

Mr Russell, my form tutor and one of the nicer teachers, would swiftly dispatch this note along with others containing similar tales to the bin as he did each morning without question.

Feeling a rush of cool air blowing slowly from the mouth of the tunnel, I tucked the note into my pocket and waited for the tube to pull in. To avoid the hoo-hah of thugs who normally congregated in central carriages, always a flashpoint for trouble, I made for the end carriage. In general, I avoided conflict at all costs, and after two blissful days of solitude, I was in no mood for the type of shenanigans that louts in the central carriage engaged in. Only when they failed to find someone there to terrify would they appear in the end carriage, where a familiar ritual would unfold. Jeered on by spineless lackeys, a dominant Neanderthal bent on conflict quickly emerged, scanning the carriage for a weak-willed passenger or a small kid. With his quarry cornered, he inflicted on him the most terrifying taunts until he was forced to flee the tube, and though I'd never been victim to such a tirade, I feared it was only a matter of time.

At Highgate Station the driver announced that due to an incident further on up the track, we would remain in the station for five minutes. A group of sixth formers from my school got on in the adjoining carriage and I watched as the girls clung to the boys, falling so easily into their laps. Boys who made it into sixth form intrigued me, they made being with a girl look so effortless, perhaps why they lacked the aggression of kids in lower years.

But sixth form was not an option for me as voluntarily devoting another two years of my life to an institution I hated was simply inconceivable. Besides, only a minority of students bright enough to cope with the intellectual rigour of A levels went on to sixth form, and I doubted I was capable of such an academic leap. In any case, like so many others in my year, I looked forward to that fast-approaching day in June when O level examinations officially ended and school turned into a carnival for the day with leavers dancing through the gates for the last time. Few knew, however, what lay in store for them. In an economy stifled by strikes, national unrest, and rising unemployment, along with four million other unfortunates, many would reflect on golden ambitions they dreamed of in school while standing in long queues at the Labour Exchange, their signature guaranteeing them a meagre weekly giro that dropped through their letter boxes two days later, the highlight of their week.

A muffled warning from the driver to mind the doors signalled our departure. The doors clunked closed only to immediately clunk back open. The driver's voice crackled back into the carriage, re-emphasising the need for passengers to refrain from blocking the doors. As we waited, sighs of impatient passengers frustrated at another delay filled the carriage. But then, suddenly, all heads turned to a disturbance by the doors in the centre of the carriage where a small group of people had already gathered. I thought it was boys messing around, but as confused shouts of genuine alarm reverberated through the carriage, passengers got to their feet and rushed to see what was happening. A nervous-looking woman opposite me sprang to her feet clearly seething at another delay.

"What the fuck is it now?" she yelled hysterically.

I followed her as she charged through the carriage, and hopping up onto a seat by the door I looked over the heads of other passengers to see a strange spectacle, a woman trapped between the doors, half of her body, including her head, outside the doors above the platform, the other half squirming inside, her arm flagging frantically. Inside, two young men worked heroically, desperately trying to free her, as did another crew on the platform outside. As they battled the doors, the young men released small grunts, constantly repositioning their feet to tighten their grip around the black rubber buffers that ran the length of the stubborn doors. Sweat glistened in the matted dark strands of their hair as the valiant young men struggled to tame doors that refused to loosen their grip on the woman. Clearly unaware of the drama unfolding in his tube, the driver issued a further warning for passengers to remain clear of the doors. More station staff arrived on the platform and offered the woman gentle reassurances that they were "nearly there." However, the woman continued to panic, her arm jerking up and down, wildly slicing the air, and then, just as someone suggested we call an ambulance, the doors hissed opened and she stumbled out onto the platform. Though clearly shaken, nodding embarrassed assurances that she wasn't hurt, she thanked everyone who had come to her aid, and as the group around her dispersed, one of the young men directed her to the other platform for tubes into central London. As I listened to her humble words of gratitude, it appeared the woman was a tourist, clearly lost, and American.

Passengers returned to their seats as if nothing had happened. Now alone on the platform, I continued to watch the woman trying to rub from her blouse the smudged streaks of dirt from the rubber buffers on the doors. Firmly rooted to the platform beside her was a large, heavy-looking case with red, white and blue luggage labels tied to the handle. A man hidden below a tabloid two seats to my left dismissively uttered a single word, "Yanks," and as the tube slowly pulled out, she looked in and our eyes briefly met.

The tube shot out of the tunnel into wretched rain, and I watched small drops of water, like tiny tadpoles, charging sideways across the windows. My thoughts turned to that afternoon, to the slog of slopping through thick and heavy mud on the cross-country run, and to the bastard PE teacher whose cruel and wicked whims had become impossible to escape. Each week, before retreating to the warmth of the staffroom to drink tea and smoke, he met us at the school gates where he pointed to distant hills which he expected us to circle, and then return to school before the bell rang. In previous years Mum had scribbled notes excusing me from PE without dispute, but in some strange sadistic U-turn, which I suspect was on advice from Dad, she had suddenly refused further issue of these much appreciated tokens of maternal love. And so, resigning myself to the inevitability of the lengthy grind of the day ahead, I sank further into my seat and watched the swathes of raindrops dribbling across the window.

At East Finchley Station a group of five or six boys from my school rushed into the carriage howling and laughing, just making it through the doors before they closed. The last one in, a chubby boy, fell against the doors on the far side of the carriage wheezing as he mopped streaming sweat from his rosy face with a handkerchief. The others slumped onto seats shouting at each other, their clipped and crude banter peppered predominantly with variations of the word *"fuck."* Two old ladies near to me repositioned their handbags, and other passengers, all too familiar with this type of behaviour on their morning commute, shifted anxiously in their seats.

Almost immediately the new arrivals began scanning the carriage for potential targets, and though I tried to avoid his stare, one of them saw me. He slowly rose to his feet and a shudder trembled through me, but luckily, after just two or three steps towards me, the driver informed us of yet further delay, politely asking passengers to refrain from blocking the doors and the boy joined his mates, jeering and clapping, jumping from seat to seat causing the carriage to rock.

The smallest among them, swinging like a trapeze artist on hand supports, released a loud fart which sent the other boys scampering up and down the carriage away from him. The chubby boy seated near the door, his face still shining under a layer of greasy sweat, clearly eager to provide his mates with laughs, stood up and squealed for their attention. With all eyes on him, he seemed lost for tricks, his small eyes darting from side to side as he thought of ways to impress, seemingly immune to the other boys' barrage of cruel jibes concerning his weight. Then, as the doors were closing, he bounced his fat frame between the rubber buffers, forcing the driver to make another, more emphatic announcement, bluntly declaring that the tube would remain in the station all day if passengers continued to block the doors. Twisting in their seats, the boys' faces glowed crimson as they whistled and laughed, pointing at the fat boy who stood smiling between the doors, thumping the air in victory, ecstatic that his performance proved so pleasing to the others.

Clearly a competitive edge within the gang, their behaviour plummeted to a new low when, from deep within his tiny chest, the smallest among them, the one who'd farted, coughed up a thick bronchial lump and gobbed it across the carriage onto an empty seat by the door. Two boys suddenly sprang up and rushed the fat boy, taking hold of him and forcing him down onto the fresh glistening wad. The others reeled as the chubby boy bounced back up to reveal a dull yellow wire stretching like warm chewing gum from his blazer onto the seat, sticking to his hands as he tried to brush it off. Disgusted by the increasing vulgarity of the boys' antics, the two old ladies got off the tube, and as the doors closed behind them, the driver issued a further curt warning about blocking the doors. The boys howled with delight once more, waving V signs in the air and shouting at the driver to fuck off. I'd had about as much as I could take. And so, when the doors opened again and the boys continued to roar as they leapt about the carriage, I got up and got off the tube.

Except for the ticket inspector smiling and nodding sympathetically at the two old ladies near the exit, the platform was deserted. I watched the tube disappear around a curve then looked back along the tracks hoping to see the dim lights of the next one chugging up the line towards me. For early summer the day was particularly cold, and though the heavy rain had stopped, a soft drizzle was falling, cloaking me in a misty film, a slow chill needling its way through my jacket into my chest and back.

For ten minutes or so, I kept my eyes fixed to the distant meeting point of the rails, willing the next tube to appear. Thinking it unusual to wait such a long time for a tube at that hour, I sought information from the ticket inspector who brusquely informed me he knew nothing. Almost certainly arriving late for school again, thoughts of yet another reprimand from Mr Russell flickered through my mind. My decision to leave the tube had clearly been a terrible mistake.

The drizzle suddenly turned into a heavy rain, and as the wind picked up, I heard muffled thuds of raindrops, like cap guns popping as they struck the corrugated tin roof covering the platform across the tracks. To get out of the rain, I crossed the old wooden bridge joining the two platforms intending to wait at the bottom of the stairs on the other side until my tube came, at which point I'd quickly nip back across the bridge and catch it. Well, that was the plan.

Only momentarily did I manage to remain on the bottom stair looking out over heads across a packed platform before I was wrenched from the handrail, swallowed by the crush, and dragged into a forest of dark overcoats. Seasoned commuters, all hustling for position, pushed and shoved me in every direction, quickly sucking me towards the centre of the platform until I was surrounded by a wall of pinstripe suits. I tried wriggling through the crush, towards the edge of the platform, hoping to follow it back to the stairs. For a small, skinny lad like me, the manoeuvre should have been a simple exercise; but whichever way I pushed, I was unable to get through, blocked on all sides.

The main obstruction was directly in front of me to my left, a short, solid man, not much taller than me, with fleshy pinkish-blue cheeks poking out above the collar of his overcoat. I whispered a polite apology and tried to slink past him, but his head disappeared into his coat. I tried again, this time apologising slightly louder as I attempted to pass. But like a leaden lump securely bolted as if part of the platform, he appeared not to hear me, which led me to think he might be deaf. So I tried again, raising my voice, only to see his chubby face rise up out of his coat, his small grey eyes fixing me with a cold stern stare, clearly indicating he had no intention of moving.

When an announcement informed me my tube would arrive on the other platform in one minute, a more aggressive approach was required. I took a deep breath and thrust myself forward, immediately feeling his frame harden, his elbows widen, stiffen then lock. My tube rumbled into the station, and with panic coursing through me, I propelled myself forward, forcing my shoulder angrily into his chest, but despite repeated attempts to pass him, he held his ground, until, quite unexpectedly, the problem resolved itself.

Having no belief in the possibility of supernatural workings, I consider myself a rational man, but when I think back to the strange sequence of mishaps colliding at every turn to thwart my journey to school that morning, there remains within me a dull flicker that a guiding force was at work that day. Even as I recollect these events for the purposes of this account, I have to constantly question my recall, not only of that day, but of the, beautiful, reckless weeks that followed. And now, so many years later, almost a lifetime in fact, in moments of quiet reflection, I think of my chubby companion who, for whatever reason, so steadfastly refused to let me pass that day, and I remain intensely grateful.

The tube for central London pulled slowly into the station and I felt that at last, my fortunes were improving. As it inched to a stop, bodies all around me began to twitch nervously. Once commuters had boarded and I was free of the awful crush, I could sprint back across the bridge and catch my tube still on the other platform.

However, the moment the doors opened I was struck with a sudden sense of terror realising I was trapped in the shifting tide of bodies. Like a formidable human undertow swiftly receding from the shore, I was dragged in one fluid movement towards the tube then tossed, rather unceremoniously, into the crowded carriage. Once I managed to find my feet, I could see into the tube across the tracks where a small group of boys from my school, almost within touching distance, sat in an empty carriage happily laughing. And then from a small speaker in the panel just above my head, the driver suggested we mind the doors.

3

Lost

Hanging on one of the walls in the Art room at school was a copy of Michelangelo's *The Last Judgement*, a graphic illustration showing thousands of doomed souls falling into hell, a daily reminder of what we had coming if we didn't behave here on earth. Wedged within the crush of bodies on the tube that morning, unable to move, and barely able to breathe, I felt like one of those poor souls in the picture.

In front of me, doused in a light perfume evocative of summer strawberries, a woman held tightly to a hand support dangling from the ceiling, her back pushing into my chest. Bouncing about her shoulders, glistening strands of bleached blond hair coated in lacquer tickled my nose. Behind me, trying to contain a cough, I felt a man's hot breath on my neck, his stomach bumping into my back each time he coughed, forcing my hips into the woman's curvy behind. Worried she might consider these unavoidable collisions inappropriate behaviour on my part, I pushed back slightly to create a respectable distance between us. Almost immediately, the man's breath quickened into a wheezing, and I felt what I guessed was his belt buckle in the small of my back, a somewhat uncomfortable predicament, but one I thought I might bear until the next stop. But then his wheezing gradually turned into what sounded like a shallow panting, I felt his weight growing heavier against me, he was much closer than need be, and I started to panic.

The tube suddenly slowed and jolted to a sudden stop sending my crotch, quite forcefully, into the woman's soft behind again. Her head fell back and wayward strands of hair glanced across my sweaty face, tickling my nose again. As I bobbed and nodded my head back and forth to free them, the man behind me took this as a sign of encouragement, and leaned in even closer. Feeling the heavy heat of his foul body so close, sweat breaking across my forehead trickled like tears down into my eyes. I felt sick. I had to get away from him, and then, fortunately, a beautiful stroke of luck arrived when a man in a tall grey overcoat to my right shuffled into the central part of the carriage freeing up a space into which I immediately slipped. I briefly considered turning to "have words" with my stalker, but within the crushed confines of the carriage, I opted not to disturb the revered silence diligently observed.

The driver announced Highgate as the next stop and as the tube slowed into the station, the desperate faces of those on the packed platform appeared. Edging towards the doors I suddenly felt a hand brush across the top of my thigh. I turned to see the same man I'd successfully eluded just moments before smiling at me, his hand slowly working its way around my inner thigh. I tried to move forward, just half a step or so, but I couldn't escape him. As his fingers pressed into my leg, the driver announced that due to a minor technical difficulty, the doors would remain closed for a minute or so. I looked behind me, towards the centre of the carriage, and mouthing silent apologies, shouldered my way back until I found space in front of a man with his head buried in the

Times. But then the doors suddenly opened and passengers came charging in, packing the central carriage, trapping me between two huge men, enormous obstacles blocking my way to the doors. As on the platform earlier, my pleas to pass fell on deaf ears. Then, as the driver asked passengers to mind the doors, the man reading the Times sprang up, apologising as he pushed past one of the huge men, just managing to escape the doors before they closed.

The tube screeched out of the station into the darkness of the tunnel and I collapsed into the empty seat. I thought of Mr Russell who had already given me several warnings about the number of times I'd been late, frequently interrupting first lessons, infractions he thought warranted a letter home. The evening I sat down with an embarrassed and disappointed Mum and Dad to discuss these matters, I gave them a solemn promise it wouldn't happen again.

I closed my eyes and tried to summon credible excuses I might successfully use that morning, picturing myself reporting to Mr Russell stammering out apologies for yet another late arrival. I even briefly considered delivering a truthful account, but as events of the morning flashed through my mind, they seemed so flimsy, absurd, ruses that would certainly appear wholly unconvincing to Mr Russell.

When I opened my eyes I was surprised to see the little man who'd blocked me from passing on the platform earlier sitting opposite. His eyes, studying me over the top of his newspaper, bore a happy glint, and when he lowered the paper slightly, I thought he did so deliberately to display the spiteful grin lodged deep within the contours of his face. Here, I thought, sitting opposite, was the reason for my troubles, but citing a random member of the public to excuse my inability to make it to school on time once more would ring hollow to Mr Russell.

He disappeared back behind his newspaper and I silently cursed him. Fumbling in my pocket for gum I found the note Mum had quickly scribbled that morning. Reading it I smiled again at her devious creation, the phantom doctor who'd *attended* to me during my *sickness*. The little man opposite me noisily turned a page of his newspaper and I looked up to see him still grinning, his eyes fixed menacingly on the note in my hand. I slipped it back into my pocket and slowly unwrapped a stick of chewing gum. Once he was back behind his newspaper I pulled out the note and read it again, and that's when the insane idea came to me. Though I tried hard to dismiss it, a devilish plan quickly took hold, worming its way through me, I was immediately consumed, I could think of nothing else and tried desperately to silence the irresistible opportunity slowly taking shape, clawing its way through me. I folded the note and stuffed it into my bag, trying to convince myself it was a venture simply too risky, one which could only result in abject failure. But dancing like a jackhammer inside me, the idea was flowering into a genuine plan, and the more I considered the content of the note, the tantalising prospect of taking this enormous risk gathered pace.

I fully understood the consequences of succumbing to such easy temptation, but I also understood how the note, potentially, offered me the opportunity of escaping the quicksand that had been dragging me down, and how it might just fix the mishaps of the day. And to boot, it would offer another delightful day free of school.

But, thinking of the promise I'd given Mum and Dad, I feared the risk of failure and continued to seek a rationale to crush such a ludicrous idea. I read the note over and over again, until I could almost recite it from memory, but I knew, deep down, I was only going through the motions of wrestling with a decision I'd already made.

The tube pulled into the next station, and when the doors opened I sat looking at the gaping hole in the carriage knowing that I still had the opportunity to change my mind, to see sense and simply head back to school.

I took one final look at the note. Written so hastily that morning, its beauty lay in what it lacked – notable omissions, specific details – exact days and dates of my absence which meant, in theory, I could use it to authenticate my absence on whichever day I gave it to Mr Russell. Even after the weekend, on Monday, for example. I checked once more for anything that might scupper this delusional yet such appealing temptation, but all I could see was the blindingly obvious: take another day off, write in Monday's date, and turn the note in then.

The doors remained open, I knew I should do the right thing to get my day back on track and return to school. I continued to struggle over what felt like such a momentous decision, but then, when the little man opposite stood up, shot me a smile, and got off the tube, quickly followed by my lewd assailant who I thought had already got off, I put the note away, sank back into my seat, and started to think of what diversions central London might offer me during the long day ahead.

At Leicester Square I vowed to avoid rush hour for the rest of my life. Squirming out from within the crush already pulling me towards the exit, I squeezed up against the station wall to watch commuters filing past. Their heads bobbed in unison amid the polite shush of awkward apologies quietly whispered for errors in a combination of dainty, well-executed footwork, slow and rapid sidesteps swiftly carrying them along the narrow strip of platform towards the escalators.

As they rolled past, I considered my options for the day. If it wasn't raining I'd go to St James' or Hyde Park, or perhaps walk along the Embankment towards the city and find a quiet spot by the river where I could draw, maybe opposite the Oxo Building or the giant disused power station a little further up.

If it was raining I'd go to the National Portrait Gallery, a place I'd been meaning to see again after a disastrous school trip there a year earlier, enthusiastically organised by our art teacher, Mr Ross, a young Scot, new to London who we all thought a little odd. He constantly declared his love for our city which, he claimed, had no rival on the planet in providing its citizens with such grand works of art. And to prove this, and possibly to inspire his young protégées to take his subject more seriously, he felt a visit to the National Gallery would open up brand new worlds for us. In this respect Mr Ross showed notable ambition, but in the mid-seventies school trips were rare, and on the morning we left, as he lined us up alongside the coach to take registration, many of the boys were clearly more animated than usual, pushing and shoving each other, making it feel more like a day off than an educational experience. And I suspect everyone, except Mr Ross, knew trouble was brewing.

He clearly had little knowledge of central London, especially during rush hour, opting to take us by coach to the gallery, which proved an innocent misjudgement on his part as we all knew that going by tube would have had us there in twenty-five minutes. After an hour stuck in bumper to bumper traffic in Camden, many of the boys, especially a very lively group in the rear of the coach, had grown restless and started to annoy the girls just in front of them who were busy holding tiny compact mirrors to their faces as they touched up their make-up. Mr Ross had already warned these boys about their conduct, advice they simply ignored, their behaviour sinking to a new low when one of the boys pissed into a plastic bag and threw it at the nervous looking new boy sitting alone, reading, in a seat opposite the girls. The bag connected directly with the side of the poor boy's head exploding and showering piss not only over him, but over the girls nearby who leapt from their seats and ran screaming down the aisle. The driver slammed on his brakes bringing the coach to an abrupt stop forcing us all to shoot forward out of our seats and into the aisle. Amid the girls' hysterical screams the driver ordered Mr Ross to the front of the coach to issue a final warning which resulted in him spending the rest of the journey sitting between the boys at the back.

We finally arrived at the gallery, and trudging up the steps to the entrance, I stopped to look out over a grey but vibrant Trafalgar Square. Nelson, the aerial custodian of the Square, perched atop his columned pedestal, black with dirt, majestically looked out over the city. At the foot of the column pigeons flapped among hordes of tourists, and beyond the Square, spiking the low cloud, the famous clock tower of Big Ben and the Houses of Parliament, iconic London landmarks many students were seeing for the first time that day.

Stepping through the two large beech doors into the grand lobby and walking slowly up the stairs towards the main galleries, my mood immediately lifted. I paused to admire the enormous paintings hanging across dust-laden walls on either side of the stairs. Overhead, a small dome, slightly concaved and painted with images of glorious Greek gods, gave the building an air of historic dignity. Continuing up the stairs I stopped again, drawn to a canvas, a portrait of a solitary girl, perhaps thirteen or fourteen, sat sewing on a wooden chair, the light from a fading fire giving her the most captivating eyes.

As I gazed at the painting, again that private desire to become an artist flickered within me. But I knew that for kids like me growing up in the late 1970s, unless you were a pop star like David Bowie or Marc Bolan, it was not well considered for boys to like art. Sacrifices made just a generation earlier, throughout Europe and many other parts of the world, by students demanding greater individual rights and a more liberal, free-thinking philosophy in a changing world, were slow to take shape in working-class Britain where old habits and prejudices clung on. And, as I stood on the stairs in pensive mood looking into the beautiful eyes of that young girl that day, I was reminded of this when a group of boys raced past me to the top of the stairs, and, dizzy with delight, jumped up and down hollering cries of victory. Then, after a brief hush, from somewhere deep within the huddle, one of the boys saw me looking at the painting.

"Oi, Green, ya poofta, what ya lookin' at that one for? There ain't no tits in that one," he squealed, provoking in his mates a wild hysteria which faded only when they stormed, laughing and yelling, through the heavy doors leading into the main gallery.

For these boys the National Gallery might as well have been Legoland, and as they ran screaming through the galleries, they pushed and shoved each other, making crude and embarrassing comments about women in various paintings. Mr Ross' feeble attempts to tame them came to nothing, and his choice of teacher to accompany us, the bastard PE teacher, did little to help matters as he lamely followed after them, grinning at their vulgar comments. Returning alone to the National Gallery excited me, especially the prospect of seeing once again the painting of that girl, and so with the day planned, I made my way up towards the exit.

A cold wind whistling into the station met me at the top of the escalators. In the grey dull light of the exit commuters gathered, reluctant to splash out into a torrential rain. Once in among them the restless shuffling began, and I was quickly nudged towards the exit where I felt the first cold drops of rain smack my forehead. I hoisted my bag above my head and leapt out into the street, the deluge quickly finding a small hole in my shoe, a shock of icy water immediately coiling around my toes. Frozen pulses of water struck my face, stinging my cheeks as I splashed through the fast-running torrents of water gushing wildly along the gutters. Though I tried desperately to keep my bag balanced above my head, it served little purpose, and such was the intensity of the rain I was already thoroughly soaked. Then, suddenly, I realised I was completely lost, so I stopped to check my bearings.

Water was dripping from every part of me, seeping through the fabric of my coat chilling my shoulders and upper back. Nothing looked remotely familiar. Then, all of a sudden, came booming cannons of thunder, furious blasts forcing me to run on, more quickly, ducking and dipping in no particular direction, splashing and slapping through puddles, each shocking clap driving me forward, making me run faster until I could go no further and had to stop. My trousers, like two wet blankets clung heavily to my thighs, and looking about me, I saw a group of people under a large canopy in the entrance to a theatre. I limped through the puddles to join them, but with so many squashed in under such a thin strip of canopy, I was unable to penetrate the interior, and as the tempest raged on, accompanied by the continuous cracking volleys of thunder thrashing about me, I dashed up a narrow street next to the theatre, turning into a smaller side street running off it where I found shelter in a small doorway at the back of the theatre.

Though it was probably only a matter of minutes before I could breathe normally, it felt like hours. Bent double and using the wall for support, I tried to catch my breath, each intake of air scorching my windpipe. Only by taking long, slow breaths did I finally regulate my breathing and manage to stand upright to look out into the driving rain running in gentle ripples across the surface of the road.

In the large glass pane of a deserted shop front opposite, I saw my blurred reflection standing in the dark doorway. Above the doorway, what I initially thought was a street sign was a weather-beaten support with the words STAGE DOOR chiselled into it. Up and down the street torn and faded posters hung limply on doors and windows of long-abandoned businesses, and I thought it bizarre that a street in central London could be so strangely quiet.

My immediate concern was to rid my body of a cold that had settled inside me like solid permafrost. I was in the most pathetic state, so cold, so lost, so dejected. It now seems inconceivable that such a day ranks easily as the best and most memorable of my life.

Although I was out of the rain, relentless frigid gusts, vicious arctic blasts raging into the doorway and swirling about me, bit into my bones, resulting in an uncontrollable shiver. No matter how much I stamped and jumped, I just couldn't stop the trembling. When my teeth began to chatter I realised I had few options but to head back to school and accept whatever punishment I had coming. In fact, the prospect of leaning against the sultry radiators at the back of the classroom as I served my hard-earned, well-deserved detention, suddenly seemed rather appealing.

I steeled myself for the onslaught of another drenching. But then, just as I stepped out from the doorway, a single shaft of sunlight cut through the clouds striking the front step of a shop further up the street. Written in large white letters and illuminated by a small light just above the door was the name of the establishment, SALVATORE'S CAFÉ. The thought of hot tea and a cooked breakfast flooded through me, and returning to school, for the moment at least, felt like a bad idea. And then, as I stepped out of the doorway, the rain suddenly stopped.

4

The Salvatores & Mercy

I opened the door to the café to feel a wonderful warm blast of heat rush over me. Such was my hurry to escape the cold, I misjudged the step as I entered, catching my toe and falling headfirst through the doorway landing on all fours. As I got to my feet, I braced myself for the sniggers and snickers worthy of such a dramatic entry, but the café was empty. Chairs were tucked neatly under freshly-wiped tables, smears stretching across table tops like big shiny smiles. I stood by the door waiting for the smiling patron to hurry out from wherever he was, warmly welcome me, and then usher me to the table at the front of the café next to the radiator. I closed the door softly behind me and lingered for a moment.

Coming from a small cupboard next to an open doorway that led into the kitchen, I could hear the faint sound of classical music, perhaps operatic, and just in front of it, at the far end of the counter, a boiler was spitting a small jet of steam. The café had the most unsettling feel, I felt like an intruder, but, already wrapped in a warm tingling blush, I stepped towards the counter to hear a hole in my shoe release a loud squelch, much like a fart. I adjusted my weight onto my heels and hobbled on, reaching the counter where I was suddenly engulfed within a cloud of glorious heat and the most remarkable smell of bacon frying.

But then I heard a noise, the deep throaty sound of a man humming. I leaned over the counter to see, hidden behind the boiler near a small doorway leading into the kitchen, the broad muscular back of a man at work, slicing, dicing and chopping vegetables as he hummed along to the music.

I gave the gentlest of coughs, hoping he would hear me. His attention, however, was fixed solely on his work and the song he was humming. On a hob behind him, thick meaty sausages slowly sizzled. I cleared my throat loudly, thinking he'd spin towards me with a smile. But again, perhaps because of his pitch-perfect humming and the heavy thudding of his chopping, he didn't hear me. I stood by the till, waiting for a pause in his preparations, ready to let rip a throaty cough that he would surely hear.

Glancing into a small, cracked mirror hanging on the till, I looked like a wretched little urchin from a Dickens' novel with strands of wet hair drooping over my eyes. I looked again at the shiny sausages spitting in the pan behind him, then at the muscles undulating in his giant back, his giant head on his giant neck bobbing from side to side. On the ceiling just above his head, like a halo amid his crown of curly black hair, a bare bulb illuminated a burgeoning shiny bald spot. Poking out above the rim of his cotton T-shirt, across broad globing shoulders, shiny matted tufts of curly black hair glistened in sweat on his neck. Beefy triceps danced at his sides as he chopped and swayed as he hummed. Such a hulking man could only possess a short and fiery temper.

When he suddenly stopped, I assumed he sensed my presence, and sweeping the hair from my eyes, I prepared to summon a smile. He placed his knife gently onto the chopping board and I remained perfectly still, watching him, waiting for him to turn. I thought perhaps he had stopped to listen to the music, now so soft I could barely hear it. But then, I was left in no doubt he was unaware of my presence when he casually dropped his chopping hand into the back of his greasy white trousers to attend to a sweaty distraction on the upper reaches of his hairy arse. Fearing he might catch me catching him in such an uncompromising position, I spun around to admire the worn and faded pictures of Mediterranean land and seascapes hanging on the walls. After a period of time I considered adequate to alleviate his complaint, I turned to see his arm, up to his elbow, still scratching away, and so continued my inspection of the café's artwork until I heard his chopping resume.

The sound and sight of those sausages made me desperately hungry, and, growing impatient, I breathed deeply through my nose, ready to issue another cough. But, about to expel the air from my lungs, he put his knife down again and stepped back from his preparation table, my eyes following his big hand, expecting to see him slip it back into his trousers. But his arms fell to his sides, swaying slightly, and as his hands twitched nervously, I thought this moment of suspended industry an ideal opportunity to win his attention. As I took a deep breath, his head fell back, the intensity in his humming increased and the muscles in his upper back started to quiver, his shoulders rising and falling as if he were out of breath. I thought he was having some kind of fit. Then, amazingly, he began to sing, softly at first, his voice quickly growing in intensity until he was in perfect unison with the Italian baritone, his rippling shoulders rolling as he sang, detailing what I assumed to be impassioned pleas of an ailing love. But suddenly, the music slowed, then softened, fading until almost inaudible, at which point he returned to his work.

I felt ashamed by my covert presence there, and looking back towards the door thought I might rectify this unforgivable intrusion by leaving and then coming back in, noisily, making sure he heard me. But just as I stepped back, the music suddenly quickened. His head started to rock and nod back and forth in time with the growing cadence of the orchestra, and he began to hum and sing at the same time, clearly enjoying the playful rhythm of the music. But then, the sound of the orchestra grew darker, his body suddenly began to shudder and he threw his bulky arms into the air, the hand holding the knife swooping wildly, slicing the air in front of him, an ever-increasing anger in his voice, a dark fury rising within him.

I had no choice but to escape. I looked towards the door again, but turned back when he suddenly pounced away from his table, his head swaying from side to side as he resumed singing, this time accompanying the soprano in her aria, his pitch, like that of a choirboy, impressively matching her note for note. And as his passion for the music soared, I imagined a new development unfolding in his song as he leapt skilfully between voices, one moment the raw passion of the baritone, the next, the gentle tenderness of the soprano. He continued like this, meeting the demands of both singers, until the trembling baritone slowed, his voice straining, each note a piercing lamentation of what had clearly become a lost cause, a lost love, until his head finally flopped forward onto his chest. The heroine in his song was gone, dead, he was alone. Then suddenly everything stopped.

In the silence that followed, as my eyes remained fixed firmly on his back, I felt like the central character in a farce. I thought briefly of the absurd events of the day – the rain, getting lost, the cold, but was startled from my thoughts, when he extended his thick arm into the cupboard, to increase the volume, and he started to sing again, an angry lament quickly growing into an angry roar, a tragic storm rising within him, forcing the muscles in his back to tighten with each shrill note. Then, as the music quickened, his entire body began to shake, his heaving shoulders swelling with each angry note, his chunky arms, with those two enormous hands, thumping the air, the sharp blade of the knife twinkling under the bare bulb as he furiously sliced at the air, and as the orchestra strained to maintain such speed and intensity, his fist suddenly came crashing down onto his chopping board sending peels hurtling all around him. For some time he remained perfectly still, and I watched him, quietly sobbing. Never had I felt as awkward as I did at that moment.

It was definitely time to leave. Once outside, I'd charge back in, perhaps kick a couple of chairs for good measure, stomp up to the counter and announce that I'd come for those sausages right behind him.

His sobbing sounded like a small, hungry pup, desperate to be fed, and as the pain lingered in his voice, with my eyes fixed firmly to the dark shade of crimson of his straining neck, I took a small step back. His trembling voice had dwindled to a whisper; I imagined him playing Romeo having just found his lifeless Juliet. But when the music suddenly resumed, he sprang back into life, pounding his knife into his chopping board then stretching his big arms upwards, shaking them at the stained polystyrene squares tiles of the ceiling, wailing his displeasure with the gods, pleading with them to bring her back.

I took another step back.

He took a deep breath and wiped his sweaty face with his sleeve. Soft, gentle strings resumed and his head dropped to his chest once more, resting there as his breathing quickened. I stopped. He'd not quite finished. Then, as he gasped in a giant lungful of air, his mighty head sprang back up to release the most prolonged and painful note, ending only when the palms of his heavy hands fell flat onto his preparation table with a final smack of defeat.

Almost halfway to the door, I didn't know what to do. From inside the cupboard, I heard the distant beat of a slow drum begin to quicken, gathering pace, suddenly transforming his sobbing cries of lament into the unmistakable roar of a mocking laughter, insane triumphant salutations of joy. This Romeo would have the last laugh, his final mortal moments mocking Death's fearful grip, and with his heavy head arching back, through eyes spilling their last mortal tears before joining his lover for eternity, he released what I hoped was his final note, an unrepentant farewell to a cruel, cruel world.

I must have been two steps, three at most, away from the door. In fact, I think I had my hand on the door handle. But like the star-crossed lovers of Salvatore's song, my fate that day was already sealed, the poignancy of Salvatore's exit into the hereafter brought to a sudden conclusion, as were my own exit plans, when I came skidding, literally, to a disastrous halt.

The moment the sole of my right foot connected with that half-cooked tomato camouflaged on the cheap, scud-marked linoleum, I knew I was in trouble. Chairs flew in all directions, one hurtling into the door, cracking a couple of panes, as I came crashing to the floor, landing in a pathetic bundle under the table nearest the door, from where, despite the booming thumps of my heart pumping violently in my chest, I could hear the sombre peals of bells hushing the opera to a close.

In the eerie grey light below the table I lay sprawled, waiting for dismemberment. I heard a tap run followed by the slip-slap of him washing his hands. Clean hands for the kill. The tap stopped and I felt the floorboards below the linoleum give as the slow deliberate steps came for me from behind the counter.

As he approached, I looked up and saw his thickset legs, solid like old oak, and I heard him breathing heavily. He was waiting for me to come out and confess. I tried to speak, to say sorry, but I was terrified, my throat parched, rendering me voiceless, my heart pumping furiously in my chest about to explode. Then a big hairy forearm reached in under the table searching for a part of me. I shuffled back towards the wall, curling into a foetal position and closing my eyes, but his hand found my ankle, locked around it, and he hoisted me out into the light.

Gulliver stood over me, pinning me to the floor with eyes like two dirty black pearls, his muscular grip still attached to my leg. Waves of desperate emotion shimmered through me and I started shaking. On the verge of tears, he pulled me to my feet and gently brushed the remaining tomato seeds from my trousers, and in soft melodious tones of an Italian accent, in broken but tender English, he asked me if I was hurt.

I looked up into warm eyes, that immediately assured me I had nothing to fear. As he finished dusting me down, I felt so deeply ashamed, and thought again of the bizarre and unrelenting rigours of that awful day – skipping school, the drenching, the frigid rain, the bitter cold – impossible events that had carried, then finally dumped me in a pathetic bundle before this kind man. It was simply too much to bear, and as I felt the tremors of fresh tears arriving, the door flew open and a woman rushed in shaking water from her umbrella.

With her eyes firmly fixed on my huge friend squatting on one knee beside me, she loosened the bow of a turquoise scarf, tucking stray strands of hair behind her ears as she approached. He stood up, placed his hand on her shoulder, and as he whispered details of my shameful performance, a sincere look of concern rose in her face.

She came and sat beside me and just like this giant man, who I assumed to be the café owner and her husband, Salvatore, she leaned towards me, and putting her tiny hand tenderly under my chin, she lifted it gently with her index finger and asked if I was hurt. I glanced into her eyes, and felt the blood rush into my face. With this beautiful woman so close, I felt awkward and asked for a glass of water. Her husband scuffled off behind the counter returning with a cool glass, then he pulled up a chair and the three of us sat together in silence. With their eyes on me, I kept mine to the floor as I took small sips. When a man entered and sat on the far side of the café, Mr Salvatore sprang to his feet and went into the kitchen. His wife tapped me on the knee and smiled before fetching a small pinafore from behind the counter, and tying it loosely around her waist, she went to take the man's order.

I got up and walked slowly to the door to see the rain driving down into the street once more. About to open the door, I felt a hand on my shoulder and turned to see Mr Salvatore pointing to the table in front of the window, the one next to the radiator on which he'd put a mug of steaming tea. Still smarting from the stinging smacks of shame, to avoid unnecessary eye contact with my generous hosts, I sat with my back to the counter and listened to the clatter of pots and pans in the kitchen, Mr Salvatore now humming along to Glen Campbell's *Rhinestone Cowboy*.

I sat for some time cradling the warm cup in my hands, staring blankly at the grey, steam-covered window stretching the entire front of the café. Though no longer cold, I felt exhausted from the physical and emotional trauma of the day. And I was so hungry, the hypnotic smell of crispy bacon and the familiar sounds of sausages popping behind the counter, too good to resist, had me bracing myself for a walk of shame to the counter to place an order.

Just as I got to my feet, Mrs Salvatore appeared with a fried breakfast and placed it on the table in front of me before resuming to her duties. Moments later she reappeared with a fresh cup of tea, and glancing at the condensation on the window, she cracked open the door allowing cool air to rush in. As I ate, I watched the condensation gradually disappear from the window until all that remained was a small grey patch no bigger than a tennis ball.

In the street outside, the occasional shaft of weak sunlight managed to pierce the overcast sky. At about midday I thought of paying up and heading to the National Gallery, but when the sky suddenly darkened and I looked across the street into the cold dark doorway in which I'd stood shaking earlier, there seemed little sense in rushing off.

Though the Salvatores remained busy in the kitchen, I sensed they were watching me. The man who had entered earlier had long gone, and I thought it strange there had been no further customers. The street outside had remained empty, the only person I saw all morning was a man with a small box in one hand and an invoice in the other. He had walked up and down the street passing directly in front of the café a number of times, even stopping at one point to look through the window. As the only business operating in the street, I assumed the package was for the Salvatores. However, the man didn't come in but instead, crossed the street, and, as he passed the doorway to the theatre, the doors suddenly flew open, and an old man dressed in a dark oversized suit stepped out. The two men chatted briefly before the old man signed for the delivery and disappeared back inside, closing the door firmly behind him.

It was at that point I noticed in a small alcove just above the doorway the small statuette. It was a figure of a small bird, its tiny head stretching skywards, its wings curled around itself as if trying to keep warm. Possessing a sense of unique dignity, I wondered how this solitary spark of beauty had ended up stuck in a dreary backstreet. Gazing at it intently, I imagined its creator, a boy paralysed in a terrible accident a hundred years ago, and confined to a lonely room above the café. His accident had brought sadness into his home, but one day, quite miraculously, he showed signs of movement in his hands. Overjoyed with what he considered the first of many steps to a complete recovery, and to develop strength in his hands, his father brought home a knife and a small block of wood and showed him basic techniques of wood carving. The boy soon regained full use of his arms, demonstrating innate carving skills, astonishing his father and sister who both truly believed he might now lead a relatively productive life.

Such was the excellent quality of the boy's work, his father saw an opportunity to develop not only his son's talent, but also the family income at the same time. Then one day, his father brought home four small marble blocks and a mallet, and the boy set to work quickly earning a reputation as a talented sculptor. But in his twenty-first year, his father died and again the walls of the boy's room closed in around him again, his world suddenly shrinking to the four walls of his room just above where I was sitting, where he remained day after day, sitting idly at the window, staring into the street below, a world inaccessible to him. In his room remained just one small unscarred marble block, which once finished would be his final piece, the little bird in the alcove above the doorway opposite.

The months after his father's death passed slowly, and though she tried, his sister was unable to provide the spark required to make him work. However, sitting at the window one night, the inspiration for his final piece arrived in the shape of a young woman he recognised lingering alone in the doorway of the theatre. She was the lead actress of the play being performed at the theatre, and each night, after the rapturous accolades had faded, he saw her in the doorway, anxiously searching the street, waiting for someone. But each night she would slip back into the darkness of the doorway beset with bitter disappointment, and in this doleful woman, waiting for a lover who never arrived, the boy found the inspiration necessary for his last work – the little bird in the alcove above the doorway.

Mrs Salvatore suddenly tapped me on the shoulder and placed a cup of tea on the table. Before returning to her work, she stood at the window looking to the far end of the street and I wondered what she was looking at. My thoughts drifted back to that lonely boy and his final piece of work, and, with the Salvatores happy for me to be camped at the front of the café, I decided to sketch the little bird in the alcove.

Immediately immersed in my work, I quickly produced a series of drawings of the bird, all with variations in shading and shape. When suddenly customers began to arrive, I thought it best I free up the table and began gathering up my sketches and putting them into my bag. But again, Mrs Salvatore arrived at my table, this time with a plate of pasta which, along with a clean serviette, she placed on the table. She then flicked through some of my drawings, smiling and nodding her appreciation before attending to other customers.

When the last customer from the lunchtime rush had left, I resumed work, making small changes to the sketches I'd drawn earlier. From time to time, Mrs Salvatore came to the table to look at my work, and as she had done earlier, lingered by the window, staring anxiously towards the end of the street, as if waiting for someone. I thought that perhaps she was looking for the little bird I was drawing and so I pointed it out in the alcove above the doorway, and she nodded her approval. She returned to admire my work a number of times that afternoon, always remaining a few minutes by the window, looking searchingly towards the end of the street.

A clap of thunder suddenly shook the window bringing with it a downpour lashing into the street, sending water rippling in waves across the surface, just as it had earlier that morning when I stood shivering in the doorway. Mrs Salvatore came to the window again, this time however, she didn't linger. Turning towards me, her face was glowing, patting me twice on the shoulder as she passed on her way back to the kitchen. I looked through the window, into the howling storm, to see what might have pleased her. Such was the intensity of the rain, I could see very little, making further studies of the little bird impossible, and so for fifteen minutes or so, until the rain eased, I continued with adjustments to those I'd already drawn.

When the rain finally stopped, I looked over to the little bird and saw something move in the doorway. Water droplets from condensation still clung to the window, running in dribbles down the glass blurring what I could see. I wiped the window with my sleeve, and sure enough, there was someone standing in the doorway, sheltering from the rain just as I had earlier. And it was someone I recognised.

At first I wasn't sure, but when I saw the black marks running down the centre of her dishevelled blouse, and the case with the brightly-coloured tags attached to the bag's handle, I realised it was the woman I saw trapped on the tube earlier that day. Perhaps the sight of her shivering in the doorway is why I rushed from the café only to find myself in front of her not quite sure why I was there or what I should say.

"I saw you from the café, over there, and I was just wondering if you needed some help?" I managed.

She sprang up, clearly startled, and as she studied me, it seemed an eternity before she spoke. I felt like running, but then she smiled and I liked her instantly.

"That is so very kind of you. Thank you. You know, yeah, I could use some help right now. I didn't think London was so big. I've spent more time looking for where I need to get to than I did crossing an ocean last night. And I'm so tired. Hey listen, that café over there, do they have coffee?"

"Yeah, I think so," I lied.

"OK. Coffee's on me," she said.

As we entered the café, the Salvatores were standing together at the counter, smiling, as if expecting us, making me feel awkward, as if I'd been caught sneaking a girl into my room.

As I led her to my table, Mr Salvatore whispered something to his wife who smiled then flicked him gently with her tea towel. Sketches I'd left scattered on the table were now neatly ordered and placed back in my sketchpad. I looked at Mrs Salvatore who acknowledged her handiwork with a mischievous little nod.

"Hi. My name's Mercy. Mercy Waters," she said as she slumped into her seat.

"I'm Bethnal. Bethnal Green," I replied, mimicking her delivery.

"Well, it's very nice to meet you Bethnal. You're the first friendly face I've seen since arriving. And I'm so tired. Where's the waitress?" she said, turning, looking for service.

Small pearl earrings bobbed on her lobes, and her hair, still wet from the rain, was a shock of black, strewn with streaks of deep red that matched the colour of her small but attractive lips. Set below steel-grey eyes tinted with specks of blue, proportioned perfectly on her delightful face, her nose reminded me of beautiful Roman statues I'd seen in the British Museum. She was stunning. And she was sitting at a table next to me.

Mrs Salvatore arrived flipping the pages of a small notepad and Mercy ordered two coffees and a glass of water.

"I'm so happy to be sitting at last. I thought I'd packed lightly but this thing seems to weigh a ton now," she said pointing to her case.

From a small black handbag she took a compact mirror, and staring into it adjusted an eye-lash, checked her hair, pushing wayward strands into place.

"God, I look like shit. I need a shower," she said, sighing as she put the case away.

She looked great to me.

I'd never seen an American up close before, my only previous encounter of one coming in my first year of infant school when a very blond, very sexy exchange teacher came for a day. And I do mean *sexy*, as even at that age I remember deep twinges of *something* that made me admire her. But at five, perhaps it was her tinny accent or her big beautiful smile, or maybe that standing next to the frumpy and matronly Mrs Anderson, our class teacher, who reminded me of my grandma, she looked so glamorous. I noticed the same quality in Mercy that had impressed me in the exchange teacher, a sense of confidence we English didn't have. Both exuded a a vivacity with warm and winning smiles, and within minutes of meeting Mercy, I felt like I was five again.

Mr Salvatore returned with our coffees, and as he put them on the table, he glanced at Mercy and winked at me, his grin widening into a broad smile. Mrs Salvatore, watching him from the counter, gave him a more determined flick with her tea towel as he passed her on his way to the kitchen.

"So what do you do, Bethnal?" Mercy asked, taking a sip of coffee.

"What do you mean?" I replied nervously.

"What do you do? Go to school? What do you do?"

Until that moment, I'd never really given any thought as to what I actually did with my life, I just got on with it.

"I go to school," I said sheepishly, immediately feeling this made little impression so I added hastily, "I draw too."

"What do you draw?" she responded, taking another sip of coffee.

"Anything really. I especially like to draw things that don't move. Things that other people might not be interested in drawing," I said, hoping this might satisfy, and perhaps, add a dash of intrigue.

"Like what?"

It felt like a test. What immediately sprang to mind, clichéd images of the obvious – chairs, bowls, flowers – all seemed too dull, but then, looking through the window, as if seeing it for the first time, I pointed to the little bird in the alcove.

"Look over there, above the doorway. Do you see that little statue? Well, things like that."

She arched her neck, scanning the doorway for the bird, and then, when she saw it, her eyes flickered gently, and, as if daydreaming, she stared at the little bird, momentarily captivated, before turning back to me.

"That is so beautiful," she said softly before quickly moving on to details of her epic adventure from Gatwick airport, elaborating on how she'd ended up in strange parts of London, and of a near-death experience on the tube earlier that day which I thought better I didn't mention I'd witnessed.

She was in London for the summer, staying in a flat owned by a friend of her father, and after fishing through her bag, she handed me a card with the address printed on it. I didn't recognise the postcode and so took the card to the counter, where Salvatore still had a cheeky smirk simmering in his face. In his hands he had an A to Z of London which he passed to his wife who pushed it across the counter to me. I nodded my thanks then leafed through the pages to discover the flat was near Lancaster Gate, and returning to the table, I told her I'd be happy to show her how to get there.

When we got up to leave, I realised I had yet to pay. At the counter, the Salvatores were holding hands, their smiles now replaced with blank expressions on sad faces. As I reached into my pocket to pay, Mrs Salvatore came out from behind the counter, shaking her head indicating that no payment was necessary. She put her hands on my shoulders, and looking at me, softly kissed the top of my head, and caressing the side of my cheek, she whispered warm words of Italian which, though I didn't understand, I knew what they meant. I hoped she saw in my face my deep appreciation for their kindness, and as her eyes began to fill, she joined her husband behind the counter. As we left, I glanced back to see them standing together behind the counter, hand in hand, watching us, and I stopped at the door to whisper thanks. Mrs Salvatore raised her hand, just slightly, and waved me goodbye.

During the short ride from Tottenham Court Road to Lancaster Gate, Mercy told me she lived in New York City with her parents, her brother, and May, her maid. She was in London to escape the heat of a New York summer which had been preceded by an unusually early spring producing record levels of pollen which had triggered in her severe allergic reactions. Her parents, on the advice of the family doctor who said that a stifling New York summer would only compound her allergic sensitivities, recommended she spend the summer in Europe. But her relationship with her parents had been strained for some time, and suspecting they were packing her off, initially she refused, thinking she could spend the first part of the summer with friends on Long Island until her parents left for their summer house in the Adirondacks, as they did each year, when she would return to the city and party. Only when her father informed her that due to work commitments they'd be staying in the city that year did she think about her European option, and decided to come to London, the nearest *happening* city.

Her flat was in a street near the station, just off the Bayswater Road. Standing with her on the pavement outside the soulless enormous block into which she was about to disappear forever, I dreaded the impending goodbye. Just an hour with her had completely erased the trauma the first part of the day had brought. As I handed over her case, I felt the dreadful gloom of my unremarkable life returning.

"Hey, sweetie? It's Saturday tomorrow, no school, right? So what time do we meet?" she said, handing me a card with a phone number printed on it, instructing me to call before I arrive.

Then, just as Mrs Salvatore had done, she put her hands on my shoulders, kissed my cheek and said, "Bethnal Green – thank you," and as my world slipped into a blinding blur, she suggested I come at noon. Then, hugging me, she added "and so cute."

"You're welcome," I stuttered, and watched her as she walked along the path leading to the main entrance to the flats.

She was met at the door by an old woman dressed entirely in grey. They talked for a while before Mercy turned, looked back and shouted for me to call her tomorrow. Impervious to the presence of the old woman who looked over at me disapprovingly, she then flashed me a wonderful smile and blew me a kiss before disappearing inside.

I sat for a while on the wall running alongside the flats in a daze, thinking of the events of the day. I had my first date with a girl, a woman, a beautiful American woman, the following day, and rushing through my mind was a question to which I had no plausible answer: how the fuck had this happened?

The events of the afternoon came to an abrupt halt when I stepped from the tube, back into the grey familiarity of my north London life, back to the reality that if the school had contacted Mum regarding yet another absence, I would be in serious trouble.

I remembered the passport photos she had asked me to get, and so in the photo booth in the station I chose the one-flash option and sat back, looking into the reflective glass waiting for the pop of the flash. As I listened to the clicking and whirring inside the machine, I wondered what Mercy might see in a boy like me. I thought of her standing in the cold doorway, then of her sitting next to me in the café, and then of her beautiful face, when suddenly the flash popped capturing an image for my passport which, for the next ten years, would remind me of meeting her. When the photos dropped, I stuffed them into my bag and headed home.

I walked slowly along the hall towards the living room, and peeking in, saw Mum busy fluffing out the cushions on the sofa.

"Oh love, you frightened me, I didn't hear you come in. Nice day at school?" she asked as she adjusted ornaments on the mantelpiece.

I gave her the photos which she held in the light at the window, studying the four pictures as if each were different. Then, after some moments, she took a deep breath, and sighed.

"Aren't you just glowing in these? You must have had a good day at school. You look positively…" but then she paused, and as I waited for her to finish, seemingly entranced by the four little windows, almost despairingly, she continued, more softly, "you look so much like your father, you certainly are becoming a fine young man, son."

5

Rejection

During dinner on Friday evenings I was normally subjected to thirty minutes or so of Mum enquiring into my weekend plans. I gave the same responses every week, moodily delivering one word grunts to indicate I'd be out with friends. That evening however, I had the impression she was more curious than usual, not quite satisfied with my standard responses. Her efforts to extract further details yielded little success, and I escaped to my bedroom where I set about sketching Mercy's beautiful face, working on a number of drawings until Mum knocked on the door telling me it was time for bed.

Not entirely happy with any of the sketches, I propped on a chair opposite my bed the drawing I felt captured something of Mercy's essence. Mum knocked again, telling me to turn off the light, and as I drifted off to sleep that night, I had the impression that something of fundamental importance had happened in my life that day.

Sunlight sliced through a crack in the curtains. I stared at the ceiling thinking of the previous day, and for a moment worried that it had all been a dream. I hopped out of bed and saw the sketch of Mercy's face on the chair. I picked it up and kissed it before cracking open my door to hear Dad downstairs whistling along to the radio and the washing machine rumbling away in the kitchen. When the phone rang, I waited for Mum to pick up, but when Dad answered I assumed she had popped out to the shops, and so darted across the landing to the bathroom crashing into a startled Mum on her way out, landing naked in a heap before her. She casually stepped over me, averting her eyes as she did so, suggesting I started wearing the bathrobe her sister, Ivy, had sent me for Christmas.

After a quick shower I was back in my room flicking through shirts in my wardrobe, finally opting for the one Mum said brought out the blue in my eyes. Before going downstairs, I nipped back into the bathroom to splash on some of Dad's aftershave. Minutes later, downstairs, as I sat at the table waiting for my breakfast, Mum leaned over me to pour my tea, and commented on how smart I looked.

"Well, just look at you this morning. You look like a million pounds. Are we going somewhere special?" she said.

"No. Just the pictures with Bradley and some other kids from school later on," I lied.

"Oh, I'm glad to see that you're friends with Bradley again. He's such a nice boy. What are you going to see?"

"Leave the boy alone, love, let him have his breakfast," piped in Dad, and as Mum scuttled back to the kitchen, he looked at me and winked.

After breakfast I returned to my room, packed my sketchpad into my bag, and after one final glance in the mirror, I ran down the stairs. With one foot out the front door and the cool air sweeping across my face I yelled goodbye, but Mum called me back to the sitting room. Standing next to each other, their elbows touching, Mum and Dad reminded me of the Salvatores the previous day. In the awkward silence that followed, as they observed every inch of me, I waited for one of them to say something.

"What?" I said, shifting nervously, "I'm going to be late."

"Here, son, take this," Dad said, handing me a five pound note, quite a sum in those days. "You might need it."

"For the pictures," continued Mum, a mischievous smirk surfacing in her face. "Have a lovely time."

Many years later, long after Dad's death, during one of our nostalgic chats, Mum told me they suspected I was meeting a girl. Had they known of the painful events about to unravel in my life however, I'm not sure they would have been as generous with their encouragement that day.

During summer months in London, the Central Line that runs east to west is little more than a sauna. After just two to three stops my shirt was sticking to my back, and so feeling the fresh, midmorning air of the Bayswater Road as I came out of the station at Lancaster Gate that day felt wonderful. Half an hour early, I checked that the phone box outside the station was working so, as per her instructions, I could call before going to the flats.

With time to spare I crossed the busy road to a park opposite and sat on a bench just inside the gates. People were out enjoying the pleasant weather, and I paid careful attention to young couples, especially those locked onto one another, their arms twisting around each other as they laughed. I thought that perhaps, later that day, I might just be walking with Mercy in such a fashion.

I thought back to the bizarre but wonderful moment I saw her shivering in the doorway, and was suddenly gripped by an unexpected anxiety. Why would she want to see me again? I was plain-looking, dull-spirited, had no discernible talent, and most likely, in her eyes, still very much a child. She was a lot older than me, and so beautiful, what could she possibly see in ordinary little me? Had I read too much into her wanting to see me again and created a schoolboy fantasy for something that was going nowhere, her invitation for a day out simply a polite act of gratitude for helping her? I thought of her packing me off home to Mum and Dad later that day, perhaps after she'd treated me to an ice cream, and I considered cancelling the whole thing. But this type of opportunity was unlikely to swing my way again, so I buried such thoughts and headed over to the phone box outside the tube station to call her.

Taking deep breaths to calm my nerves, I stepped into the phone box. As I fumbled in my pockets for the card with her number thinking of the first words I should say to her, panic struck when I realised I'd lost the card. Emptying my pockets and spilling the contents of my bag to the floor, I frantically checked the inner lining of my bag, then my pockets again to find nothing. Thinking the card may have slipped between the pages of my sketchpad, I held it up and flipped through the pages, leafing carefully through each individual page before slumping to the side of the phone box embarrassed and humiliated.

I repeated the same search two or three more times before finally accepting I'd lost the card, and with few options but to return home, I trudged the short distance to the tube station, flashing my ticket at the inspector who grabbed hold of my arm, informing me I needed a valid ticket to use the tube. I looked in my hand to see her card stuck to the back of my tube ticket and quickly raced back to the phone box.

I dialled each number slowly. Before releasing the final number, again I thought of my first words, and as the dial whirred back round, I listened to the clunks and clicks of the call as it connected, counting the rings, anticipating each one to be the last before I heard her voice. However, my excitement soon dwindled when she failed to answer and the ringing persisted, dull thuds churning on and on, echoing monotonously in my ear, the receiver slipping in my sweaty palm.

I thought perhaps I'd dialled the wrong number, so I dialled again, carefully checking each number, making sure each was correct. I held the phone tightly to my ear only to hear the same agonising ringing, and after hanging up, decided to wait five minutes then try again.

Pacing anxiously back and forth outside the phone box, I tried to dispel from my mind a fast-emerging conviction, that she was ignoring my call, didn't want to see me, that her invitation had been offered on a whim, and her brief London life had already moved on to bigger and better things. But though I'd spent barely an hour with her, one underpinning aspect of our meeting was a sincerity that she possessed, a truth of which I had no doubt. I returned to the phone box and dialled again, willing her to pick up, but once more heard only a familiar, monotonous ringing mocking me. A sinking sensation of rejection plummeted through me, and I felt a physical hardening in the pit of my stomach, as if an immovable weight was resting inside me.

I decided to walk the short distance to the flats where, like a voyeur, I stood staring up at the hundreds of windows twinkling in the sun. I thought I saw a movement in one, a face peeking out from behind a curtain, and convincing myself it was her, I waited, watching the door through which she'd entered the day before.

But she never came, and after fifteen minutes or so, it was finally time to go home.

At the station, I took a last look at her card before I threw it away. As my hand hovered above the bin, by simply letting go, I would expel all hope instantly, releasing me from any further tangled agony, and I could return to a mundane, but certainly less complicated existence. Besides, there seemed little point in prolonging the inevitable. But then, as memories of my fledgling love affair flashed through my mind for the last time, I heard the phone ringing in the box outside the station.

I slipped the card back into my shirt pocket and stood outside the phone box listening to the dull clang of it ringing, looking up and down the street for anyone who might be arriving to take a call. I decided to answer it, and so heaved open the door, but with one foot inside and my hand on the receiver, the ringing stopped. I lifted the receiver anyway, only to hear again the droning hum of the dial tone, and reasoned, that as I was there, I might as well dial her number one last time.

With the receiver resting on my shoulder, I listened again to the eternal clodding of a phone ringing. I thought of her sitting in her flat watching the phone, waiting for the ringing to stop. I closed my eyes and let the receiver fall from my shoulder to crack against a glass pane on the side of the box, where it dangled about my knees emitting a distant muffled ringing.

Then, suddenly, an enormous ear-shattering crash exploded all around me. I sprang upright to see the source of this explosion, an angry-looking girl outside, her wild stare terrifying me. Chewing furiously on some gum, her face, hard, unforgiving, a contorted fury emanating from eyes just inches from mine, looking at me through the smeared panes of the box. She sucked on a cigarette cocked between two heavily-ringed fingers, taking impatient drags, waiting to crack another pane with her weapon of choice, a key tightly secured between her thumb and index finger. As she waited, she took a step back and folded her arms, rage continuing to swirl in her fierce eyes. I felt for the wiry metallic cord connected to the receiver, quickly pulling it up and raising the phone to my ear, pretending to talk, nodding to her that I'd nearly finished.

The brutal ringing of the phone in Mercy's empty flat persisted, and when the beast outside struck the glass once more and I saw fresh displeasure plastered across her ugly, impatient face, I was somewhat reluctant to come face to face with this scary girl and so I spoke more loudly, gesticulating as if someone was actually there. I kept up the pretence longer than I really wanted, occasionally peeking out to see the girl talking to herself. I just wanted to be home, be back in my room, back to the simplicity that was my life, and decided to count to five, hang up, then leave. One… two… three… four… fi…

"Hello."

The rapid sounds of pips demanding payment startled me at first, but I immediately recognised Mercy's voice. Forcing a coin into the slot, I heard her say "hello" again, the sweetest "hello" I've ever heard.

"Mercy, it's me, it's Bethnal," I finally managed.

"Hello?" she said again. "Oh, sweetie, hi. What time is it? Oh fuck, honey, I'm sorry, it's gone twelve. Oh shit. I'm *so* sorry. Where are you? Oh, fuck. Are you outside? Oh shit, honey. I'm so sorry. Listen, sweetie, can you give me fifteen minutes? I'll meet you downstairs, in front of the flats. Is that OK? I'm sorry, I overslept."

"It's OK. Everything's OK. I'll be there waiting. Take your time. See you in a bit," I responded, hung up, and then stepping from the phone box, I held the door open and smiled as the girl pushed past me and squeezed inside.

On the short walk to Mercy's flat, I questioned how, even for a moment, I could have doubted her sincerity, and, as any shortcomings about my own inadequacies faded away, I knew I was ready to give this a go.

6

Resurrection

The doors of the main entrance to the flats suddenly burst open and Mercy rushed up the narrow path towards me. The smooth and sexy curves of her hips swivelled in a pair of tight black trousers, and with each step her breasts rose and fell under a white cotton blouse. Her hair was slicked back, and she dazzled me with her smile as she approached. When she threw her arms around me, I inhaled, for the first time, the light and sensuous scent of a woman.

She grabbed my hand, and pulling me towards the main road, apologised for sleeping in, telling me of her meeting with the old woman the previous evening.

"You saw the old woman who met me at the door, she takes care of the building. She told me she was expecting me a lot earlier so I gave her a brief rundown of my day to that point thinking this would keep her happy. I was so tired, I just wanted some sleep. But no, she invited me in for a cup of tea which was the last thing I wanted. I think she really just wanted to inspect me. Anyways, I didn't want to get off on the wrong foot with her and so I accepted, and, can you believe it, she kept me there an hour telling me about how wonderful Mr Roberts is, he's my father's friend, the owner of the flat, before eventually showing me to the flat. I had a good look around the flat then called my folks who weren't at home. I left a message, just to say I was here, unpacked, and went to bed. Can you believe it, I thought she must have put something in the tea, 'cos I felt so wired when I got into bed, I couldn't sleep. Well, when my body needs to sleep I like to give it what it wants, so I took a sleeping pill. I guess, what with jet lag, getting lost and the Grand Tour of London's subway system yesterday, I was bushed. Did you try calling this morning? I did hear a phone, but I thought I was dreaming. By the way, I dreamed about you last night."

I felt a prickly heat rising in my neck.

"Hope it was good," I responded, a daring hint of the devil in my reply.

"Mostly. Look, there's a café. Come on, I need caffeine."

We sat for a while drinking coffee on the same bench in the park where I'd considered cancelling our meeting earlier. The sun was shining in a cloudless sky, the sort of day Londoners yearn for during summer months, and we watched children screaming as they scampered in and out of the park's majestic fountains which sent jets of water shooting high into the air, covering us in a light mist, making little rainbows appear in the air before us.

We finished our coffees, and as we walked along one of the many paths criss-crossing the park in the shade of enormous trees, like vigilant guardians towering above us, she wanted to know about my background, my family, in fact, anything to do with me. I didn't have much to tell, and so gave her a heavily-abridged version of Dad's epic journey to London, revealed I was an only child, and that was about all there was to my rather dull existence.

Her life however, was super exciting. She told me about New York city, of buildings and bridges, of frigid winters, and as she talked, I realised I knew little of what America was really like, having always imagined that it was a place where the sun shone constantly, and beautiful girls, like those in my favourite TV programme, *Charlie's Angels*, kept the streets safe. It seemed a very happy place.

She was in London to earn accreditation for a Master's degree in *Urban Planning*, starting her course the following week at the University of London. I had absolutely no idea what that was, and as she casually reeled off the names of many famous British architects, most of whom spent their professional careers seeking a commission to design a central London park like the one we were in, I just nodded as if I understood what she was saying. Her knowledge of London, the city in which I was born but of which I clearly knew little, was impressive. And as she bewitched me with more detail of her clearly very interesting existence, I couldn't help but notice in the shady patches below the long branches, young couples wrapped around each other, stealing kisses and laughing.

"What an absolutely beautiful park, such pretty flowers," she said, drawing my attention away from the manoeuvres of young lovers scattered below the trees.

Neatly-cut green verges running along the paths acted as borders behind which small shiny flowers danced softly in the breeze. I'd like to have informed her of the various native flowers we stopped to admire, but unfortunately, on nature walks in primary school we never quite made it as far as the woods. Mrs Rice, our teacher, thought collecting leaves, twigs and branches that blew into the playground sufficient pieces of the natural world to perk our curiosity. This of course made "nature walks" dull and uninspiring, the only flashes of excitement coming when we found dead things like small rodents hidden amongst the foliage which we threw at the girls who ran screaming to Mrs Rice. Though I came up short in identifying those species within those perfectly-tended flower beds, I hoped that at some stage in the day, I might say, or do, something of note, something that might impress her.

Near the centre of the park we stopped to rest under a tree with a lumpy, knotted trunk, its long branches, thick and strong, stretching out over us, shading us against the increasing heat of the sun. Mercy slumped down against the trunk, kicking off her shoes and wiggling her toes in the air. Unsure if this was her way of saying that perhaps something more physical was on the cards, I remained on my feet, uncertain of what I should do, doubting again whether I was equipped for what was potentially a life-changing moment, my first *real* sexual encounter. I'd not yet known her a day but worried that if I didn't act, she'd move on to another, more reliable boy, one who fully understood her cues. I tried desperately to recall details of those loss-of-virginity stories I heard most mornings before registration, about how these boys had wooed, charmed, impressed, any detail to help me in that moment of need. But all that came to mind were sound bites concerning either tits, or the jackpot, penetration.

Magnetised by her beauty, I felt Neanderthal, wanting to pounce. I suddenly realised another way in which school had failed me, and no doubt millions of other boys who found themselves in this situation. In my final year, about to step into manhood, I still had no idea about the *wheres*, *hows* and *whats* of love. Why hadn't I been given a list of useful words and phrases of how to deal with the mechanics, movement (and positions) of first sexual encounters? And who was the genius who deemed cross-country more important than this type of guidance – it's not as if we still had to chase them to fuck them!

A bead of sweat trickled down my spine, I knew had to do something, but never imagined that panic such as this was part of the build up to one of life's greatest moments. I was out of my depth, my heart was pounding, just as it did after cross-country. With her eyes closed and her hands resting on her lap, she was so calm. She'd done this before, a woman of ample experience.

I felt so inadequate, and could think only of escape. When it appeared that she was sleeping, the idea of fleeing seemed the most practical course of action. Dotted throughout the park were hundreds of thickets, each, potentially, a place to where I could run and hide, from where I could wait and watch her wake to find me gone. The chances of meeting her again in a city the size of London were slim, and in the unlikely event we did run into each other, I'd take a mildly embarrassing moment over the shameful ineptitude I felt at that moment.

And so, with no time for second thoughts, no regrets, my decision final, it was time to go. In the unlikely event she gave chase, I'd outrun her. OK, time to go, on the count of five, no turning back, still a boy, not quite ready for this stuff yet. Five, four, three.... And then suddenly, hidden high on a branch in the dark foliage above us, a bird released an angry squawk, and noisily flapping its wings, flew out of the tree, and Mercy woke up.

"Oh, honey. Are you still standing? Come, sit down here," she said, patting the worn tufts of grass next to her.

I dropped down beside her and leaned against the trunk, careful our shoulders didn't touch.

"That's better," she said smiling, and then she took my hand in hers, patted it a couple of times and left her hands resting on top of mine.

A girl had never held my hand before. My first *real* touch of a girl. With her soft, gentle flesh on mine, I prayed I wouldn't fuck things up. No rushing things, no inappropriate moves, rely on natural instinct to guide me (not the Neanderthal option).

And of course what I should have done is enjoyed the moment, smiled, closed my eyes and savoured this tender intimacy. But with her hands on mine, a strange warmth had begun to flow through me, and though I might have just managed to disguise my emotional state, shuffling in my jeans, my stiffening cock would prove more of a challenge.

She looked at me and I cracked a nervous smile, hoping she was unaware of my cock pinging into any available space in my jeans.

"Your hands are very sweaty, Bethnal. Are you OK?" she said suddenly.

"Yeah, I'm fine. It's just so hot today," I lied.

"Sweetheart, you think this is hot. You should be in New York in the summer. Over ninety degrees, and that's in the shade. Forget that. Give me this any day. This is perfect, just perfect," she said closing her eyes once more. "Just think back to this time yesterday," she mused, "what a miserable day, trolling around the city in the rain. Until I met you."

I felt myself blushing.

"Isn't it so strange how things happen?" she continued. "Just two days ago, we had no idea of each other's existence, and here I am with this cute little British boy who's showing me around his city. What more could a strange girl from out of town ask for?" she said, my cock suddenly shifting again in my jeans.

Her use of the word *cute* to describe me both bemused and embarrassed me. *Cute*? What did that mean exactly? A baby's *cute*, so is a puppy. Was I in a category of things only to be played with, to be cooed at, to be petted and swooned over in maternal fashion? I hoped not. Again, dark thoughts of her offloading me at the tube station later that day descended. Then, just as I was resigning myself to the category of *cute*, a new problem arose.

"Do you mind if I lay down for a while?" she said, and in one natural sweeping movement she extended her legs horizontally, swivelled around, and landed her beautifully-made head directly in the middle of my lap.

She glanced up and smiled at me, then closed her eyes and commented on what a wonderful afternoon she was having. Her head was resting gently on my thigh, but an inch and a half from my throbbing cock. I was so excited by her milky-white breasts quivering slightly against the fabric of her blouse, little pert nipples tempting me to run my fingertips over her neck, down across the smooth skin above her breasts and under the soft cotton. But suddenly, in a severe state of panic, a strange state of paralysis took hold of my arms, I was unable to move them. And when she moved her head, just slightly, I felt my cock pulse, shifting in my jeans towards the soft skin of her cheek.

I managed to put my hands to my sides and close my eyes, taking deep breaths, hoping her head wouldn't make any sudden movements. Her fragrance reminded me of my early childhood, of Mum's big-breasted friends who when waiting for her as she got ready for bingo, would chase me around the house, hoisting me into their arms, kissing me with their big lips, traffic-light red, leaving me with cheeks smudged pink until the following morning when Mum washed it off.

I opened my eyes and considered for a moment that this was my cue, that she wanted me to touch her, to softly massage her shoulders. But I noticed her breathing had slowed, that she was asleep, which I admit was a relief. For the moment, at least, I could relax and yet despite my anxiety, I looked down on her, to savour my first moment of real physical intimacy with a girl. A memory that has never left me. However, the manner in which this moment of intimacy ended is quite bizarre, by what happened next.

"Well, you gonna feel my tits or what? I've been giving you the come-on all day. Look kid, I'm almost blowing you, and you just sit there. Come on, Bethnal, get a grip. Carpe Diem, the iron's glowing hot, strike it before it cools. Come on, my *cute* little British boy, go ahead, I'm yours, enjoy yourself," she teased, rolling onto her back, staring at me impatiently, then nodding provocatively towards her breasts and calling me *cute* again, a cue that had me lifting my T-shirt over my head as she slipped out of her slacks to reveal silky black knickers, and I moved towards her, finally about to touch the soft skin on her stomach, and before sliding my hand slowly up towards her breasts, I heard myself saying, "Thank you, God."

"Bethnal? Are you OK? Bethnal?"

I woke to find Mercy standing over me, her hand gently nudging my shoulder.

"I guess we both dropped off," she said, smiling, and seeing us both fully clothed, I realised, rather disappointingly, that I'd fallen asleep.

"Yeah, me too," I said.

"Come on, let's run," she said, playfully, clearly invigorated from her rest.

"Run?" I said, thinking it not quite the type of foreplay I had in mind.

"Yeah, run, you know, on legs," she repeated, and then, with mischief gleaming in her eyes, continued, "I'll give you a big kiss if you catch me."

A kiss – that was more like it. But when I started to get up, it appeared not all of me had nodded off. Deep within my jeans, my cock, as hard as flint and still thinking of Mercy, was ready to launch to the front of my jeans the moment I stood.

"You go ahead," I said playing for time, "you'll need a head start," and picking up her shoes, with a playful look in her eyes, she skipped off.

With her back to me, I sprang to my feet and made necessary adjustments, then set off, quickly finding a stride that had me closing on her. She gave little screams as she glanced back at me, and I anticipated the moment my hand touched her shoulder, of hearing her gentle sighs of submission as we fell laughing and panting hysterically into the long grass trying to stifle our giggling as we searched for each other's lips.

"Are you coming, slowpoke? Come on, chase me, *cute* little English boy," she shouted, almost mockingly, as she raced ahead.

With my eyes focused on her firm buttocks, a couple of firm plums, ready to mount, I gathered speed, thinking that for such a marathon effort, I'd require more than a kiss.

But as I accelerated, she did too, with seemingly little effort, and I found I was no longer gaining ground on her, the distance between us remaining more or less the same. In fact I think at one point she might have looked over her shoulder and slowed a little.

I pumped my arms faster managing to reduce the distance between us, then, just as my fingertips were on her shoulder, I launched forward, and as my legs left the ground, as if finding a lower gear, she burst forward and I came crashing to the ground, skidding to a halt, instantly feeling the friction burns stinging my hands.

She stopped to examine the humiliation left in her wake, breaking into fits of uncontrollable laughter. I looked at the raw pink flesh of my palms, and thought of the motto our old French teacher always used as he circled the room slinging our failed test papers back at us. No doubt an expression his teachers had beaten into him, he reminded us that if we heeded these words, that in our bleak futures, when things didn't go as planned, we might just find suitable remedies for the trauma we had coming in our lives. I got to my feet softly reciting to myself his wise words: *When at first you don't succeed, try, try, and then try again.* And with renewed vigour, determined to catch her, I was off.

But the chase was brief. She rounded one of the dense thickets (into which I was planning an escape earlier), and disappeared. I heard a sudden movement within, the crack of a twig. She was near, I could sense her, and so I slowly circled its thorny perimeter, squinting through the wiry branches into the interior where dust particles swirled in the narrow rays of sunlight penetrating the dark heart of the thicket. Every few steps I stopped to listen, looking for shadowy life within. And then, surely, a movement. A flash of her white blouse. She was close.

I found a small hole leading to the interior, and with one foot in and sharp brambles already flaying my arms, suddenly, from behind, and with some considerable force, a pair of hands sent me sprawling headfirst into the bush leaving me helplessly hanging, trapped and tangled within the sharp thorns. I waited for the mocking jeers of what would surely be angry boys celebrating an ambush, but swivelling to the left, just slightly, I looked up to see Mercy standing with her arms folded, smiling at me.

"Honey, you're gonna have to do better than that if you want that kiss," she said as she pulled me up, brushed me down, and declared what fun she was having.

We spent the remainder of the afternoon strolling aimlessly through the narrow side streets of Chelsea, admiring old houses more like small country cottages, all beautifully decorated with pretty flowers in hanging baskets.

We caught a bus to Hyde Park, and the moment Mercy saw the Serpentine sparkling in the afternoon sun with couples in rowing boats, she dashed off. By the time I caught up, she was standing next to a small boat holding its oars. Though I'd never rowed before I took them from her, insisting that I row, hoping to demonstrate proficiency in at least one activity before the day was out. Fortunately, I took to it quite easily, and with just a few pulls on the oars we were under clear blue skies in the middle of the lake with water lapping against the side of the boat and a soft breeze blowing across us. I let the blades lie flat on the water and we surveyed majestic London all around us – the Houses of Parliament, the Post Office Tower and magnificent spires of churches stretching high into the sky.

Mercy kicked off her shoes and using her bag as a pillow, stretched out along the length of the boat, resting her hands on her stomach and closing her eyes.

As she lay before me, I questioned again if she could really be the girl for me. Dad often told me that when things don't go as expected, that I shouldn't force them, that for every experience in life, "the right time is the right time." I reflected on the events of the day, thinking again that perhaps for her, our day was nothing but a pleasant day out, and that I was simply too eager, that I wasn't ready for that *something* more, that she wasn't *the* one that this encounter was just a dry run to give me the experience necessary to pull off *the first time* without the terror I'd experienced earlier. Had we met a month earlier, I would have shirked a second encounter, preferring instead the safe and solitary route of loneliness. I knew nothing of first love, even less about her, but for the first time in my life I knew that in this case I had to take a risk, trust my instinct. The thought of suspending this first experience of love felt unnatural. She was the one, I was certain of this. A voice inside rebuked me for doubting her, urging me to throw caution to those fearsome winds of doubt and pursue this unexplored path. I thought again about what Dad had said, about the 'right time'. That time had arrived.

I spent the next hour as she slept sketching her, trying to catch in my drawing the essence of her beauty, and in years that were to follow, as time dulled the memory, I would occasionally pull from a chest in the attic the drawing I sketched that day. Simply to remember her.

When she woke, I rowed us in, and as I was paying the attendant, she called. I turned to see her talking to a couple, thrusting into the man's hand a camera. She tugged me to the water's edge and wrestled me into a number of different poses, searching for an embrace worthy of our first photo together. The moment she pulled me to her, planted her beautiful lips on my cheek, the camera flashed. Shockwaves of delight reeled through me, and after thanking the man, she took a small tissue from her bag and gently massaged the lipstick from my cheek, giggling as she smudged it into a little pool of pink.

We hopped on a bus at Hyde Park Corner for the short ride up Piccadilly where we jumped into the hum of jostling Soho. After a stroll up Shaftesbury Avenue we cut through the narrow side streets of Chinatown and Leicester Square and took photos of each other below the flashing neon lights of the billboards in Piccadilly Circus.

We had dinner in a splendid Italian restaurant in a small street just behind the National Gallery where we made plans to meet the following Saturday. Six days seemed like an eternity, and though I knew a midweek meet for me impossible, I suggested it all the same. But she had a busy week lined up at the university and appeared excited by the days ahead. I could only think of the numbing tedium of school, and how my time there now seemed all the more pointless.

7

Rediscovery

"Bethnal? It's twelve o'clock. Are you OK in there?"

Mum was outside tapping softly at the door. The clock on my bedside table confirmed the hour.

"Bethnal?" she called again.

I cleared my throat.

"Yeah," I said.

"Are you OK in there, love? It's twelve o' clock. Are you OK?" she persisted.

She tapped again.

"What do you want for breakfast, love?" she said, mumbling something about it being time for lunch.

"Toast."

"Do you want tea?"

"Yeah."

"Well, get a move on, love," she said as she thumped back down the stairs.

I thought back to the previous day and realised that things were now different in my life. I now inhabited a new world, one with a beautiful companion. I threw back the covers and hopping from the bed, searched the floor for my underwear. Looking in the mirror I saw a strange aspect in my face, something I'd not seen since my childhood – happiness.

Dad had popped out for the newspapers and I thought it better to wait until he returned before going down. He often stepped in when Mum was too intrusive, and I sensed she would be requiring details of the previous day. But I was determined that changes in my life would remain private, and when I heard the front door open, I thought Dad had returned and so went down and sat at the table, waiting for Mum to bring me my breakfast. But Dad hadn't returned, the door opening was Mum putting out the empty milk bottles. She brought my breakfast, and as I watched the butter slowly melting into the toast, I could feel her behind me, hovering.

"What are those scratches on your arms?" she said lifting one arm from the table.

"What?"

"Those scratches? How did you get those? They look sore."

The scratches from our high jinks in the park stretched like long wounds down my arms. What could I tell her? The truth? I thought for a moment how that might sound.

"Well, Mum, let me explain. I've met this woman from New York City who I've fallen deeply in love with, and, to be frank, (I'd look and wink at Dad if he were there at that point) I'm trying to get into her knickers. But she's playing hard to get, and yesterday, you see, she pushed me into a bush, her unorthodox version of foreplay I suppose. Don't ask me what I was doing looking into a bush. Anyway, must be an American thing, you know what Yanks are like. I admit, it wasn't amusing at the time, though on reflection, I can now see the funny side. It was just a bit of fun, I suppose. Well, anyway, *mater*, that's how I got all scratched up. Oh, by the way, as she's a stranger in our country, and she mentioned she'd like to drop by some time, I've told her that she can come and stay with us, well with me, in my room, while she's in London. In fact, that will be her at the door now."

And then the sound of the doorbell startled me from my monologue. Mum rushed to the door to let Dad in who'd forgotten his key. He tapped me softly on the back as he entered the room, and handing Mum his jacket, a little out of breath, he slumped onto the sofa, the Sunday papers landing on his lap with a thump.

"Morning, son. Sleep well?" he asked shaking open the paper, but before I had the chance to reply, Mum had some unfinished business.

"Well," she continued, "how did you get those scratches on your arms?"

Dad looked over at me, at my arms.

"We were mucking about yesterday, in the park, and I ended up in a bush," I said, crunching into my toast.

"Who pushed you in a bush?" persisted Mum.

"Tom," I lied.

"I told you about that Tom, I don't know why you go around with that boy. You know what happened to his older brother with all that robbery business and, believe me, that Tom is on the same path as him, you mark my words. It's probably better you stay away from him in future," she said.

With her inquisition on hold, as she did each Sunday, she joined Dad on the sofa and flicked open the *News of the World*, licking her thumb before turning each page, rooting out the latest national and international scandal.

As I ate my breakfast I listened to her soft disapproving sighs escalate into small fits of exasperation as she scanned the newspaper for gossip. From time to time, she read aloud updates on preparations taking place up and down the country in honour of the Queen's forthcoming Silver Jubilee anniversary, cutting articles out and circulating them at weekly meetings with women on our street's committee, the group responsible for our party on that big day in June. Sitting happily together on the sofa I looked at them, trying to imagine them as young and in love. But then Mum dropped a bombshell.

"Bethnal, we've been invited over to Ivy's house for Sunday lunch today. She says she's really looking forward to seeing you," she suddenly announced.

Dad looked up sharply from his paper.

Mum's sister, Ivy, lived only a couple of miles away but we rarely visited her, and for good reason. Like me, Dad didn't like Ivy, she criticised everything and everyone, and during afternoons spent with her the air turned toxic, drawing Mum in to engage in malicious gossip, provoking her to say things which under normal circumstances, she would never say. After one such visit, Dad had returned home infuriated, openly venting his dislike for the woman, describing her as "being from the gutter." Mum countered with familial obligations to a sister who lived alone, and, as dutiful husband, Dad always continued to accompany her when required, stopping short however of offering a retraction in his opinion of Aunt Ivy.

But I couldn't face a trip to Ivy's that day and had to let them know.

"Can I give it a miss? I've loads of homework to finish before tomorrow," I said, Dad's eyes flashing towards me, both of us knowing that I'd cut him loose on this occasion.

In the silence that followed I waited for Mum to round on me. Rubbing the scratches on my arms, I knew I had to remain firm.

"OK. There's some ham and cheese in the fridge, make yourself a sandwich. There's Coke in the cupboard above the sink. Wash up after yourself," she said, casually flicking a page, leaving me a little stunned by this strange and unexpected response.

I went into the kitchen and, amid the shuffle of newspapers, I heard them whispering.

"Well, I'll get started with my homework I think. Tell Ivy I said hello," I said, returning to the living room, both peeking over their newspapers.

"OK. I'll tell her you were asking after her, she'll be pleased," Mum said, and nodding my thanks I made my way out of the room.

"Bethnal?" said Dad, calling me back.

"Yeah?" I replied, turning towards them.

As they stared at me I thought they might want particulars of my changing life. They provided me with everything for nothing in return, but some things, like details of my new love, I'd never share with them.

"We're happy you're taking more interest in your schoolwork, son," he said, Mum concurring with the faintest of nods.

And that was all he said.

An hour or so later, I could hear them downstairs getting ready to leave, Mum telling Dad to change his shirt followed by his slow plod up the stairs, one I'd come to recognise over the years. In fact I was familiar with exact pitch variations in the creak of each stair, and knew if it was Mum or Dad coming up. Mum's step was sneaky, barely audible, but the third step from the top always gave her away, producing such a distinctive unavoidable creak, always warning me of her proximity.

In their bedroom I heard hangers clanging and Dad muttering as he rifled through his shirts.

"The brown one?" he shouted down the stairs.

"No, the one I brought you last Saturday," mum replied.

"But it's still in the packet."

"Well bring it down and I'll run the iron over it. And while you're at it, bring down that tie I bought you for Christmas, it'll go nice with that shirt."

"I'm not wearing a tie. It's Sunday."

"But you haven't worn it yet, it'll suit you down to the ground."

"I've worn it to work."

"But I haven't seen it on you. Just bring it down and get a move on, we'll be late," Mum insisted, and as he passed by my door I heard him ripping the plastic packaging, swearing under his breath.

Shortly after, I heard them in the hall putting on their coats.

"Bye, Bethnal. There's food in the fridge, we'll be back at about six," Mum shouted.

"She means five, son. See ya soon," Dad added, closing the door behind them.

From my window I watched them walking down the path, Mum just behind Dad rearranging the collar of his jacket, then putting her arm through his.

With no set plans for the long afternoon, I decided to tidy my room thinking that when Mum inspected it the following day, she'd see I'd put my time to good use. Starting under the bed, I was somewhat intrigued by what I might find there, and lying flat on my back, I stretched my arm into the darkness initially only managing to find a dozen or so fluffy balls of tissue. On my second attempt I was surprised and pleased to find an old library book, one I'd given up for lost quite some time ago. I rubbed the dust from its cover to see its title, *Italian Art*, and a marble sculpture of a young girl. I opened it and saw the big red stamp indicating it was three years overdue. Then, as I leafed through the pages, I remembered how this came to be the first book I ever checked out of a library.

Mum has always been an avid reader of romance novels and makes a trip to the library every two weeks or so. Accompanying her there three years before, she asked me if I'd like to check out a book, and, as usual, I said no. As she potted about the Romance section, I walked up and down the aisles killing time when I saw, amid the musty smells of old worn leather books at the rear of the library, a book protruding from a shelf. I was immediately drawn to the white marble statue of a young girl reclining on a chaise longue, unashamedly showing her breasts. I assumed that if the book displayed such magnificent breasts on its cover, then surely there would be more inside. And so, I checked up and down the aisle to make sure I was alone, then pulled the book from the shelf.

As I flicked through the pages, I was thrilled to see more of what was on the cover, neat little beauties displaying their wares in a number of different ways. But I was also intrigued by other sections of the book, more specifically a section devoted to detailing effective techniques in charcoal sketching. We had just started experimenting with charcoal drawing in Art, and inspired by the moment, and the girl on the cover, I decided to check it out.

With the book under my arm I peeked around the end of the aisle to see Mum talking to the librarian who was thumping a stamp on the inside covers of books Mum had piled before her. I approached the desk slowly, hoping they wouldn't think a book showing a beautiful young girl with beautiful breasts might be a little too racy for a boy my age. In the event of expected protestation, I would support my supplication by quoting the History teacher who, when introducing us to Renaissance Italy, had said something along these lines: "Italy in the Renaissance is arguably the most important era in the development of man in western democracy. It was a reawakening of human ingenuity in the realms of literature, art and all aspects of life, where at last we could look deep into ourselves through beautiful art and begin to appreciate the contribution of our species to the world we live in." And besides, the book was on the shelves of a public library, not the top shelf of some smutty newsagent.

I walked slowly to the check-out counter where the librarian was busy pulling well-worn cards from small drawers under her desk, stamping on them expiry dates before inserting them inside the front covers of each book. I tugged at Mum's sleeve and handed her the book. As she looked at the cover I studied her face, waiting for that disapproving frown which I knew so well, the one which would scupper any chance of my being alone with the book in my bedroom. She flicked through the pages, then glared at me. I promised to return it in good time, and, after a moment's thought, she placed it alongside her books, tits-down, and needless to say, *Italian Art* never saw the shelves of the local library again.

A month or so later, Mum received a letter from the library informing her that her card had been suspended. She badgered me daily to return the book, but I had no idea where it was, I thought it lost, either at school or on the tube. When she asked about it, I just shrugged, fobbing her off with excuses, hoping the problem would simply *drift* away. So, it wasn't until that Sunday afternoon that I finally got around to actually opening the book.

And I understood immediately what had drawn me to the book. The polished marble statue of the beautiful maiden on the cover was so alluring, she knew nothing of inhibition, caring little for either praise or condemnation. My eyes inspected again the curvature of her fine supple breasts, but other parts too, admiring the graceful way she held out her arm as she lay reclined across a chaise lounge, the contours of her legs clearly visible below a thin shawl draped across the lower half of her body, her gentle curves, her equilibrium, the fine detail in the artist's craft. I knew that artists in the sixteenth and seventeenth centuries were normally commissioned by wealthy families and members of the aristocracy to produce art according to their bourgeois tastes, and so I wondered who the artist was, and why he had created such a beautiful piece. Perhaps because of my own emotional fragility at the time, I concluded his inspiration for preserving forever the beauty of this young girl could only have been love.

I flicked to the section on preparatory sketches, to discover a series of drawings detailing preparation for different parts of the sculpture on the cover. I learned also of those responsible for its creation, especially intrigued by the young girl on the cover, a member of a very important, high-ranking family in Rome, led by an enterprisingly *free spirit* in the form of her outrageous uncle who cared little for public morality. At his behest, the family had commissioned the piece with the uncle personally interviewing artists from around Europe, finally plumping for a young Venetian who shared his belief that good art had a dual obligation to push boundaries of morality and to stand the test of time.

The process and the degree of skill necessary to produce the sculpture astounded me. Years were spent on small preparatory sketches, and within the pages of the book, hundreds of drawings, small preliminary sketches, showed how the artist had carefully studied each part of the model's body, detailing minute features on fingernails, fingertips, limbs, and various other parts of her body, before beginning work on the huge marble block he had personally selected from the small Italian town of Carrara, just north of Pisa.

I was suddenly filled with a new sense of inspiration, wanting to draw like the artist in the book. I clearly had so much to learn, and with this beautiful maiden as inspiration, I set to work immediately, copying body parts directly from the book into my sketchpad. On completion of each drawing, I compared my efforts to those in the book, assessing areas of my work that required improvement. As my pencil glided across the page, I thought of Mercy, my muse, who had reignited passion in me, not only for sketching, but also for life.

When I heard the front door open and my parents talking in the hall, I thought their premature return a bad omen, and that Dad's patience with Ivy had finally snapped.

"Bethnal, we're home. Are you there?" Mum yelled up the stairs, nothing in her voice to suggest she was angry.

I cracked open the door to hear them in the living room talking, noting no discernible friction.

"Yeah," I shouted back down the stairs.

When I heard Mum in the kitchen filling the kettle for tea, only then did I realise that I hadn't eaten, and heard her come pounding through the living room to the bottom of the stairs.

"Bethnal Green. You get down here now," she hollered up the stairs.

Downstairs, Dad was sitting comfortably in his chair scanning the newspaper.

"Hello, son. How's the homework coming along?" he said, not sure if his enquiry was genuine or he was just winding me up. "It's good to see you showing such interest in your studies," he continued.

"How was Ivy's?" I enquired.

"Oh, tolerable, just tolerable," he said, flicking a page of the newspaper.

"She made a lovely roast, and the pudding was just like my mother used to make. She really did make every effort. We'll have to invite her round," Mum piped in from the kitchen.

Dad looked up from his paper, folded it awkwardly, then threw it on the floor beside his chair.

"Not if I can help it," he said in a low voice, looking at me and winking, then shouting through to the kitchen for his tea.

Mum came into the living room carrying a tray laden with steaming tea and ham rolls. Placing the tray on the table, she prepared me a plate then took Dad his tea before sitting with me at the table to recount events at Ivy's. As I ate, I pretended to listen, but I was eager to get back upstairs to continue drawing.

With tea finished, Mum switched on the TV and moved to the sofa. I remained downstairs for a while watching a game show with them. Mum adored game shows, responding to all questions even if she didn't have a clue. When she got a question right, she laughed, almost humbled by her intellectual superiority, and when contestants got questions wrong, she commented on how thick they were. For half an hour or so the show was mildly amusing, but the programme that followed, a dismal soap set in a village in middle England, signalled time for me to return to the solitude of my room, to my drawings.

On entering the room, I was impressed by the work spread out across the carpet. I collected several drawings together and after pinning them to the walls, stood back to admire my afternoon's labour. Hands, arms, fingers, eyes, lips, beautiful pieces of the maiden covered every space available on the walls. For a stranger stepping into my room, these drawings would have appeared a mere assemblage of bizarre body parts tacked to the walls, but for me, in each one, quite surprisingly, I saw not only the maiden, but also, in a strange but pleasing way, Mercy. Though at first I doubted the resemblance, the more I examined the drawings, the more striking the similarities between the two became clear. Their bodies, the suppleness of their lips, the shape of their breasts, in each sketch I'd subconsciously merged the young maiden and Mercy, to the point they were indistinguishable from one another. And as my eyes continued to skip from sketch to sketch, the more I examined the images, though inspired by the marble maiden on the cover of the book, the individual parts I had produced were most definitely those of Mercy.

Before going to bed that night I decided to work on one more sketch, the image of a solitary hand. I worked for half an hour or so before crawling into bed thinking of the following day, the start of a tortuous week, five more long pointless days before I saw Mercy again. I drifted off to sleep hoping Mercy would join the virgins in my dreams that night, but I suddenly woke with a start. Mum was always so annoyed with me if I asked her for my PE kit on the morning that I needed it, so I hopped out of bed and went downstairs to remind her I needed it the following day.

The living-room door was ajar and grey flickering images from the TV bounced into the hallway as I softly descended the stairs. I entered the room quietly to see Dad sat next to Mum on the sofa with her hand in his. The moment they saw me at the door, he released it, and after quickly reminding Mum about the PE kit, I ran back up the stairs.

Back in my room I looked again at the hand I'd started sketching, comparing it to the one in the book. I opened a fresh page in my pad and began a new sketch, one which required no guidance from the book. Though only briefly, in the half light of the living room, I'd seen Dad's hand wrapped tenderly in Mum's, and that's what I drew before going to sleep that night.

8

Coping

I awoke to see the sketches stuck to the walls all around me. Once again, I was up before the alarm had rung, and in the bathroom I stared at the smiling boy in the mirror who didn't look like me, but someone else, someone who had a purpose in the world. It was going to be a very arduous week, so I was determined to use this unexpected spring of optimism in my life to carry me through the day and, if possible, the entire week.

For the first and last time, I was first to arrive at school. I thought I'd hang out in the Art room but it was locked, so when I saw the janitor coming out of the music studio, though I was trying to avoid Mr Martins, the Music teacher, I decided to wait there until registration. Mr Martins was a good teacher, but he'd recently been complaining, constantly, of my apathy, that I was "wasting a talent," that my "application" to his subject was sorely lacking. He was right, my interest in music had faded, which had clearly disappointed him.

I wasn't sure if I had any real talent for music. When I was six, while attending their first parents' evening, my parents received glowing comments regarding my skill as an artist. They were then amazed to be told I was musical, and that just before Xmas I'd almost effortlessly learned how to play *Away in the Manger* on guitar, quickly followed by *London Bridge* on the recorder, and that I had been selected as a member of an elite group within the school considered *gifted*. My shocked parents sat before the music teacher unsure of what to say as she lauded me for my "innate talent" and "good ear" for music. I suspect most parents were blinded with similar praise for their child that evening, but Mum and Dad, unaccustomed to any form of flattery, were easily swayed. When I moved on to secondary school and they received similar reports of my "untapped talent" in music, they deemed it wise to invest in private music lessons.

Dad was the driving force behind developing this untapped talent. As a child I never understood his insistence on me learning an instrument, an issue which created on-going conflict between us. Years later, shortly after his death, I learned of his love for music when I took ownership of a large trunk that had sat in the corner of the living room behind his chair (which I had been forbidden to go near) for the entirety of my childhood. When I moved into my first house, as I heaved the trunk up to the attic, curious to its contents, I broke open the lock to discover hundreds of records Dad had collected over the years. Alongside popular artists of his youth such as Frank Sinatra, Dean Martin and Mario Lanza, there were records by Miles Davis and Ella Fitzgerald. But what surprised me most was the number of classical records in his collection. Mum revealed that his favourite composers were Mahler and Mozart, but his collection included many other notable composers such as Beethoven, Bruckner and Britten, among other more obscure, composers. She also told me that he had once confided in her that his only regret in life was that he had never learned how to play an instrument, that as a boy he was led to believe that playing a musical instrument was something lads didn't do. However, shortly after he married Mum, he started to collect records and played them when he was alone in the house. When I learned of the contents of the trunk, and what they had meant to him, I was very moved, and understood his reasons for pushing me to play an instrument, simply to provide me with an opportunity he'd never had.

In my final year of primary school, my parents attended open evenings at secondary schools in the area. Their choice of school for me was sealed when Dad stepped into my school's Music room to see every instrument the school possessed polished and on display. It was easily the biggest and best equipped music room of all the schools they'd visited, and so with the next five years of my life mapped out, they arrived home enthusiastically detailing the wonders of my new school, and informed me I had to decide what instrument I wanted to learn.

Guitar seemed the most logical choice, not because of my mastery of *Away in the Manger*, but because of a super teacher, Mr Lossaso, a wonderful man who had once let me hold his guitar and strum the strings. As infants, we sat crossed-legged most afternoons star struck, gazing up at him as he strummed away on his guitar singing to us songs of peace and love. He was easily the most popular teacher in the school, especially for girls who smiled and blushed as he encouraged them to sing along, their bodies swaying through every chorus. Even at that innocent age I noted how they swooned as he played, and so when it came time to choose an instrument, I hoped a guitar might prove as attractive on me as it did on him.

However, my dreams of wooing the girls with a guitar were short-lived. When I went to sign up for guitar lessons, I was informed classes were full and that I would have to choose another instrument. I stubbornly refused, it was guitar or nothing. But Dad was determined, not letting my belligerence dissuade him, and in my first week of school he took a morning off work and accompanied me to a meeting with my first music teacher, a pale creature with dirty fingernails whose name escapes me. The only two instruments with slots available for instruction that term were the double bass or the violin. I'd never even heard of a double bass, and when the music teacher dragged one out from the dark recesses of the storeroom and I saw it was bigger than me, I reluctantly opted for the violin, an instrument I considered incredibly ugly, one I thought only *strange* kids took up.

For six months or so, I struggled to produce any type of noise remotely pleasant to the ear, my slow fat fingers clearly not designed for the nimbleness required of a violinist, a fact I drove home each evening over dinner which normally ended with me storming out of the room in tears screaming that I hated it. But Dad stood firm, insisting I persevere, and in a spirit of compromise said that if I saw the year out and felt the same way in September, he'd sign me up for guitar classes. I agreed.

In May of that year, however, Mrs Emerson, the new music teacher arrived. A tender and patient lady with a perfectly round bottom, under her smiling tutelage she told me that I'd made excellent progress in the short month she'd been teaching me. With gentle reassurance she persuaded me to play a solo piece, "just a short piece," at the school's end of term concert. She also convinced me that my fingers were "made for the violin," her kind words coinciding with me producing melodic and recognisable chord transitions, and though I didn't tell Dad, I began to enjoy these lessons, so much so, that from time to time, I would voluntarily swing by the Music room for extra practice.

With Mrs Emerson at my side, I practised the piece over and over, and as the day of the concert approached, I was growing incredibly nervous. On the evening itself, below the harsh and unforgiving spotlights, I managed to claw my way through the performance, then felt so awkward stood uncomfortably alone on the stage as roars of applause from those packed into the hall prevailed. When I searched the crowd for Mum and Dad and found them, their faces glowing, Dad wiping tears from his eyes, directly after the concert I signed up for violin lessons the following year.

And so that morning before I entered the music room, hoping Mr Martins wasn't there, I listened at the door before cracking it open to find the room empty. I sat at a desk thinking I'd look back through some of my sketches until registration.

"Mr Green. Well, well. What brings you to the music department this term, let alone this morning at such an early hour?" said Mr Martins who I hadn't seen sat at his desk.

"I've been ill, sir. Been practising at home," I lied.

"Is that right?" he said.

He got up, smiled, and walked to the cupboard where instruments were stored. Unlocking it, he said "didn't you need this?" and from inside he pulled out and handed me my violin. Noting my embarrassment, he assured me the curtains hadn't totally fallen on my music career and asked me what piece I'd be playing for my final composition, a live recording sent off to be scrutinised by examination moderators. He surmised correctly that I'd given no thought to it whatsoever, then before rushing off to do his "bloody playground duty," he shuffled through some papers on his desk and handed me a sheet containing a list of concertos, one of which he suggested I choose. But before he left, he asked me what I thought to be a strange question.

"Are you OK, Bethnal? You look, somehow, different," he said, then finishing his sentence, "you look, well, awake."

"Sorry, sir. I've been ill. That's why I've not been here. You can ask my form tutor if you want," I responded, not quite sure what he was trying to imply.

"No, no, I believe you. It's just unusual that you, anyone for that matter, might show any sort of enthusiasm for, well, music," he said, before rushing off.

Earlier in the year, we'd studied Baroque music, listening to various recordings of Vivaldi's *Four Seasons* in class. With his name the only one I recognised on the list, I tentatively selected one of his shorter concertos thinking that perhaps, with a modicum of effort, I might just scrape through the exam. I put the list in my bag and until registration flipped through the pages of *Italian Art*, again struck by the beautiful image of the girl on the cover, and her uncanny resemblance to Mercy.

Registration was normally a low-key affair with most students, their heads on their desks, trying to sleep. Others sat slouched around the classroom speaking in whispers, waiting for Mr Russell, our form tutor, late for registration as usual.

The moist odour of teenage adolescence hung heavily in the air and the livewire of the class, Ashley Smith, by far the most irritating boy in our class, was in particularly high spirits. Over the years most of us had learned to ignore him, especially girls who had long since tired of chasing him away. Standing by the door laughing loudly to himself, something he did most mornings, a group of the girls nearest to him at the front of the room, used to his weird behaviour, did their best to ignore him. His mistake that morning however, was pulling an aerosol from his blazer pocket, "accidentally" spraying a cheap mist among the girls. Bessie, the meticulously primped, no-nonsense big-breasted hard girl of the class, who wafted through school in an odour unique to her own specifications, was not be messed with that morning. She suddenly appeared from within the mist, and with impressive speed and accuracy, hurled her geography textbook at Ashley who slumped to the floor when it struck him with a heavy smack square on the side of his head, a small poppy-coloured bruise appearing just as Mr Russell arrived.

"Good morning. Everyone be quiet. Ashley, get up off the floor and get to your seat," he said, as he sat behind his desk.

Mr Russell taught history and we liked him because he spoke to us frankly, he told us exactly what we might expect out of life. Sometimes during his lessons, when he saw in our faces how little we cared for Luddites or Agrarian Revolutions, he shifted his discussion to a topic that kept us awake, more often than not concerning "awkward" issues relevant to our lives, moral dilemmas we might face in the next few years. He didn't use deflection strategies employed by most teachers who refused to answer questions they felt were "no-go" areas for classroom discussion. In fact, he was keen to debate controversial topics of the time such as underage sex or abortion.

I remember one amusing incident, when Kylie, the cheeky coquette of the class, Bessie's best friend, tried to embarrass him by asking him why boys wank so much. Sitting on the edge of our seats in a silence rarely witnessed in any of our lessons, we awaited his answer. An awkward silence hung in the room as he considered his response. He rose from his chair, slowly rounding his desk, then sitting on it, he looked around the room, his eyes finally settling on Kylie who sat squirming in her seat. For a moment, we thought that perhaps her question had overstepped the mark, but then, quite seriously, he said he would happily discuss the ins-and-outs of male masturbation if she were willing to enlighten us on the female perspective. As the class erupted into fits of laughter, the mortified Kylie sat blushing in the corner.

The map pinned to the wall behind his desk in the History room detailed a road trip he'd taken across America with his girlfriend, Sara, shortly after leaving university. He'd highlighted in a luminous yellow the route they'd taken before Sara abandoned him in San Francisco for a woman who, according to Sara, "held the key to her life." We suspected that key came in the shape of LSD, and the general consensus amongst us was that he, too, had spent a good deal of time in the late 1960s savouring the delights of what San Francisco had to offer.

His responses to our questions, especially regarding those "tricky" questions in 1970's Britain, mainly to do with sex, were blunt, and we respected him for this. I remember clearly, one particular day, just before the bell rang, when he concluded one of his stories with such impassioned candour, making it clear to us all that not talking about sexual relations openly, was irrational, anti-academic, harmful, not only to our development, but to a greater extent, to the development of the nation. He also urged us to think for ourselves, impressing upon us that decisions we made in life should always consider the welfare and concerns of others. As students filed out of that particular class, I remained behind, thinking about what he'd said, wondering how much of an impact his honesty had on kids like Ashley, Bessie and Kylie.

"Ashley, get me the register. Quick, the bell's about to go. And what's that mark on the side of your face?" he said, fresh howls of laughter hurrying Ashley from the room.

As he waited for the register, Mr Russell checked uniforms, politely informing individual students what to amend in order to remain within the requirements of an acceptable school dress code. A stickler for correct school uniform, the headmaster held form tutors directly responsible for any student who violated school uniform policy. Each morning, as Mr Russell's eyes landed on Bessie, a girl whose emerging identity was expressed in her own, provocative modifications to school uniform, he sighed, shaking his head, knowing that advice coming from a man his age, she could only ignore.

Ashley returned with the register just as the bell rang. As students spilled into the corridor Mr Russell asked me to remain behind, and once we were alone, asked me if I had a note for my absence. I suddenly panicked, and fumbling through my bag for the note, I realised I'd completely forgotten to write in the date as I'd intended. But fortunately he read it quickly, threw it in the bin, and told me to run along to my first lesson, so I skipped off, assuming that was the end of the matter.

My efforts to approach school positively began to flag during maths in period two. In our third lesson, French, I had lost all interest and sat at the back of the room by the window, daydreaming. When the French teacher, Mrs Trickett, enthusiastically announced the lesson objective for the day: how to say and spell, in French, the various parts of the body, I was mildly amused and thought back to the previous afternoon, and the sketches now pinned to my bedroom wall. But school being school, any enjoyment was short-lived. And so when Mrs Trickett drew simple stick figures of a man and woman on the board, highlighting gender variation by giving the woman a triangular body, armed with my newly-honed skills in shaping body parts, especially those of a woman, drawing matchstick men and women felt childish and insulting.

She tapped away at the board, snapping various sticks of chalk as she labelled then enunciated each body part aloud. I looked outside, across to the wall running the length of the playground, a net stretching along the top to stop balls from going into the house next door which the school owned. Behind the wall at the back of the house was a garden accessed via a rickety gate where the wall ended at the far end of the playground. Students were strictly forbidden entry to the garden, and to the swimming pool which took up most of it. On the first day of every new school year, all new students were threatened with expulsion should they enter the garden, a warning severe enough for most students.

Rumours gave what lay behind the wall in the garden great mystique, the oldest and most exciting was that a young couple were found dead at the bottom of the pool in the nineteen fifties, and after months of investigation requiring rigorous interrogation of all members of staff, including the Headmaster, it appeared the teenagers had committed suicide.

But the rumour that excited us most was that, from time to time, teachers would escape behind the wall to fuck. I found this particularly exciting because, based on an experience during the summer term of my second year, when I often stayed behind for music practice, I was almost certain that this was indeed the case. I remember passing the gate on my way home one evening I heard what sounded like teachers beside the pool, drinking and laughing. I lingered by the gate for some time, looking through a gap between the gate and the wall, and though I never actually saw anyone fucking, I heavily suspected sexual frolicking was the cause of such merriment.

"Bethnal Green, mon dieu! Would you get on with your work and stop daydreaming," shouted Mrs Trickett from the board, feigning her stern Gallic look of disapproval.

When she turned back to the board, my mind drifted back to behind the wall, and I imagined some of our teachers gathered around the pool for their end-of-year party given by the Headmaster in appreciation for their hard work throughout the year, many of them awarding him rare compliments, grateful for his generosity in providing free alcohol. From inside the house the sound of Jimi Hendrix floated into the garden, as did the wafting odour of marijuana. The pool was soon full of our teachers, laughing and screaming like the children they berated daily for such behaviour. Mr Russell was quick off the mark, trapping Ms Fiori, the melon-bosomed Italian teacher, in a corner of the pool, his head burrowed enthusiastically between her breasts.

"Would you please get a move on, Mr Green, you've yet to draw a thing. Come on, hurry up, I want to move on to something else," said Mrs Trickett who'd crept up to startle me.

"Yes, Miss, I'm thinking," I replied.

"You're not here to think, you're here to copy," she said, curtly, as she shuffled back to the board, her fat arse jumping from side to side below a polyester skirt she was clearly too big for.

I looked back towards the wall, hoping to rekindle the action in the pool, in particular Mr Russell's progress with Ms Fiori, but the lingering image of Mrs Trickett's quivering rear-end made this impossible. However, perched up on the wall was a black cat, its neck stretching over its shoulder, nodding and bobbing as it licked its back, its fine silhouette elegantly set against the blue morning sky, as if posing. I spent the rest of the lesson sketching its lithe little frame, until it disappeared into the garden behind the wall as doors crashed open and kids charged into the playground for morning break.

After break we had English, a lesson that always failed to inspire, mainly because of the unfortunate soul who taught us. Ms Geragthy, a pretty, young, Irish woman fresh out of college, was in the wrong job. She spent the majority of our lessons on the rack, her persecutors three boys whose only objective in English was to destroy her. Only in her lessons did this trio sit at the front of the classroom from where they tormented her, making her cheeks flame and her soft, curly hair, an odd mix of ginger or blond depending on how the light fell on it, seem unmanageable when she was under pressure.

Perhaps because of the courtesy and respect she had given us in her debut lesson, these boys thought she was a pushover, constantly mocking her, their often hostile comments making execution of her well-prepared lesson plans impossible. She sought advice from one of the more experienced teachers who recommended a number of ways how "to keep the little bastards quiet," but his suggestion of adopting an "iron fist" approach was not a technique that came easily to her. In her second lesson, trying to exact a level of control, she raised her voice to the three boys who just sat back rocking in their chairs, laughing at her. For a month or so, she did her best, before finally succumbing to defeat, reluctantly accepting that "learning to cope" was an aspect of teaching they never covered at teacher-training college.

The year wore on, wearing her out, her enthusiasm for her trade dwindling with each class, and we began to see in her the lethargy we recognised in most of our teachers. Her lessons became dull and predictable, a series of in-class writing tasks she never got around to marking. Sometimes, as we were scribbling away, I watched as she stared vacantly through the window, perhaps acknowledging that her decision to enter the noble profession of teaching had been a catastrophic error in judgement.

On that morning however, the boys began their attack the moment she entered the room. Though I'd always observed their behaviour with a detached sense of apathy, on that day their insults I thought especially cruel and spiteful, reviving a matter of some controversy on which the previous lesson had ended. They claimed Ms Geraghty had made comments she certainly hadn't, their mockery soon plummeting to comments bordering on personal insult. In a supportive spirit of female solidarity, I hoped one of the girls, Bessie perhaps, might sense Ms Geraghty's difficulty and turn on the boys. But she didn't, and, like me, she sat back and sleepily observed them torment her. And then Ms Geraghty finally snapped.

As the rest of us got on with our writing, the boys continued to needle her with subdued whispers she did her best to ignore. But, about twenty minutes into the lesson, a piercing shriek shook us in our seats, the boys suddenly stupefied into an abrupt silence. I looked up to see Ms Geraghty staring at us, her wild blue eyes throbbing in her crimson face, and as the last echo of her roar faded from the room, each of us remained locked to our seats, our eyes fixed on the mad woman before us, her tempestuous eyes, wide and insane, scanning the room for any sniffle of dissent, like a bull before a scarlet cape, breathing loudly through her nose, ready to strike.

"That is it!" she screamed, slamming her hand violently onto the desk of one of the boys.

For one so slight, normally of such gentle demeanour, she managed to summon remarkable strength, forcing the legs to shake as her hand connected with the top of the desk. With her palm flat on the desk, her eyes held us in an unusual state of suspended obedience, a revered silence reminiscent of when we were innocent eleven year-olds in senior school for the first time. She'd reached the tipping point, her dreams of making a difference in our lives through the beautiful voices in English literature crushed, in tatters, and as she glared around the room, mesmerising us with those fierce Celtic eyes, I could hear the dull and muted sounds of happier, more successful learning experiences coming from other classrooms in the corridor outside.

"Bethnal Green," she said, making me flinch, her strange voice several octaves lower than normal, chairs screeching as they scraped across the floor towards me. "Go immediately to Mr Jones' office. Tell him he's needed in room fourteen," she commanded.

The trio stared at me, their eyes questioning my loyalty. They knew the heavy-handed Headmaster, Mr Jones, was, simply put, a brute. But the boys that day deserved everything they had coming.

Minutes later, walking along the corridor I listened for the re-emerging spill of noise to follow me from my classroom, but none came, and nearing the stairs leading up to the Headmaster's office, I met Mr Russell.

"Everything OK, Bethnal?" he enquired.

"The Headmaster is needed in our room," I said, reluctant to provide details.

"English?"

"Yes, sir."

"Usual suspects?"

"Yes, sir."

"OK. Run along then."

"Yes, sir."

But about half way up the stairs, he called me, and so I stopped and turned. For a moment, he didn't say anything, just stood staring at me.

"Is everything OK, Bethnal?" he enquired once more.

"Yes, sir," I repeated, his gaze making me uncomfortable.

I turned once more towards the Headmaster's office, but he called me back again.

"I have to go to the Headm…" I said.

"I know where you're going. I mean, is everything OK with *you?*"

"With me, Sir? Of course it is," I repeated, trying to hold his stare.

"It's just that Mr Martins said he saw you this morning, very early, in the music room. It's very out of character for you to be in school so early," he said, searching my face for any flutter of deception.

"I just woke up early, Sir. I couldn't get back to sleep and decided to come in as I didn't have anywhere else to go."

"OK. Good. That's fine," he said, and nodded me on my way.

At the top of the stairs I stopped to think about what he'd said. Prior to that day Mr Russell had spoken few words to me, and now he was suddenly taking what appeared to be a genuine interest in my life.

As I stood before the Headmaster's door, I thought of how he delivered-school assemblies, sternly informing us how we should conduct ourselves in his school, and how, after each gathering, teachers deferentially bowed their heads as he strode out of the hall. I looked up at Mr Jones' door, the letters of his name in large block capitals high up, painted in a glossy white. I paused before knocking, thinking about how hard I should strike the door. I prayed for him not to be there.

I put my ear to the door and listened, then knocked, timidly, three times. Tok. Tok. Tok. On that third knock, my heart began to thump when I heard the heavy rumble of a chair move inside. I counted the footsteps as he approached the door, then heard him shuffling into his gown. When the door swung open, he appeared from behind a cloud of smoke, towering over me.

"Who are you and what do you want?" he said.

"Bethnal Green, Sir. There's a problem in room fourteen. Ms Geraghty's class, Sir," I said nervously, averting my eyes as he took a pull on his cigarette, inhaling sharply on hearing her name.

"Return to your room. Inform Ms Geraghty I'm on my way," he ordered.

Skipping back down the stairs I met Mr Russell again who nodded at me as I passed him.

I entered the classroom and informed Ms Geraghty that the Headmaster was on his way. In the same, unusually low voice in which she'd ordered me to fetch him, she instructed me to leave the door open and return to my seat.

Ms Geraghty continued to hold us tightly in her grip as we waited for the Headmaster. With the exception of the trio sitting submissively in their chairs, their eyes searching the floor below their desks, wild looks of excitement flashed between the other students. In the silence that followed, we listened to the busy taps on chalkboards coming from other classrooms, suddenly replaced by the faint clicking sounds of the Headmaster's footsteps, the clicks of his studs growing louder as he approached. Ms Geraghty got up, and with her arms folded, walked to the window, then casually back to the front of her desk, where, trembling slightly, she straightened the bottom of her blouse.

When the Headmaster entered, his work was swift.

"Which ones?" he demanded, his eyes failing to meet Ms Geraghty's.

She pointed to the trio.

"Come," he said, and with their eyes fixed to the floor, the boys trudged out of the room behind him.

Ms Geraghty closed the door, and as we turned and looked at each other, speculating in small groups what would happen to the boys, she returned to her seat, a wily grin rising in her face.

"Now, where were we?" she asked as she wrapped stray strands of hair behind her rosy ears. "Ah, yes, that's right. How to build tension in creative writing," she continued.

As we sat upright in our seats, she walked up and down the aisles passing out copies of the Gothic short story we were unable to finish in previous classes, a story that I quickly lost interest in.

And I wondered just how I might survive the long week ahead.

9

Diversions

Ms Geraghty had sacrificed so much to achieve the ordered diligence that was the drone of students taking it in turns to read of eerie windswept castles. Once I had read my paragraph, detailing creaky doors and things going bump in the night, I decided to take a break, and as I made my way to the door, Ms Geraghty nodded me permission to be excused.

On my way to the toilets I briefly considered skipping afternoon lessons. After English it was break time, then double geography, a lesson which might prove bearable depending on how well Mr Boodle was managing the hangover he had most Mondays. We knew the severity of his "migraine," as he often called it, by the manner in which he entered the room. After particularly punishing weekends, he slouched in, dark rings under his eyes, not saying a word. He would then pull from his bag a reel of celluloid which he attached to the projector, switched off the lights, and we'd watch documentaries of exploding volcanoes, tsunamis and other such natural disasters, as he nodded off at the back of the room. I decided to stay for geography and reassess matters at lunchtime.

Teachers looking for skivers like me, often patrolled the toilets during lessons, some even peeking under doors. So when I entered the stall, I closed the cubicle door behind me, dropped my trousers to my ankles and sat slowly down onto the icy seat. I leaned back onto the thin pipe running up the back of the wall to the hissing cistern above to check for new graffiti that covered the walls.

Despite stern warnings from the Headmaster in assemblies, the walls of the cubicles were covered in graffiti. Based on the numbers of amusing vignettes, irreverent graphic cartoons lampooning teachers, quite clearly I wasn't the only boy with artistic talent in the school. From time to time the Headmaster would check our pockets, looking for those talented rascals who used him as a centrepiece for their work. One such example was on the back of the door, a caricature showing Ms Richards, an unattractive heavy-set Latin teacher, generally hated by students and staff alike, grappling with the inner thighs of one of the dinner ladies, while she, herself, was being fucked from behind by the Headmaster.

The same trio featured on the wall too, just above the toilet paper where a budding surrealist had participants bent into positions humanly impossible. Clearly aware of his target audience, which included boys in the first and second years, he'd included large arrows labelling body parts in question for clarity - *cunt*, *dick*, and *tongue*, with brief explanations as to what they were and where they went, laboriously entitling his piece: *Jones sticking his dick in Richard's smelly cunt while she has her tongue in the dinner lady.*

The door also functioned as a message board for rival football fans consisting mainly of insults between Arsenal and Tottenham fans. A lone West Ham fan had scribbled his loyalties high up on the left side of the door, and below it, daubed thickly in a heavy black marker, a blunt response of *fuck off cockney cunt.*

As I scanned the rest of the cubicle, it was clear the school had a disproportionately high number of *cunts* either studying or working there. Considering his wife taught PE at the school, and his daughter was in the first year, I thought it highly unlikely that the music teacher, Mr Martins, was a *gay cunt*.

I thought I'd check out the cubicle next door, but as I bent down to pull my trousers up, standing at the urinal trough that stretched the length of the wall outside the cubicles, I saw a boy's feet. I listened as his zip descended and the splash of his jet hit the wall. After shaking himself dry, he cleared his chest of heavy phlegm, expelling it with a slap against the urinal wall. I thought he might shuffle back into one of the cubicles when he released a couple of rapid, trumpet-like farts in quick succession, but after a loud, unapologetic burp, he zipped himself up and trotted off back to class.

In that final year of school I had the impression my body was changing almost daily. With the toilet seat comfortably warm, I thought I'd stretch the break a few more minutes by conducting a brief examination for the slowly emerging man in me, an activity I normally reserved for the safety and privacy of my bedroom. With each inspection I always discovered something new, thicker and darker hairs appearing on my body, and on that day, I saw for the first time, a thin line of dark hair, like a faint shadow, slowly making its way from my cock to my belly button.

As I continued my inspection, I thought of Mercy, of her exceptional beauty, of our first day together when she was lying in my lap with her eyes closed. And then, quite unexpectedly, in one swift involuntary movement, my cock shifted up and sideways onto my thigh, quickly rising until it was fully erect, then twanging out towards the door. I'd been out of class longer than expected, and growing anxious, I hoped my erection would dwindle if I re-read some of the messages on the walls. It was then that the unthinkable, the dark and daring possibility of taking it in hand, came to mind. But masturbating in school was absurd, a line I couldn't cross, until, of course, I looked down to see it looking up at me, as if smiling, as if saying, "yes, you can."

On my way back to class, the bell rang for break. Classroom doors flew open immediately filling the corridor with kids charging in both directions. I sat for a while in the empty room, the stale odour of teenage sweat still clogging the air, thinking of the fun I'd just had in the toilet.

It seemed I'd discovered a way of making the week bearable, that trip to the toilets during Ms Geraghty's class on that Monday spawning an ingenious way for me to deal with the tedium of those long days at school. In short, over the next few days, when a lesson became too dull, I slipped out to the toilets to "think of Mercy," and by breaktime on Wednesday I was seeing school in a whole new light. I'd quickly established a system to limit teacher suspicion of my absences, remaining in lessons for the first ten minutes, a period in which they showed greatest enthusiasm for their craft, thus minimising the chance of my request being denied. Then, at about the fifteen minute mark, when any meaningful instruction had finished, I sought permission to be excused, and was skipping off down the corridor again.

On Wednesday after school however, I was in a state of panic, thinking this happy distraction was producing some very disturbing side effects. I'd listened to the *Summer Concerto* from Vivaldi's *Four Seasons* a number of times, and with practice, thought I might do it justice. But that afternoon, as I practised for my final violin examination, my fingers felt unnaturally slow, unable to produce the right chords, and I thought the worst, fleeing the Music room convinced that this loss of agility in my fingers a direct result of my hand being so firmly cupped around my cock for most of that week.

On my way home, by the gate to the garden at the end of the playground, the black cat I'd seen preening itself on the wall earlier that week suddenly leapt out in front of me. Stopping momentarily, it jerked its head to display a muffled lump of bright yellow feathers hanging from its mouth, a tiny budgerigar, limp and dead, its neck drooping to the side of the cat's mouth. Its glazed eyes stared unapologetically up into mine, its small fragile quarry a stark colourful contrast against its tight black jaw. I imagined the gruesome final moments for the small bird, wondering why anything so beautiful deserved such a violent end, and then great terror tore through me when I thought that perhaps, this small unfortunate creature might be our bird, Harry.

When the school secretary saw me in such a state of alarmed dishevelment as I entered her office, she immediately waived school policy concerning student use of the school phone and dialled our number. As I waited for Mum to answer, I pictured her in the garden, tears streaming down her face, her eyes searching the sky for her little bird to return. The ringing seemed interminable, then, just as I passed the receiver to the secretary, she answered.

"Mum!" I said, listening carefully for sobs, looking at the secretary stood next to me, staring anxiously at me.

"Hello? Bethnal? Everything alright, love?" she said.

"Mum, is Harry OK?"

"Yes, he's fine, love. Why do you ask?"

"Oh, nothing. I'll tell you when I get home."

"OK, but get a move on. I've got your tea on. It's fish fingers tonight, is that alright?"

"Yes, Mum, that's great. I'll be home in half an hour," I said, relieved Harry was still with us.

But I've digressed, not purposely so. But maybe so. Details of what happened on the Friday afternoon of that week I hesitate to share, simply as the incident that unfolded still ranks as probably the most embarrassing of my life.

10

Red-Handed

In hindsight, I was rather foolish to introduce a competitive edge to my grand scheme, the *project*, which rather cockily, I'd begun to call it. Quite early in the week, I'd starting setting targets for the number of visits to the toilets I could successfully pull off in a day. Despite my fears about side effects I'd had on Wednesday after school, I arrived back in class just before home time, flushed with pride at having managed three successful "appointments" that day. I set myself a more ambitious target of four visits the following day, Thursday, which I easily smashed with two lessons to spare. The following day, Friday, I set myself the unimaginable target of five "appointments."

On Friday morning, I got off to a great start, easily managing two visits before break. With a couple of lessons before lunch, and three in the afternoon, I saw no reason for not meeting my objective by the end of the school day.

I'd managed to extract from Mum the previous evening a note excusing me from cross-country that afternoon, which meant spending the afternoon sitting in classes of the year below me. However, in the first lesson after lunch, I was having second thoughts about carrying on. I was meeting Mercy the following day, and, in the unlikely event of her planning to strip me of my virginity over the weekend, I thought it better I "save myself" for her.

In the final lesson, Religious Education, with just forty minutes to the bell, I sat staring at the second hand on the clock above the blackboard clicking round, each click a second closer to meeting Mercy. But five minutes into the lesson, with the teacher unconvincingly detailing more irrational tales of unnecessary suffering, I changed my mind, and on the fifteen minute mark, I was off for my final appointment of a very stimulating week.

On the way to the toilets, I paused to peek into a classroom to see Ms Geraghty slumped in her chair, a blank look of hopelessness stretching across her face as listless students read from the same Gothic story she was using in our class. Turning the corner at the bottom of the corridor, I ran into Mr Russell, his coffee splashing across my shoulder, immediately seeping into my shirt.

"Sorry, sir," I said, wiping coffee from my hands.

"Bethnal. What are you doing out of class?"

"Toilet, sir."

"Be quick, and hurry back."

"Yes, sir. Sorry, sir," I said as I watched him head up the stairs to the staffroom.

A fundamental requirement for a successful visit required me being alone. Under such conditions, I could be in and out in three to four minutes, but when interrupted, I would wait until the intruder had gone at which point I simply picked up where I'd left off. Only on one occasion that week, when a boy came in and sat in the cubicle next to mine, was I unable to see things through. Thinking that perhaps he was in there for the same reason as me, I tried to proceed in silence, but as my legs stiffened and my breathing became heavy, I worried he'd hear me and so I gave up and returned to class.

So that afternoon, when I entered the toilets, I made a quick sweep of the other cubicles before getting comfortable in my favourite end cubicle, ready for the grand finale of the week. What I should have done is simply knocked a quick one out and return to class. But I made a rash judgement, foolishly trying to prolong procedures with a technique I'd been developing for some two to three months, which until that afternoon, I'd toyed with only in the privacy of my bedroom. In short, it was a technique that produced the most thrilling sensation, but required a great degree of self-control. The trick to achieving the best results was when I felt that shuddering delight from inside my cock, that first wonderful twinge of rising ejaculation, I would stop, take a series of deep breaths, and wait, suspending climax, and bask for a moment in the delicious shiver running through my body.

However, the manoeuvre required discipline, the temptation always there to simply finish it off, the line between success and failure so fine. With just one stroke too many, procedures would rush to a close. But with the right timing, and controlled discipline, I could take myself to the very edge of climax, delaying ejaculation by just a stroke or two, producing a far thrilling release sixty seconds later. However, development of this technique was still in its early stages, and so I have no idea what possessed me, on that afternoon, to experiment with a procedure I had yet to adequately master.

With my legs spread, slumped back on the pipe of the cistern with my school shirt and jumper wedged up around the top of my chest, I thought of Mercy, naked, in school, clicking her way down the corridor in sexy high-heels, on her way to join me in the toilets. I listened for those short, sharp clicks of her sexy red stilettos echoing around the toilet as she entered, walking slowly until she was outside the cubicle. Wearing only sunglasses, her hair tied up in a bun exposing the beautiful softness of her neck, I could hear her short sigh-like gasps, gradually rising into deeper, sharper breaths before she tapped the door. I instructed her to ask me *nicely* to unlock the door which she did, her desire to enter and finish me off quickly taking hold of her, and in frenzied desperation to get at me, her tapping slowly grew into a manic slapping. But before I released the latch, she had to tell me, once more, whisper through the door, why she wanted in. I put my ear to the door to listen to her, to hear why she wanted me, then released the latch and the door swung open.

But she didn't rush in, she just stood in the frame of the door her legs shoulder width apart, watching me admire her, her tongue slowly emerging from between her cherry red lips. When she caught sight of my stiff cock, she fell to her knees, her hands landing softly on my straining thighs. Then, she took hold of me, my body stiffening as I felt her soft skin and the warmth of her short breaths, soft exhalations of deep desire on my stomach, her lips, her exquisite lips, so full, so warm, parting, slowly, lowering her head onto me.

"GREEN! GREEN! Are you in there?" the voice demanded, the rapid thumps on the door startling me, terrifying me, so completely disorientating me that I lost my balance and tumbled sideways off the toilet, landing on the floor, wedged between the bowl and the wall.

I saw the tips of Mr Russell's shoes under the door, twitching impatiently as he continued his violent banging, almost forcing the door from its hinges.

"Green, come on out, I know you're in there. Out!" he continued, the echoing crash of his hand beating the door, bouncing off the walls, rendering me speechless.

I struggled to my feet, desperately trying to think of a reasonable account for these extra-curricular diversions. But this sudden shock of my form tutor catching me wanking had my head in such a spin, I didn't know what to do. My cock however, still very much in party mode, was immune to the alarm the rest of its owner was experiencing, and as I straightened myself up, glistening threads of viscous jism, dancing jets of joy, shooting in all directions around the cubicle, rushed out of me.

"Green! Green! Come out. Now! I want to talk to you!" he screamed, each welt of his hand on the door growing more furious. "I know what you're doing in there. So out. This second!"

I grabbed some toilet paper and quickly wiped *evidence* from the walls. Even if he threatened to drag me to the Headmaster, I'd admit to nothing, I'd deny any accusation of being caught in such a shameful act.

"Green, are you coming out or am I to fetch the Headmaster?" he continued, this serious breach of school conduct pushing the normally mild-mannered Mr Russell to his limits.

"No, sir. Yes… sir. I'm coming out," I replied, straightening my uniform, wiping any remaining traces of semen from the walls then flushing streams of toilet paper down the toilet.

When I opened the door, our eyes met.

"Step out here. Now," he ordered.

He stepped into the cubicle, looked into the toilet and then behind it. Lifting the seat, he hopped up to inspect the cistern, trying to remove the lid which was attached to the wall. He stepped down and out of the cubicle, breathing impatiently.

"Bethnal," he said, his voice softening, a ploy to extract a truth I'd never reveal.

"Yes, sir," I replied, feeling tears rising in my eyes.

"Look at me," he demanded, and I did as he asked, noting a fleeting look of concern in his face. "Now. Tell me what's going on?"

Determined not to confess to such disgraceful behaviour, I bowed my head and said nothing.

"Bethnal, look at me," he repeated, and when I looked up, a tear fell from my eye, my lower jaw beginning to tremble.

He rested his hand tenderly on my shoulder as I wiped my eyes with the sleeve of my jumper.

"Son, don't cry, we can work this out," he said, gently raising my chin with his index finger. "I've just got to ask you a few questions, some very important questions that you must answer truthfully. And then we'll clear this whole mess up. Do you understand me, Bethnal? It's very important that you tell me the truth."

"Yes, sir," I replied, sucking in air, trying to stop my body from shaking.

"Bethnal, it's been brought to my attention this week, by various members of staff, that you've been spending rather a lot of time excusing yourself from their lessons. Mr Martins has informed me that you have uncharacteristically been showing up very early in the Music room when most days you struggle to make it to registration. Bethnal, something has clearly happened to you, and I want to know what it is. I want to know *what* is going on."

But what could I say? How could I admit to him, to any teacher, that I'd been playing with my cock all week? Head bowed, I had little option but to remain silent.

"OK, Bethnal. Let's do it like this. I'll ask you some questions, and you simply say yes or no. But you have to tell me the truth, OK?"

I shrugged a muted sign of agreement.

"Something has happened to you lately hasn't it?" he began confidently.

"Yes," I sniffled.

"Good. Now, is everything OK at home?"

"Yes, of course," I replied, unsure of his implications concerning my perfect home life.

"You're getting along OK with your mum and dad?" he ventured, at which point I understood the gist of his questioning.

"Sir, everything is fine at home," I responded, wiping my nose with a sleeve.

"Are you sure, son?"

"Yes, sir. Why shouldn't it be?"

"OK. Now, is it true that when you make it back to your classes from these absences, would it be fair to say that you've been in a, let's say, happier mood?"

"Yes, sir."

"OK. Listen. Whatever your answer to the next question is, I give you my word, son, it's only going to be between me and you and I promise that I'll help you sort it out. Do you understand me Bethnal?" he said, clearly the question he'd been leading to all along.

He placed his hands on my shoulders and asked me to look him in his eyes. Steeling myself for the most embarrassing question an adult, no less a teacher, could put to a fifteen-year-old boy in the hazy developmental stages of personal exploration, I looked up at him. As he sought the right words to use, a young kid suddenly charged into the toilets, skidded to a halt, then dashed back out the moment he saw Mr Russell.

Mr Russell composed himself, then looking me directly in the eyes, took a deep breath. Again he sought the right words to broach the delicate topic of masturbation.

"OK, Bethnal. Tell me straight. Are you, in any shape or form, indulging in the recreational use of any banned substances?"

I stood staring at him blankly, unsure of what these words meant. His question sounded serious. A trick perhaps? He hadn't used the word masturbation. But I'd confess to nothing, certainly not accusations I didn't understand.

"I, I, I, don't know what that means, sir," I replied.

"Are you doing drugs, lad?"

Only then did it all make sense. That's what he was looking for. He was under the wonderfully wrong impression I was skipping lessons to do drugs. The serious nature of his questioning, his search of the toilet – he thought I was doing drugs. I'd never even seen a drug. I suddenly realised he had absolutely no idea what I was actually up to; he had no inkling of the thrilling wank marathon I'd been having all week. But how could he have imagined *me* doing drugs? Were all of my teachers under the impression that the quiet boy, Green, was nipping off to the toilets to load up with drugs during their lessons? I had to assure him that I wasn't.

"No, sir. No, sir. I swear to you I'm not. No, sir. No, I'm not," I said protesting my innocence.

"OK, son. I believe you. Relax, relax. But still, I'm at a loss as to why you are spending so much time out of lessons. Can you shed some light on this?" he said, trying to smile.

All I could think of was how wrong he was to think I'd been taking drugs. I needed a credible excuse to successfully draw a line under this not-to-be-repeated mishap, and as I stood looking at his shoes, trying to think, I sensed a wry tone in his voice when he began to pursue a line of questioning on a matter wholly unrelated to my predicament.

"What's that on your collar?" he said stepping towards me, a widening grin making his eyes glow as he studied my collar.

"Coffee, sir. You spilled it on me in the corridor," I replied smugly, hoping to offload some of the guilt onto him.

"No, it's not coffee," he said, his eyes firmly fixed on a particular part of my collar as he pulled me in front of the mirror.

Squinting into the mirror, I saw the glistening shiny pendant resting just below my chin on my shirt collar, its smooth grey sheen, with the dull look of chewing gum, a small moon about the size of a fifty pence piece, a wayward bullet of fresh cum, slowly sinking into the fabric of my shirt. As blood coursed up through my body into my neck, neither of us knew what to do or say, but then he started to laugh, a menacing laugh that seemed to bounce off the toilet walls, and issuing me a warning to remain in lessons, he ruffled my hair and I sprinted out into the corridor, the sound of his laughter drowned by the sweet sound of the bell ringing for the weekend.

11

Wow!

Standing in the darkness on the upstairs landing, I was growing impatient as I listened to Mum and Dad downstairs. I wanted to call Mercy from the phone in the living room, but that evening, as Dad got ready for his nightshift, he seemed to be taking longer than usual. When Dad worked nights, Mum always walked with him as far as the shop on the corner of our street where she kissed him goodbye, then popped into the shop and bought a bag of her favourite mints that she slowly crunched through while watching TV later that evening. When at last I heard the ruffled swish of coats and the latch of the front door click open, I shot into my bedroom and from my window, watched them walk off up the street together. I rushed downstairs, switched off the TV and carefully dialled the number.

"Bethnal?" Mercy said.

"Yes, yes, it's me. How did you know?" I said, gripping the receiver with both hands.

"Honey, I've been waiting all week for this call!" she responded.

In his cage just above the TV, Harry chirped and flapped his wings.

"Hi," I managed, "just calling about tomorrow. We said about eleven o' clock. Is that, is that OK?"

"Sweetheart, could we make it more like, say, one. I got some errands to run in the morning?"

"Yeah, that's great," I said, "I'll wait for you outside at one then. OK?"

"Sure, sweetie. How was your week at school?" she enquired.

"I'll tell you tomorrow," I said, "my mum's here and she's got to call her sister. So, I'll see you tomorrow. OK?"

"OK. I'll look for you out of the window. Looking forward to it. Bye."

I hung up, and thought of her calling me "sweetie" and "honey," talking to me as if she'd known me for years. I thought of calling her again, quickly, but with Mum on her way back, I couldn't risk it, so I sat in Dad's chair and looked out into the garden, thinking back to a time in primary school when I was unexpectedly praised by my favourite teacher, her kind words leaving me in a humbled state of mild embarrassment, just as I felt hearing Mercy telling me she'd been "waiting all week" for my call.

Mum came in carrying a plastic bag, walking straight through to the kitchen. I heard a small hissing pop as she opened a bottle of Coke.

"Do you want a drink, love? They get dearer by the day up at that shop. I can get Coke for half the price down the Holloway Road. They think I don't notice, but I do you know. Have you been on the phone, why's the TV turned off?" she said, coming into the living room and handing me the glass.

"Wrong number," I said, slurping down a mouthful of Coke.

"Are you OK, dear? You look a little flushed," she said, leaning over me and feeling my forehead.

Harry flapped excitedly in his cage.

"You are, you know. I think you've got a temperature. Wait there, let me get some aspirin," she said, hurrying off to the bathroom.

"Maybe you'd better stay in bed tomorrow, love. Looks like you've got something coming on again," she said, returning with two aspirins which I swigged down with a large gulp, assuring her I was fine.

"I just need some rest. I'll be fine in the morning. Anyway, I have plans tomorrow with friends. I'm going to head on up," I said, and rushed up to my room.

I slept soundly that night, and the following morning after a quick bath, I returned to my room and tried on every shirt I owned. I'd never had problems getting ready to go out before, but looking at the shirts in a pile under the mirror, none seemed right. I took the only shirt left hanging in the wardrobe, the one I wore on special occasions, wriggled into it, and though still not quite right, knew it would have to do. I went down the stairs quietly, and, with one foot out the door, I shouted my goodbye. But as on the previous week, I was summoned back into the living room where Mum and Dad were standing side by side, somewhat ceremoniously, as if about to present me with a prize. Their eyes darted from my crispy clean shirt to my smooth shiny hair, slicked back with a generous wad of Dad's Brylcreem.

"Yeah?" I said.

"Have a good day, son. Give us a call if you're going to be late," said Dad, stepping forward and squeezing a ten-pound note into my hand, Mum's eager eyes twinkling for details of my day. But that's all that was said and so off I went.

At Lancaster Gate the sun was high in the sky, pouring its wondrous warmth into beautiful London. Sitting on the wall outside the flats, I noticed a black cab parked on the other side of the road. At first I thought it was empty, but then the plump, crimson face of the taxi driver appeared in his window, an unlit cigarette dangling from his mouth.

"You gotta light, mate?"

"No, I'm sorry. I don't smoke," I replied.

"I dint ask you if you fuckin' smoked, I asked if you 'ad a fuckin' light," he said, wheezing, and as he disappeared back into his cab, I heard Mercy call my name.

"Bethnal," she called again, and I turned to see her skipping along the concrete path in a white weightless summer dress, dipping at the front, her breasts shuddering provocatively below the thin cotton. She took my hand, pulling me back towards the main entrance to the flats, where the doors were propped open by two picnic baskets.

"Help me with these," she said, passing me one of the heavy baskets.

I assumed we were heading for the park just off the main road, but at the bottom of the path, she crossed the road, and after briefly speaking with the chubby taxi driver, he rolled out of his taxi and helped us put the picnic baskets in the boot. Then, she flung open the back door, and smiling at me, nodded for me to get in. She gave the driver further instructions before hopping in beside me, her dress flying up, giving me a sudden glimpse of her thighs as she landed on the seat.

"That's everything," she said to the driver, slamming the door behind her.

Then, like an excited schoolgirl, she took my hand in hers, shuffled up next to me, leaned over, and kissed me on the cheek, this playful, innocent kiss reaffirming what I'd been feeling all week, what I'd suspected since the moment I met her. I was in love.

As we headed west along the Bayswater Road, I nodded and smiled as she told me it was her first ride in a London taxi and that she'd got up early to shop at a local market. I was still consumed by that kiss, thinking how much I wanted to make love to her.

I thought it odd when the taxi dropped us off outside a Victorian cemetery. A black wrought-iron fence stretched the length of the block, and peering through it, I saw the tops of grey headstones, just about visible, peeking above unkempt vegetation. My initial impression was that the cemetery had been long abandoned, but with hordes of people streaming through the entrance, two enormous iron gates, and along a central thoroughfare dividing the cemetery, a promenade, about the width of Oxford Street, this clearly wasn't the case.

Parents with pushchairs talked among themselves as they unleashed dogs that scampered into wild shrubbery creeping everywhere. Children screamed, charging in on bikes and scooters, racing up the central thoroughfare which stretched as far as the eye could see. Estimating the exact size of the cemetery was difficult, but just visible through the ubiquitous unruly overgrowth were the warped and crumbling red-brick perimeter walls. Walking through the gates, it soon became clear that the charm of the cemetery lay in its beautiful state of crumbling disrepair, long abandoned to unrelenting elements from above and shifting nature below.

As we made our way along the path, I was surprised to see so many graves packed so tightly together, many of the headstones twisting up and out of the earth as if in pain, while others had toppled completely to dissolve within knotted shrubs, some reduced to what looked like small grey bricks. Those headstones that had weathered the elements more successfully belonged to Victorians wealthy enough to commission skilful artisans whose extravagant craftsmanship, of such finesse, had produced a range of impressive designs, from small statues and simply-carved epitaphs, to crypts the size of small houses. Many were adorned with what was clearly a popular choice, flamboyant, life-size, trumpet-tooting angels feigning ostentatious fanfares to the dearly departed.

And so, within this fading beauty, the cemetery had the feel of a big city park. Joggers running, cyclists riding, and even at one point, swerving in and out of strollers, a posse of in-line skaters gliding past. Children snacking on crisps and chocolate soon found playmates in an expanding army of elusive squirrels, the most enterprising ones among them standing upright on hind legs, their bushy tails twitching, rigorously assessing each child before snatching morsels and darting off into the shrubbery.

Mercy paused at the grave of a famous suffragette, explaining exactly what the word meant, using words like "pioneers", "forward-thinking" and "courageous". She compared the Women's Movement at the turn of the century in Britain to the more recent Civil Rights Movement of the 1950s and 1960s in her own country. Like Martin Luther King, who I had heard of, the woman buried before us had also fought for liberation, and Mercy read to me the inscription summarising the woman's fascinating life but rather tragic end. And then, as we turned back to the path, we found ourselves surrounded by a small mob of squirrels.

Mercy immediately slumped to her haunches, stretching her arm to them, declaring them all "so cute." They darted back and forth around us, their little noses quivering, and when one of them sniffed at the basket I was holding, Mercy slipped her hand inside and pulled out a piece of bread. As crumbs spilled to the ground, the squirrels got excited. Ever alert for signs of foul play, they flinched excitedly, their nervous little heads quirking as they eyed crumbs sprinkled below her hand. Then one squirrel, much smaller but clearly more adventurous than the rest, slowly approached her hand. Up on its hind legs, its tiny nostrils flaring, it gazed directly into Mercy's eyes. As the two of them held each other's stare, the other squirrels fidgeted, anxiously watching their courageous little sister so close to Mercy's hand. Mercy glanced up at me, thrilled by the little squirrel's curiosity, but then, as she turned back, the squirrel shot off behind a headstone. Mercy sprang up, wiped her hands, and suggested we explore one of the many smaller paths leading towards the perimeter wall where I could just make out solitary figures, their small heads rising, dipping and disappearing in and out of the dense foliage.

As I followed her along one of the narrow paths, the screams of children on the central path behind us slowly faded. In the wild and rugged beauty in this part of cemetery, there were far fewer headstones. Those remaining were small, worn down into small stubs and wrapped in wiry strands of unruly, relentless vegetation pulling them down into the earth. Looking about me at scores of butterflies fluttering in the soft breeze, occasionally settling on small clumps of brightly coloured flowers, we could have been deep in the heart of England.

As we approached the perimeter wall, the path seemed to disappear. Mercy continued to push her way through the wild overgrowth and I wondered if she knew where she was going. When we reached the wall and it appeared we were at a dead-end, stretching her arm back towards me, she took hold of my hand and whispered that we were "almost there." My eyes ran the length of her white and slender arm, all the way up to the tip of her shoulder, slightly reddened in the increasing strength of the sun.

But when we arrived at the wall, she suddenly released my hand and disappeared into a gap between the wall and a large, sturdy bush. I dragged the picnic basket behind me as I followed her through, pleasantly surprised to arrive into a small clearing with well-worn grass, roughly the size of two double beds and shaded by branches stretching from a tree on the other side of the perimeter wall behind us.

"What d'ya think? Perfect for a picnic?" she said, wiping the creases from her dress.

"Perfect," I replied, smiling at her, wondering how on earth she had discovered such a place.

She pulled a large red and blue plaid blanket from the basket and tossed it into the air, whooping excitedly as it descended, its edges unfolding flat onto the grass. She hopped onto its centre, and on her knees, smoothed out the ripples until the blanket was as flat as a table top. She sprang up, and in one fluid movement, kicked off a shoe which shot like a bullet against the wall. She then kicked off the other, falling back as she kicked out, and the other shoe flew up into the tree remaining lodged between the branches which had us rolling around the blanket laughing uncontrollably. Not to be outdone, I loosened my laces and kicked out, hoping my shoe would join hers in the tree, but my other foot slipped on the silky blanket, and as I came crashing down, my shoe flew high into the air and over the wall.

She jumped up, and on tip toes, looking over the wall, she searched for the shoe. I assumed fetching it would be easy, but I discovered that on the other side of the wall, the perilous tracks of the tube network ran above ground, and as I searched for the shoe, I heard the familiar rattle of the tube coming from down the line. As it sped by, a sudden slap of wind struck our faces, then we watched as the undercarriage spat out a mangled piece of leather. We fell back onto the blanket, rolling around, again laughing hysterically, and when we finally stopped, I could see in her eyes that she was up to something.

"I want you to do something for me," she said, teasingly, spreading herself across the blanket and patting a spot beside her.

My heart began to thump. My *time*, I sensed, had finally arrived.

"Wait. Before you get comfortable, do me a favour, sweetie. In the basket there's a bottle of wine, next to it, a corkscrew. Let's crack it open," she said.

I fumbled through the basket for the wine then turned to see her sitting up, her arm stretched towards me. As she unscrewed the cork, I thought her plan to ply me with wine before having her wicked way with me very ingenious, and as she filled my glass, my hand trembled.

"I want to make a toast," she said, and holding up her glass, she paused, searching for words to fit the occasion. "Here's to life, that it may be long, healthy, happy and meaningful. Cheers," she exclaimed, and after clinking our glasses, I took a long pull from the glass.

"How is it?" she asked.

"How is it what?" I replied.

"The wine."

"It's good. I've never had wine before. Well, no, I did try some white wine before, but not red. Yeah, it's good, I like it," I said, nervously downing the remainder of my glass which sent a sudden flush running through me, making my face warm.

"OK. I want you to do something for me. It's going to require a little work, but you look up to it. And besides, it will be a new experience for at least one of us," she said, coyly.

As she shifted herself into a number of positions on the blanket, I poured myself more wine, watching as she rolled around. I thought of how girls had the innate ability to tease, Nature's absurd evolutionary twists and turns short-changing us boys, programming us to think of sex as much as possible from about the age of twelve onwards. Girls held the keys to our engines that always seemed to be revving, and watching her squirm around the blanket, I felt what I hoped were tremors of sexual tension running between us. But, again, I couldn't be sure, and briefly considered a proactive "quick-strike" approach, a rudimentary manoeuvre that simply required me to hop on her. However, self-doubt, that ever-present demon resting on my shoulder, whispered that her intentions were innocent, that man-handling her would be a catastrophic move, I'd destroy the moment, she'd probably run off, and I'd end up going home shoeless, ashamed, and worst of all, still a virgin.

I poured another glass of wine, gulping it down quickly.

"Whoa! Slow down, honey, this ain't soda. You gotta take this slow. I'll have to carry you outta here if you keep putting it away like that," she said, refilling my glass and winking at me. "Besides, I need you thinking straight for what I want you to do for me."

"Well, just tell me, what do I need to do?" I said, impatience nervously whining inside, her cheeky smile goading me.

"OK," she said, "I want you to sketch me. Now. Here. I've never been sketched before, a first time for everything, huh?" she said, winking at me again, and falling back on to the blanket, she closed her eyes.

I pulled my sketchpad from my bag, and as I sharpened a pencil, I looked up to see an enormous cumulus cloud move in front of the sun, and just behind it a Jumbo Jet straining in its descent into Heathrow airport, just a few miles to the west of us. I watched as it disappeared into the cloud, re-reappearing directly over us, thinking it could have been the plane that had brought her from America, and that perhaps, at that moment, another "Mercy" was looking down on the verdant patchwork quilt of little England, floating in to bring life to another lucky English boy. As it disappeared behind us, I saw in the distance, another plane descending, and in quieter moments much later that afternoon, lying next to her, listening to her breathe as she slept, I watched plane after plane slowly descending into London, feeling happier than I'd ever been.

Once I was ready, I instructed her how I wanted her to lay, shifting the angle of her body so her head was just in front of my knees, the rest of her body stretched out across the blanket, offering me a delightfully unrestricted view of her breasts. After a few stroking swoops of my pencil, I was immersed in my work, and in the silence of the next hour or so, I traced every part of her, hard-wiring her beauty into my memory forever.

As I was putting the finishing touches to it, she began to stir.

"How much longer, I want to see it?" she said.

"Just a little longer," I replied, "there's something missing, something I have to include. I need just a little more time. A few more minutes," I replied, not entirely sure what that something missing was, but acutely aware that I wanted so much for her to like what I'd drawn.

She wanted more wine, so I rummaged through the basket, pulling out from under what appeared to be enough food to feed a small country, a burgundy bottle, a wine from the Dordogne, somewhat bigger than the first. When I turned to pass her the bottle, she was kneeling upright in the middle of the blanket, the shoulder straps of her dress hanging loosely at her sides, the top half of her dress rolled down to her waist revealing her bare breasts. With the help of my crotch, I just managed to catch the bottle as it fell from my hand before she swiped it from me and opened it.

"I thought you might need a little more inspiration," she said as she popped the cork, filling our glasses, then stretching out once more across the blanket and closing her eyes.

My glass shook in one hand, my pencil in the other as I stared at the curves of her perfect breasts. Hoping to slow the wild pounding in my ears and to stop the involuntary shaking of my hands, I downed my wine, taking long steady breaths as I tried to calm myself.

My skin was burning, the sweat seeping out of me making my pencil slip between my fingers. I poured more wine, taking nervous swigs as I tried not to look at her breasts. I realised that this was my cue, the moment, the *time*. I had to act, but I was still shaking, and overcome with an infantile sense of inadequacy, I pulled the pad closer to my face, so when she opened her eyes she wouldn't see the shambling wreck before her.

But I couldn't resist peeking over my pad to see those breasts, within such easy touching distance. I continued to shake and looked up into the sky, searching for more planes sailing in, for any distraction, anything to help me stop trembling. When I heard the shallow breathing of her sleeping once more, I was grateful for such a generous, timely respite, but knew I was teetering on the edge of the most important event of my life, and I simply wasn't measuring up.

I continued to monitor planes floating slowly over us into Heathrow until the pounding in my ears began to fade. I then picked up my pad to add some final touches, but it was suddenly snatched from me and I looked up to see Mercy on her knees, the wild look in her eyes telling me protestation was useless.

When she pounced, she had me on my back in one swift movement, hovering over me for a moment before swooping down and plunging her tongue into my mouth, a warm fleshy tail swishing its softness over mine, simultaneously producing, in equal measure, distress and desire, forcing from somewhere within me a soft groan of pure, desperate delight.

Her strength surprised me, making even the smallest contribution to foreplay impossible, and as her hips began to writhe across my belt, grinding in small circles, she released short soft gasps. Her tongue suddenly swept down across my face, finding the smooth skin behind my ear, never before touched by anyone other than myself, each touch of its tip zapping my body, forcing my back to rise and arch, pushing my midsection into her. Then she raised herself up, just slightly, and momentarily weightless above me, she pulled the shirt from me and I felt her tireless tongue gliding across my chest. She rose up again and released my arms, taking my hands and directing them onto her breasts. This manoeuvre proved particularly problematic as I felt myself coming. From somewhere, I found the strength to haul her from me, rolling her onto the blanket, then moving quickly, assuming responsibility, copying her techniques, first running my tongue across her neck and mouth, then down over the soft skin on the upper reaches of her chest, in search of what I really wanted, her soft breasts in my mouth. Feeling the warmth of her breasts on my face, my tongue sought her nipples, small pips, each touch of my tongue producing in her soft yelps, and in me, a strange sense of pride that I was pleasing her. But I had to pause, again. I was about to come, and as I sat up to catch my breath, giggling like a schoolgirl, she was suddenly on her feet, flipping me onto my back once more, and falling to her knees between my legs, she pulled at the zip of my trousers, tugging at it so recklessly I worried she'd catch in its teeth the throbbing virgin prize within. Only when I felt the cool air swirling around my nakedness, and her small hands resting on my thighs just above my knees, did I finally surrender. Looking up into the blue sky, I saw another plane sailing in, and I felt her tongue moving slowly up the insides of my stiffening thighs. That magical moment, when my cock was in her hand, forced my body to twitch and shake, almost violently, and when I felt the soft warmth of her mouth around me, my virginity rushed into her and the sound of my gratitude sent birds flapping from the trees.

Moments later, we lay next to each other panting, sweating, speechless, trying to catch our breath. She took my hand in hers and gripped it tightly, then turned to me and whispered: "Bethnal, now I'm going to fuck you."

And that's just what she did.

12

Knock, Knock

In the weeks following that wonderful day in the cemetery, I was incredibly happy. I had boundless energy, even completing cross-country runs with relative ease, prompting the bastard PE teacher to joke that I should consider joining the team. However, the long days between weekends were hard. Yearning to be with Mercy, I constantly fought temptation to show up at her flat unannounced. So when she had to visit Highgate Cemetery one Wednesday afternoon for a paper she was writing as part of her course, I said that I'd meet her there. Living only a mile or so from the cemetery, I'd passed it hundreds, if not thousands of times, but had never gone inside, so thought this a good opportunity to take a look. Besides, exploring another cemetery might just result in another afternoon delight.

I bunked the final two lessons of school and waited in a park I knew well, next to the cemetery, the one Mum and Dad regularly took me to as a child. It was a fine day, and sitting on a bench near the swings, I watched bulbous white clouds passing slowly in a gentle summer sky thinking how lucky I was. Mercy's world colliding with mine opened doors for me that summer, doors that have remained open. She stoked in me a sense of wonder, of curiosity, about a world wider than the one I inhabited, about who

I was, and what I was worth. Sometimes, in moments of quiet reflection, I realise that what she gave me was truly quite extraordinary. Simply because of the remarkable person she was.

But our time strolling in the cemetery that afternoon was brief. After collating her notes and taking some photos, as we walked back to the tube station, she detailed the demands of her assignment, and seeing her so engaged in her studies, I thought that perhaps I should make more of an effort in mine.

I started the following day, staying behind at school to practise the concerto for my final examination, *Summer* from Vivaldi's *Four Seasons*, selected primarily for its brevity. I'd listened to it over and over again, believing familiarity would help me produce a rendition worthy of passing the examination. When I played it, I thought of Mercy, and it evoked in me a sense of desperate longing to be with her, but it also stirred more in me, a sense of strange yet delightful liberation, especially if my playing went well.

One lunchtime, as I brought the concerto to a close, Mr Martins stepped out from his office, clapping as he walked towards me, a broad smile lighting up his face, then insisted I play the concerto at the end of year concert. Initially I protested. No other students from my year were performing, but his flattery proved persuasive, and though the concert was some weeks away, I was so anxious about performing in public, I practised constantly. I was buoyed by the remote possibility that Mercy would accompany Mum and Dad to the concert, and, sometimes as I practised, I imagined myself backstage, peeking through the curtains to see the three of them sat together, chatting excitedly, waiting for my performance to thrill them, to bring tears to their eyes.

Other lessons had begun to border on interesting too, especially English, where the frazzled Ms Geraghty had been replaced by Mr Wilson, who, unlike other teachers, seemed to know what he was doing. In his first lesson, sensing the trio at the front of the class was trouble, he separated them which earned him the immediate respect of the whole class.

His selection of short stories and poems transformed the class, instantly engaging us. The way he read poems, walking slowly up and down the aisles, was pure performance, and I especially remember one lesson, one in which he glided around the room reading aloud Marvell's *To His Coy Mistress*, reciting the poem as if he'd written it himself. During his delivery, he would sometimes pause, silent interludes key to understanding the voice in the poem. What excited us most though, were subtle changes in his intonation as he read the poem, suggesting its subject matter might have something to do with sex. After his first reading, he asked us to comment, to say anything we wanted about what *we* thought Marvell was trying to get at. The unusual hush that followed suggested Mr Wilson's choice of poem had been lost on us all. As he paced along the aisles waiting for any form of response, we sat in a curious silence, all of us lacking even a flicker of self-belief. I suppose, like me, others had a vague suspicion the poem had something to do with sex, but no-one would dare say. So when Jenny and Mary, girls who normally attended to their nails during lessons, began to giggle, Mr Wilson sought their enlightenment.

"Yes, Jenny?" he enquired.

Jenny looked at Mary.

"No, you tell 'im," she said, yielding to Mary, whose neck reddened as she shifted uncomfortably in her seat.

"Do I have to?" continued Mary, squirming.

"Yes, come on, tell me what *you* think it's about," urged Mr Wilson, moving to the corner of the room where he waited for her response.

"Well, sir. We just thought it's about. Well…"

"Come on, Mary, out with it. It's about what?" he said.

"Well, Sir, about…"

"Shagging!" shouted Jenny, impatiently, the class erupting into jeers, cheers and whoops.

Mary turned on Jenny, playfully slapping her on the arm and calling her a bitch. As hysteria rocked the room, I felt embarrassed. I too had thought the poem's broader themes had something vaguely to do with "shagging." But shagging had rarely strayed from my mind since meeting Mercy, and I had dismissed it as a possible topic of exploration, or the inspiration for such old and eloquent poetry. So when Mr Wilson continued, I was both surprised and pleased.

"Exactly, Jenny," he said emphatically, "but could you possibly use more formal language to say what you've just said."

"What's that mean?" she said, a serious look descending on her face.

"Could you say it another way? I'm not sure the word *shagging* appears in the Oxford English Dictionary," he continued, the class cheering again at his use of the word.

Mary responded loudly, mocking a posh voice, "Making love, sir."

"Thank you, Mary. Shall we read it again?" said Mr Wilson, smiling, and a hush ran quickly through the class as our heads dropped towards the poem, each of us eager for details of exactly what the narrator wanted of this young girl.

On the way home I read the poem again. I thought about the poet, Marvell, a young man who had written his poem so long ago, describing, almost perfectly, my early desire for Mercy, convincing myself that he, once, must have loved a girl the way that I loved Mercy.

Every waking moment informed me of my changing emotional state, and hanging on the inside door of the wardrobe in my bedroom was a full-length mirror in which I witnessed the physical changes. I carried out daily inspections of my rapidly changing body, noting that certain muscles in the upper half of my body had broadened, and, quite astonishingly, though in the early stages of development, I appeared to be acquiring pectoral muscles. Arguably, the most pleasing part of my anatomy showing signs of growth, however, was my cock, which I estimated had grown by at least a full inch since meeting Mercy. Weaving its way up towards my belly button, pubic hair was now clearly visible, and smaller black hairs had begun to sprout on my stomach. These changes, especially my lengthening cock, I believed a direct result of making love, and so each Monday following my weekend with Mercy, I rushed home from school anticipating new changes, staring at my cock in the mirror, convincing myself that, in the not too distant future, I'd be hung like a horse.

During the week, I called Mercy every other night at around seven or so. I couldn't call from home so I used public phone boxes which, in 1970's Britain would often be a very frustrating experience. Like me, teenagers up and down the country, on the verge of whispering those first, unforgettable, warm words of love they wouldn't dare say in person, were well accustomed to declaring their affections from within the squashed confines of these piss-stinking boxes, hardly the ideal setting for such romantic declarations. Apart from the general, filthy disrepair of these boxes, difficulties that came with making a call were numerous. The main problem was that calls required lots of coins, so I made sure I had lots of them, checking each one for even the smallest flaw, the slightest kink, as I knew from experience, from struggling to force the most pristine of coins into the narrow slot as payment for the call, depending on the vicarious whims of that particular box, it might easily be declined, resulting in immediate disconnection.

If you were lucky enough to get a connection, you had to remain on your toes, your call interrupted every three minutes by pips warning that to continue the call, you had to insert another coin. And almost always, despite my meticulous preparations, when the pips arrived, so did a spasmodic attack, and in a wild panic, I'd rummage through my pockets in search of a coin deemed fit to be accepted, knowing that disconnection was just a pip away.

And so, even armed with a mountain of shiny, perfectly-minted coins piled neatly next to the slot, like I always had, the experience was rarely romantic. Undying fidelity was often promised above a whistling wind blowing in through broken panes that vandals had kicked in, the phone company doing little, if anything, to maintain these phones. In order to limit problems thrown up by such an archaic system of communication, I'd scouted the neighbourhood for the best box and found one not far from our house which, more often than not, was empty when I needed it. From inside that box, I spent many a memorable evening talking to Mercy of many wonderful nothings. Today, all these years later, when I visit Mum, I often make an excuse to slip out and walk by it. If it's empty, I step in, just for old time's sake.

But of all the calls I made from that phone box, the briefest is the most memorable. Even before I said hello, Mercy excitedly told me that she needed to see me, immediately, that she had something to "run by me." Thrilled and intrigued with this midweek summons, I arrived at Lancaster Gate where she was waiting in a particularly chirpy mood, cradling my face in her hands, kissing it a number of times before we marched off to the flat to 'make plans'. Over dinner, I sought clarification immediately.

"OK. Out with it, what's going on?" I said playfully.

"Oh, Bethnal. I've got the greatest surprise for you, for us. Oh, it's going to be fantastic," she enthused.

"OK. So what is it then?"

"I can't tell you. It wouldn't be a surprise would it, silly."

"Oh come on," I replied, "I know you well enough now, there's no need to drag this out. You said you wanted to run it by me. So, here I am – get *running*," I continued.

"Well, first, I want you to tell me a couple of things about yourself and then we'll go from there."

"What sort of things? I've told you my life story already, there's not much more I can tell you."

"What I want to know is the number of countries you've been to."

"Countries?" I said, not having to think for long. "None, I haven't been to any, I've never left England, apart from a day trip to Wales with the school. Does Wales count? Mum and Dad are taking me to Spain soon though, we just got our passports. Anyway, what's this all about?"

The moment I mentioned passports, she looked up from her plate excitedly, curling her legs up towards her chest on the chair, mischief unfolding in her beautiful eyes. I knew things happened when and how she wanted, so I waited, holding her stare, watching her swirl wine in her glass.

"How would you like to come on a journey with me?" she said.

"What do you mean a journey? A journey to where?"

"Well, it's going to be a surprise. I thought about it today and wanted to discuss it with you. But I need to start making plans immediately. I need you for four days over the weekend at the end of the month. Can you swing it?" she said pragmatically.

"Well, maybe, but where are we going?" I persisted.

"I can't tell you, that's the surprise. And you don't need money. You just need to be available. All I need to know now is that you'll come, and I'll book the tickets tomorrow," she said quickly.

A four-day absence without giving full disclosure to Mum and Dad would be tricky, if not impossible, but spending four uninterrupted days with her was too good to pass up. She leaned across the table and took my hand.

"Come on, let's do it, it will be so… so much fun. Plus, it will be so romantic. Oh come on Bethnal, live life, say yes. Just say yes."

"Yes," I said, and she sprinted around the table and threw her arms around me.

Shortly after, as we cleared the plates from the table, I continued to pester her for destination details, but she was resolute, repeating that if I knew where we were going then it wouldn't be a surprise.

Once we'd finished in the kitchen, she switched on a small record player and the soft sound of a soprano filled the room.

Taking my hand, she led me to her bedroom where a candle on the small bedside table was flickering in the semi-darkness of the room, throwing shapeless shadows across the ceiling and walls. As the dulcet tones of the soprano filled the flat, she removed my clothes and we made love as if it were the first time all over again, her tongue seeking unexplored areas of my body, forcing me to twist and turn until we were both entangled in the knotted sheets, and when I saw a small book on the bedside table, and the five large capital letters clearly visible in the dim light from the candle, I realised she was taking me to Paris.

When I arrived home later that evening, the light in the hallway was off and the door to the living room closed. Mum only ever switched the light off when they went to bed, it was still early, and only during the winter was the living room door closed. Something was wrong. Stood in the darkness of the hallway, I could feel a strange presence hanging in the house, and listened for a moment at the door before going in.

When I entered the room, Dad, a lonely figure deep in thought was sitting in his chair, staring blankly through the window out into the darkness of the night sky. Mum was on the edge of the sofa holding a knotted tea towel, a helpless, haunting look in her face, her blank, apologetic eyes fixed on Dad. For the first time, I was witnessing an alarming disharmony between them which I assumed, was of my doing.

"What? What is it?" I asked, softly.

They sprang to their feet, as if embarrassed, leading me to the sofa where they sat either side of me, Mum nervously trying to explain.

"Son. It's your father. Well, we've had some terrible news. Robert, your father's brother..." she said before pausing, her fingers pulling at the knots in the tea towel, looking over at Dad.

"Son, your Uncle Robert has been diagnosed with terminal cancer. We received a call this afternoon from Michelle. The doctors say he'll be lucky to survive a month," Dad continued, his voice wavering slightly.

In the silence that followed I didn't know what to do or say. I felt those boyish feelings of inadequacy I'd done so well to offload since meeting Mercy, begin to re-emerge. I thought of how wonderful the evening had been, of making love to Mercy, of discovering the destination of our forthcoming trip together, then, learning so suddenly of the desperate plight of Uncle Robert, such joy colliding head on with such sorrow made processing such opposing disparate emotions difficult, and I began to cry. Mum took me in her arms and held me until I stopped, and clearly shattered by such conflicting emotional events of the evening, she suggested I go to bed.

The following morning I heard Mum in the hall seeing Dad off as she did most mornings. When I arrived downstairs, everything appeared normal. Tea and toast were waiting for me on the table, the radio was on, and as if the tragic news of the previous evening hadn't happened, Mum was rearranging objects in the room. Wiping invisible crumbs from the tablecloth around my plate, she finally sat down, and tapping her fingers on the tablecloth, sighed.

"What is it, Mum?" I asked.

"Are you OK love? We were terribly worried about you going to bed in such a state last night."

"Yes, I'm fine, really, don't worry about me. How's Dad?"

"Well, that's what I wanted to talk with you about. You know Robert is his only brother. Anyway, Dad's not gone to work this morning. He's gone to stay with your uncle. He'll be gone at least a week, maybe longer, so we'll just have to cope on our own for a while. I told him we'd come and join him in a week or so. I think it's the least we can do."

I thought of leaving London, of leaving Mercy, for a week, missing two weekends, perhaps more, in all likelihood ruling out our trip to Paris. No, it was simply impossible, I couldn't leave now.

"No. I can't go. I can't," I blurted out, unsure of reasons I'd give for so swiftly failing in my duty to family.

Visibly startled by this unexpected outburst, Mum looked at me, her eyes searching my face.

"No, I can't go," I continued, "I've got so much going on at school at the moment, stuff I can't miss. Stuff I've been working on for so long, I can't miss any more school," I blubbered.

"You," she said, "turning down an opportunity to miss school. This is not like you at all. What sort of stuff are you talking about?" she enquired, getting up from the table to fluff out the cushions on the sofa.

I needed a credible lie, but I was useless with spontaneous improvisation, clearly evident from what fell irretrievably from my lips.

"I've got cross-country," I said.

She knew only too well of my intense distaste for sports, especially cross-country. What the fuck *had* I just said? How often had I run back and forth between her and Dad pleading for a note to excuse me from games? To counter such nonsense, I needed something, quickly.

"I've been selected for the cross-country team. Really, I have," I said.

But I could see she was having none of it. She knew I was up to something, so I sought a more credible line of deceit.

"And the end of year concert?" I continued, "How can I perform in that if I don't put in the practice time? You told me yourself that you and Dad and… that you and Dad were looking forward to coming to see me play."

She got up and went into the kitchen. An uncomfortable lull followed, I couldn't gauge her mood. She filled the kettle and hummed to herself softly.

"So what is it you're playing at the concert?" she shouted through to me.

"Vivaldi."

"Viv who?"

"Vivaldi."

"Who's she?"

"It's a he, and he's a famous Italian composer."

Another pause. A trap? She continued humming.

"Why don't you play something English, we might recognise it then," she said.

"I'm sure you'll recognise it. It's a very famous concerto. One that everyone knows."

More silence. More humming.

"What's it called?"

"What's what called?"

"The song by Viv someone."

"Vivaldi."

"That's her."

"Him."

"Well, what's the song called?"

"It's not a song, it's a concerto."

"A what?"

"A concerto. A piece of music. I'm playing it on my own."

A tap ran.

"Aren't there any words, then?"

"No, it's just for violin. You do remember I play the violin, don't you?"

"No words? Is the whole concert going to be just music? Not sure if the parents will enjoy that. You sang the first year you were there, remember, with the rest of your class. Is there no singing then?"

"There'll be singing, but it will be all the younger kids singing. The older kids don't sing. They'd get the… they'd be made fun of constantly, and they don't want that."

"So what's it called then?"

"What I'm I playing?"

"Yeah."

"Four Seasons."

"How long is it?"

"The part I'm playing is about three minutes."

"All four seasons in five minutes, that's about a minute a season. We'll look forward to it then."

"I'm playing for three minutes and only a short piece from the *Summer* part of it."

"Well, I hope it's cheerful. What with everything we got coming with Uncle Robert and all, we'll need cheering up. Just don't play anything that sounds depressing. So when is this concert? It's not coming up is it?"

"No, it's not till the end of term, about another month or so, I'll let you know in good time."

"I hope so. We'll look forward to that," she said, as she came back into the living room, rearranged some cushions on the sofa then put her coat on. "We'll miss not having you with us, but if you're so busy with school *stuff*, then I know Dad'll understand. Besides, you're big enough now to look after yourself. He'll be pleased you're playing at the concert, it'll give him something to look forward to, raise his spirits a bit. We'll probably come and watch the cross-country now the weather's picking up. Your dad'll be pleased you're taking such an interest in sports too. You'll be captain of the football team next! Come on, don't dawdle, get a move on, you'll be late," she continued, picking up her handbag and checking its contents.

And before leaving, she pecked me on the cheek and placed my freshly-laundered PE kit on the chair next to me, sauntering out of the room and down the hall humming, a smirk rising in her face.

13

Awakening

Standing on the worn thin strip of ancient carpet running up the centre of the hallway outside her flat, I brushed the creases from my shirt, rang the bell, and waited, thinking that at some point that day I'd tell her I knew we were going to Paris. I rang again, and with my ear to the door, listened to a dull buzzing inside. I waited a minute or two before ringing a third time, keeping my finger on the bell and tapping the door, calling to Mercy through the letter box. I then began knocking loudly, rapping with increasing intensity, breathing a deep sigh of relief when I heard the click of a light switch and her call my name.

When she opened the door, concealed within the heavy folds of her dressing gown, she tried to smile, but couldn't disguise the drawn look of pale fatigue in her face.

"What's the matter? How long have you been like this?" I asked, trying to hide my distress.

"Oh, it'll pass. I just feel so run down. I get like this sometimes. Don't you worry yourself hun, I'll be up and running in no time. I think I'm going to have to take a rain check today. I'm sorry, hun, I was so looking forward to it. I had a great day planned too. We'll do it next week, huh?" she said, her voice unfamiliar, raspy.

Her lifeless face was a mere shadow of itself. Her forehead glistened under a thin layer of perspiration, and on entering the living room I saw a ruffled blanket strewn across the sofa where she'd been sleeping.

"Of course we will. Don't worry," I replied.

I wrapped her in the blanket, and the moment she lay on the sofa, I noticed she could barely open her eyes, her face twitching when she tried to speak. I suggested she try to sleep, and put another blanket over her.

In the kitchen, she had little food, so I returned to her with some water and told her I wouldn't be long, that I was popping out to the shop.

As I rushed down the stairs, I thought of her alone, suffering, and had to fight back tears. On my return I was relieved to find her in bed asleep. I drew the curtains, and as I unpacked the food in the kitchen, I thought of Dad at the bedside of his only brother, and when I heard Mercy cough, it suddenly felt as if I were surrounded by sickness and death, that all joy in my life had suddenly ceased.

I knew little of Mercy's family, the only time she had talked of the "folks back home" was one afternoon after we'd made love. Oddly, the only person of note I recall her talking of with any real affection was May, the family maid, who, from what I gathered, performed duties normally expected of a mother. She told me that when she was a very small girl, she would help May prepare family meals, and on their way to a museum or the cinema, they would cut through Central Park so she could feed the squirrels. One time, May even took her to see the New York Philharmonic where Mercy saw her crying.

Suddenly I heard Mercy call and I rushed to her. Though still asleep, she was breathing heavily, saying something I couldn't understand. Her forehead was burning, sweat was pouring from her, so for some time I remained at her side holding a cold flannel to her brow. Just when I thought she was beginning to relax, she suddenly called out again. This time I heard what she said, she was calling for May. I took her in my arms, whispering to her, reassuring her that she wasn't alone, and for the next hour or so, I wiped sweat from her face until she fell into a sound sleep.

She woke late in the afternoon, and though still clearly fatigued, she could sit upright. She managed a weak smile which brightened her face a little.

"How do you feel?" I said, taking her hand and putting it mine.

"Thirsty," she replied.

"I've got just what you need," I said, hurrying to the kitchen and returning moments later with a tray laden with soup, apples, and a large glass of water.

"God, what time is it?" she asked as I lay the tray across her lap.

"It's five-thirty," I replied.

"God, five-thirty. How long have I been sleeping?"

"All day," I said, handing her a soup spoon, nodding at the bowl.

She sipped at the soup, which I made her finish, then I placed a small plate of sliced apple in her lap.

"Thank you," she said, yawning.

"You're welcome. Now, get some more sleep. That's what you need," I said as I rearranged the pillow behind her.

"I will, I promise, but you don't need to stay here, honey. I'll sleep through the night. I know I will. I'm just so tired. I get like this sometimes, and when I do, all I can do is sleep. That's what my doctor says. Sleep. I'm fine, I promise. Your mom will be wondering where you are."

"No, I'll stay a few more hours, I'll give you some dinner. I'll…"

"No, hun. Thanks. I'll be fine now. Thank you *so* much for taking care of me. I really do appreciate it. But I'm just going to sleep now. Why don't you come by and check on me tomorrow morning and you'll see, I'll be much better. Really, hun, I just want to sleep now, I don't want to worry about you worrying about me."

"OK. But I'll be back tomorrow morning, and I'm going to take the key with me so I can let myself in. OK?" I said reluctantly.

"OK," she nodded, and smiled.

"There's water on the table if you get thirsty. I've left my phone number on the table. If you need anything, just call. OK?" I said, kissing her cheek.

On the way home I thought of Dad, of the depth of despair he must have been feeling sitting next to his dying brother. And of Mum, who felt Dad's loss as much as him. I realised how lucky I was to have them, how much I loved them, and once again, I was close to tears. I decided that once Mercy was back on her feet, I'd tell her of Uncle Robert, that Paris would have to wait as I had to leave London for a while, to be with Mum and Dad up north.

After a restless night and a quick breakfast, I rushed to her flat the following morning. Turning the key in the lock, I slowly cracked open the door to inhale the rich aroma of freshly-made coffee. I found Mercy sitting up in bed, a coffee cup resting in the palm of her hand, a book open on her lap, looking much improved. I leapt onto the bed and kissed her on the cheek.

"You look much better," I said, holding her hand, relieved to see some colour back in her face.

"I feel a lot better. I guess I must have been a real mess yesterday. Thank you so much for looking after me. I've been awake a couple of hours, I made some coffee and toast. Thank you so much for buying food. I even managed a shower this morning."

"What are you doing?" I asked, looking at a stack of books on the bedside table.

"I've got to get some work done before tomorrow. I also wrote a letter to May, I told you about May didn't I? I had a dream about her last night. By the way, I need your address. I realised I don't have it," she said.

Thinking it better not to mention May, I spelled out the name of my street and she copied it into her address book.

"Hun, I'm afraid I need more rest today. When I get sick like this, I just need to rest, I know the rhythm of my body and I know I need another day. You wait and see, I'll be ready to take on the world tomorrow."

"I was planning on spending my day here, with you," I said, immediately sensing the improbability of that happening.

"Thanks honey, but you really don't have to waste your day cooked up inside with me, I'll be fine. Anyhow, I'm going to be right here all day writing letters, reading and sleeping, so I can get fixed up good and proper." Seeing the disappointment in my face, she continued. "Listen, why don't you stop by Wednesday night? I'll cook you dinner, we'll make a *real* evening of it," she said, mischief rising in her eyes, this teasing offer of another midweek visit compensating for the blow of my impending departure. "I want to tell you about our trip, too," she added, walking me to the door.

I thought it best I wait until Wednesday to tell her I probably couldn't make the trip. I kissed her, and before leaving, insisted we talk later that day by phone.

At home, Mum was busy in the kitchen preparing the Sunday roast, my favourite meal of the week. She said that with only the two of us for dinner, there was no need to extend the table, a laborious task Dad undertook each Sunday.

I sat on the sofa and she came and sat next to me, fidgeting. In her hands, her tea towel twisted into knots, her eyes darting back and forth across the carpet. I suspected she'd had news from Dad, details of Uncle Robert's ailing state. I didn't want to rush her, and sat patiently as she told me that she felt it best she join Dad sooner rather than later. I felt such a wrenching disappointment about leaving Mercy, especially so soon after her being so sick. But she wasn't quite finished.

"What is it, Mum?" I asked.

Then she informed me, almost apologetically, that since I'd only met my uncle a couple of times, and with exams coming up, that both she and Dad felt it better that, under such circumstances, I should remain at home and that she alone would join Dad "when the time came". The truth is, I was secretly thrilled that I didn't have to leave London, and though I made half-hearted protests, the matter was settled, and she shuffled back into the kitchen stating that the decision was final, that "Dad knew best."

Monday and Tuesday flew by. On Wednesday evening I had to be at Mercy's by seven, and so to avoid the horrors of crossing London during rush hour, I bunked the last lesson in order to get an early start. Arriving home, Mum required an explanation for why I was home so early. I told her that students performing at the end of year concert had been given the last lesson off as we had to be back at school by half past four for final preparations. She mumbled something about me missing dinner, then after quickly changing clothes, I was on my way to Mercy's.

Though notorious for its unreliability, I'll be forever grateful to the London Underground system. Not only were its shortcomings responsible for Mum and Dad meeting, but its complexity led to Mercy getting lost on the day of her arrival which, indirectly, led her to me.

That evening, when I turned the corner onto the High Street on my way to the tube station and saw bumper to bumper traffic running in both directions, I knew the Northern Line was suspended.

At the entrance to the station an angry crowd had gathered, hurling questions at a besieged employee, holding him personally responsible for the closure of the station due to a suicide at King's Cross. His face fraught with despair, sweat trickling from greying sideburns and a growing impatience in his voice, he stuttered out repeated apologies for the delay.

I pushed to the front of the mob to find myself beside a young olive-skinned girl, perhaps Spanish, her polite enquiries drowned by the angry voices all around her. When she finally managed to ask about alternate routes into central London, her request delivered with such gentle courtesy, her timing, however, proved rather unfortunate, arriving just as the employee's patience expired. Any impression she may have held regarding high standards of British courtesy and civility were surely shattered when he took one last drag of his cigarette, tossed it to the ground, then wiping sweat from his forehead, took a deep breath, and looking directly at the girl, but addressing us all, emphatically announced, in a voice loud enough to be heard by his colleagues working hard many stops down the line at King's Cross station, "There's a fucking bus stop over there, catch the fucking bus," before disappearing into the station and slamming closed the partition behind him.

The bus for Notting Hill edged towards Camden Town in a series of shunts, punctuated by long periods when it remained stationary. At Tuffnell Park, a rumour that the Northern Line was running again suddenly swept through the bus and most of the passengers got off. With time to spare, I stayed on, continuing my journey to Lancaster Gate without further incident, arriving at the flat to find the door ajar. The living room and kitchen were empty, and so I thought Mercy had popped out, but then I heard a noise in the bedroom. I opened the door slowly to see her spread naked across the bed, the healthy glow of her skin a clear sign she was well again. After making love, I wanted to stay in bed, wrapped around her the entire evening, but she had other plans, hopping up out of bed, declaring it was time to eat.

While she prepared a couple of steaks in the kitchen, I set the table, placing on top of the cotton place mats, shiny white china plates before lighting candles, one for each corner of the table. She came in and drew the blinds, then before returning to the kitchen, clicked on the record player. I sat at the table listening to the needle scrape the outer edge of the vinyl, and the moment that first note rose into the air, I knew it was Vivaldi, his *Four Seasons*, sounding nothing short of magical, better than any version I'd heard before. So inspired by the beautiful music filling the room, I thought of the end-of-year concert and that perhaps it was time for Mercy to meet Mum and Dad. But then, suddenly, the needle found a scratch on the record, slid to the centre of the disc and ejected itself.

Over dinner she assured me that she'd made a full recovery, that, in fact, she had more energy than usual. Based on her boundless agility in the bedroom shortly after my arrival, this was clearly the case.

"You really shouldn't have gone to all this trouble," I said.

"Of course I should. You practically saved my life on Saturday. This is the least I could do. Besides, I felt so bad at not being able to spend the day with you. I think you probably guessed that from when you arrived this evening," she said, her face colouring slightly in the soft candlelight.

"Listen," I said, "if that's the welcome I get every time I visit, then I'll be dropping by daily," I joked.

Seeing her radiant smile again, images of her so weak flashed through my mind.

"I was really worried about you, I really was. You looked, well...." I paused, "well, kind of really ill. I didn't know what to do."

An anxious look appeared on her face.

"Anyway, look at you now, you're back and lovely again. Lovelier! You're absolutely gorgeous," I continued, a blush rushing into my face.

"Oh, hush," she said, giggling, dabbing her lips with her napkin.

"So, where are we going then?" I asked, re-directing the conversation to a more playful topic.

"What do you mean?" she countered, toying with me.

"The trip? Where are you taking me?" I replied.

"Oh, that," she said, faking an air of forgetfulness. "Well, as a matter of fact, I have it all prepared," she continued as she poured more wine. "We're not going this weekend but the next, a little sooner than I thought. I hope you can fix not being in London on Friday or the following Monday cos we're travelling those days. Now, you need to be at Victoria train station by six-thirty Friday morning or I'll be leaving without you. You don't need to pack much, just a pair of dress pants in case we eat somewhere nice, and some blue jeans should do. Oh, and don't forget your passport," she said smugly.

"OK. But where're we going?" I probed.

"I'm not telling you," she said. "I won't even tell you if you guess, so don't bother trying. I think you'll enjoy it though, a trip you'll hopefully remember. So, you can sit back and literally just enjoy the ride, cos you'll find out soon enough," she said, falling back into her seat and smiling.

We spent the rest of the evening engaged in small talk, and when I finally told her about Uncle Robert, I was touched by the sincerity of her concern for people she'd never met. But the moment she learned that Mum was at home on her own, she insisted I go home to her. As we stood at the door, I nearly told her that I loved her. But saying something so meaningful for the first time was more difficult than I thought, and moments later, sat on the wall outside the flats, I wondered why I struggled to tell her what was plainly obvious to us both. I thought that perhaps I'd missed the "right time" to tell her exactly how I felt about her, and on my way home on the tube, I took small comfort by vowing to myself that she'd hear these words from me in Paris.

The living room felt cold and uninviting when I entered. The TV and gas fire were off and Mum was sitting in Dad's chair, something I'd never seen before. In the weak light from the lamp next to the chair, she looked so lonely. She'd never spent an evening alone, certainly not since she'd met Dad. With him away and me behaving in a strangely erratic manner, it dawned on me she was seeing a brief glimpse of her future, when the men in her life would be gone.

She hopped up when she saw me, running into the kitchen to fetch me the sandwich she'd made earlier. We chatted for a while, then she said that I should go on up to bed, that she was waiting for a call from Dad.

On my way up the stairs I thought of how lonely she'd appeared when I came in. I stopped halfway up and returned to the living room, and, as I'd done so many times as a little boy, I kissed her goodnight. She smiled and whispered, "Goodnight, son."

The following morning, the phone ringing had Mum hurrying from her room. I waited for the sound of stifled sobbing as she learned of Uncle Robert's departure, but when I heard the kettle whistling, as it did every morning, I went downstairs to see who'd called.

"Morning," I shouted through to the kitchen.

"Oh, morning, son. What are you doing up so early? Are you poorly?" she replied.

"No, the phone woke me up. Who was it?"

"I know, wasn't that strange, I suppose it was a wrong number. As soon as I picked it up and said hello, they put the phone down. I thought it might have been your father, but I'm sure he would have called back if we were cut off. Not to worry, if it's important they'll call back. Do you want some beans with your breakfast?" she said, stood at the kitchen door tying the strings to her apron.

As I ate breakfast, I was thinking of the previous evening, of making love to Mercy. Such a super night, and she was looking so well, completely recovered from the fever of the previous weekend. Just as I took a generous pull on my tea, Mum caught me off-guard.

"So, how did it go last night?" she said, just as the tea entered my mouth.

The sharp intake of air sent me into a sudden fit of coughing and Mum rushed over to me, slapping my back until I regained use of my windpipe.

"Practice? How was the practice for the concert?" she repeated, a frown rising in her face.

"Fine," I said.

She sat in Dad's chair, his tea mug cupped in her hands on her lap, then looked vacantly out into the garden.

"Think it's going to rain today," she said.

As I got up from the table, she asked me to wait a moment, she had something to tell me.

She informed me that as I was old and responsible enough to look after myself for a while, that she'd be joining Dad the following day. I know I should have felt sad and upset, but the only thing running through my mind was staying overnight with Mercy, waking up and making love first thing in the morning.

"Bethnal?" she said, startling me from the thoughts.

I tried to catch the thread of the last thing she said.

"When will you be leaving?" I enquired.

"My train leaves tomorrow, at six, from Euston. I don't know how long I'll be gone, but I may be gone for as long as a week. Maybe more. It depends," she said, tugging at a loose thread hanging from the hem of her dress.

I thought of Paris, and worried she might change her mind, I suddenly felt the need to reassure her I would be fine.

"I've been invited on a trip next weekend," I said, her eyes suddenly brightening.

"A trip? Who's invited you on a trip then?" she said, her eyes narrowing, shifting her body towards me.

"Camping. I'm going camping. I'm going camping with Billy Brown. You remember him. He's the one whose mother you spoke to for about an hour at the school gate every day when you used to come to pick me up. He's invited me to go camping with him and his dad," I said, hoping I didn't sound too desperate.

"Oh, that nice boy. Billy is his name? It's been such a while since you've mentioned him, I didn't realise you were still friends with him. Funny enough, I thought I saw his mother in Sainsbury's, it must be six months ago, maybe longer, I'm sure it was her. Well, I was just about to say hello, but she just walked straight past me, she mustn't have recognised me, I did have my hair different then, but she did seem very...cold," she replied.

Billy's mother had probably blanked Mum as Billy's time at our school had come to an abrupt halt when angry fathers started showing up in the school office almost daily, threatening to castrate the "problem" child who continually scared their daughters by flashing his "parts" at them. Despite the school's obligations to protect the rights of this *troubled* boy, his expulsion was finalised when the Maths teacher caught him unawares, measuring his little erect member in the book cupboard at the back of the classroom.

"Oh, well, that's nice. Puts my mind at ease, knowing you'll be in the hands of a responsible adult. That does make me feel better," she said, patting me on the head and pouring me more tea.

14

Bonjour!

"Just a few more days," she said, "after the weekend, Tuesday." Then on Monday she changed her departure date to Thursday. I thought she might not leave at all, that she'd still be here Friday, ruling out my trip to Paris.

On Tuesday evening, when she staggered in from the shops carrying bulging bags, I felt confident she would be leaving Thursday. On Wednesday evening I felt guilty when she came in with a shiny new pair of camping boots she'd bought "special" for my weekend adventure in the country. After dinner that evening, she produced an "emergency" list of people's phone numbers "to remain by the phone," that I should call "just in case," taking me through each name on the list, reminding me exactly who each person was. The remainder of the evening she spent ironing virtually every piece of clothing I owned.

I was sad but relieved to see her leave Thursday morning, but managed to make it to school on time, and after yet another uneventful day, bunked the last two lessons and went home to pack. With my suitcase open on my bed, I wasn't sure what I might need, so I piled everything Mum had meticulously ironed into the case. I then dragged it downstairs leaving it by the front door ready for my early departure.

After an early dinner, I went to bed, setting the alarm for five o'clock, placing the clock on the chest of drawers on the opposite side of the room, a successful strategy which had me up on time and wrestling my suitcase along the High Street, arriving at the tube station just as it opened.

I arrived at Victoria Station ten minutes early, where, as instructed, I waited under the giant clock. Trains arriving into the station stuttered to a halt, their engines hissing as they cooled, and as doors flew open along platforms, I was surprised by the sheer numbers of commuters spilling from them at such an hour to scurry across the sparkling, freshly-buffed tiles of the station floor, and disappear out of several exits scattered around the station.

"Hi, hon, you ready for a trip of a lifetime? It looks like you are," Mercy said when she arrived, hugging me then looking at my case. She added, "We're going for the weekend sweetie, not a month."

We bought frothy cappuccinos then boarded the Dover train. I put our cases on luggage racks above the seats then sat opposite her.

Leaving England for the first time made me feel nervous, but I felt in safe hands being with her.

The train clunked its way out of the station, and as I was looking down the steep embankment into the small rectangular gardens of terraced houses, the carriage door suddenly flew open and a young man and woman with bulging backpacks squeezed in to join us. They helped each other out of their packs then introduced themselves, Randy and Cindy, American college students backpacking around Europe. Though I didn't participate in the conversation that followed, I did listen closely, hoping Mercy would let slip details of our destination, to simply reconfirm what I already knew. The couple recounted details of their adventures since arriving in Britain from their home in Illinois. They were in the UK to trace ancestry in Scotland before they hitched to Wales, and were now beginning the European leg of their trip, to Montpelier in southern France. Like us they were heading to Dover to catch a ferry to Boulogne, then the train onto Paris before hitching south to Montpelier.

With this couple in tow, my vague romantic plans of standing on deck with Mercy, holding her hand, watching as my country slowly disappeared, were slowly fading. When the conversation shifted to their respective studies back home, I lost all interest, looking through the window to admire the beautiful emerging greenbelt south of London, its luscious green fields dotted with sheep.

I suddenly thought of Mum and Dad at Uncle Robert's bedside, and the enormity of my deception suddenly terrified me. Then, as if sensing my concern, I felt Mercy's hand on my knee, her smile reassuring me, reminding me of the wonderful diversions my first trip abroad might bring.

After thirty minutes or so the train began to slow and people dragging suitcases filed past in the corridor outside the carriage. We couldn't have reached the port, we were barely out of London. The young man informed us we were approaching Gatwick, the airport into which they'd flown for the start of their European adventure.

"Well, I hope you guys have a good time," Mercy said, getting to her feet and pulling her bag from the luggage rack. She turned to me and smiled, cheekily informing me that "the plane wouldn't wait for us."

An insatiable excitement crashed through me as I dragged my case behind her into the airport. When the terminal doors swung open, I entered a frenzied, alien world, the enormous hall of the terminal building where hundreds, maybe thousands of people were shuffling in all directions. On benches, using their bags as pillows, people slept as others dashed past them with trolleys loaded with cases. From skylights high in the ceiling, narrow shafts of platinum sunlight fell across a large constantly-changing display board, and as its large white letters and numbers changed, it sounded like birds flapping through the airport. We were soon in among people gathered below it waiting for details of their flights, squeezing our way through to the check-in desk where Mercy asked me to remain with the bags as she collected our boarding passes.

As people speaking French joined the queue, Paris felt that much closer. The woman at the counter summoned me, checked in our bags, and handed Mercy our boarding passes which she tucked into an inside fold of her handbag. As we waited in line at security, the woman from the check-in desk appeared before us shaking Mercy's keys that she'd left on the counter. In perfect French Mercy thanked the woman, at which point I thought it silly not to declare our destination.

"We're going to Paris, aren't we?" I said.

For some moments, Mercy just looked at me, her eyes giving nothing away.

"Yes. We're going to Paris," she said, smiling.

"I've never been on a plane," I confessed.

"A first time for everything," she said, and stepping towards me, still smiling, she pulled me towards her and whispered, "and sweetheart, you better hold onto your socks, this is going to be a whirlwind."

Greeting us in both English and French as we boarded the plane, two pretty stewardesses in navy uniforms, with similar wide smiles and sparkling blue eyes giving me the impression they might be twins, directed us up the aisle. As we made our way to our seats, overhead compartments clattered shut, and as I looked up and down the enormous vessel, no other passengers appeared to share my concerns regarding the danger of raising into the air such an enormous object made of heavy metal.

Our seats were over a wing, and hopping into the window seat, I twiddled the various knobs on the inside of the armrest. Mercy sat in the aisle seat, pulling a toothbrush and a small tube of toothpaste from her handbag, tucking them into the pouch on the back of the seat in front of her before fastening her seatbelt.

An American couple struggling out of coats in the seats behind us stopped one of the smiling stewardesses and complained about the heat in the cabin. Moments later, as passengers fanned themselves with laminated emergency landing procedures, a dull groan resonated through the cabin as the captain announced his apologies for the stifling heat, assuring us that technicians were currently working hard to fix the problem.

When the last of the overhead compartments slammed shut, stewardesses strode up and down the aisles counting passengers, a sudden hush running through the cabin as the captain announced final preparations for take-off. I leaned over, and shaking Mercy, excitedly told her we were about to take off. She smiled, yawned, and then pulling around her the thin blanket provided by the airline, she closed her eyes.

As the plane shunted back, I listened attentively to emergency landing procedures, my concerns about this heavy object defying gravity still smouldering. The pretty stewardesses gave stellar performances, and I gripped the armrests trying desperately, but unsuccessfully, to recall what I must do "in the unlikely event of landing on water," and exactly how I should inflate my life vest, "stored under your seats" once we'd made the emergency landing into the English Channel.

The plane slowly reversed away from the gate and I felt vibrations from the engines humming softly below us. It came to a sudden halt and the captain announced, 'READY FOR TAKE OFF', a truly magical moment which had the stewardesses shuffling along the aisles to the back of the plane where they strapped themselves into small fold-down seats.

As the plane taxied towards the runway, Mercy was sleeping soundly, her head flopped onto her shoulder. For her, the novelty of being shot into the air at five hundred miles an hour had long gone. I could barely contain my excitement. I was nervous, excited, scared, and looking through the window at the large silver wing shuddering, it looked a little frail, a bit too thin. We came to a sudden stop, and for a minute or so, the cabin was quiet. But then, suddenly, from the rear of the plane, the enormous roar of engines firing sent vibrations shivering through the plane and it surged forward, powering along the runway, making strange noises in the undercarriage, thrusting me back in my seat, the wing shaking violently, surely about to break off.

When I glanced over at Mercy, she was still sleeping. Across the aisle I saw a nun with her head bowed, her eyes closed tightly as she blessed herself. Well-worn rosary beads dangled loosely from under her white knuckles clawing at the armrest. As the plane roared and shuddered forward, surely running out of runway, I watched her, hoping the Hail Marys she was reciting would come in handy. Then, just as I thought time was running out, the front of the plane tipped up, almost effortlessly, and I fell gently back in my seat, and through the window, I looked down to see the slowly shrinking houses.

We suddenly entered a thick bank of cloud, dense grey candyfloss swirling all around us, then hit a small pocket of air causing us to drop momentarily. The sudden gasps throughout the cabin signalled what I thought was our descent into the Channel. A more determined whirring from the engines did little to allay my fears, but did assist in our continuing ascent, until we were soaring in the most perfectly beautiful blue sky and looking down on a thick, flat mass of grey cloud stretching as far as the eye could see.

When the seatbelt signs pinged off, people got up and began pulling things out of overhead compartments. Mercy was still sleeping, and the nun, her prayers suspended until the tricky business of our descent, was now preoccupied with the snack trolley being slowly wheeled up the aisle.

Some twenty-five minutes into my maiden voyage, it seemed like we'd just taken off, the captain announced the start of our descent into Charles de Gaulle airport. The plane bounced and dropped as we hit more pockets of turbulence, and as we dipped below French clouds and I saw French fields partitioned neatly into small squares divided by small roads snaking into the distance, to certify that we were indeed descending into France, I checked the miniature lorries and cars moving slowly on the wrong side of the road.

Despite the bouncy descent, the brave stewardesses made their way up and down the aisles making final checks. As the wheels dropped out of the undercarriage, I thought the hydraulics may malfunction, but they proved to be in fine working order, and as we touched down, the wheels screeched and the plane shook frantically before slowing and finally coming to a stop. As we taxied to the gate, I saw the nun bless herself, then slip her rosary beads into a small pouch below a fold in her habit. My first flight had been everything I imagined it would be, and in a few days' time, I looked forward to my second, the flight home.

Seatbelt signs pinged off and passengers leapt up to wrench bags from overhead compartments. I tapped Mercy's arm to wake her, but she didn't respond. I gently shook her, whispering that we'd arrived. She opened her eyes, glanced at her watch then smiled before closing her eyes and falling back into her seat. I shook her again, whispering that it was time to get off the plane. She cleared her throat and mumbled something I didn't understand. In a more urgent tone, I tried to stir her, telling her again that we'd arrived.

"No, we haven't," she whispered, opening then closing her eyes.

Not sure what to do and hoping a stewardess could help, I looked up and down the aisle. But then I felt Mercy tugging at my shirt. She pulled me to her and whispered words clearly symptomatic of what could only be a declining, possibly delusional state. I stepped into the aisle, looking at her, shaking my head, waiting for her to tell me she was joking. My heart was hammering as she pulled me back into my seat, just as the captain welcomed us to Paris.

"Ladies and gentlemen. Welcome to Paris, Charles de Gaulle airport where the temperature outside is not too different from London, a very comfortable twenty-seven degrees. I do wish you a pleasant stay in Paris, and for those of you with connecting flights, please seek a member of staff in the arrivals lounge where they will be happy to direct you to your gate. We do value your custom and when next you decide on air travel, either business or pleasure, I do hope you consider flying with us again." And then following a muffled sound in the cockpit, he continued. "And for those of you continuing on to New York, I kindly request that you stay in your seats, we have to pick up approximately ninety passengers here and then we should be on our way. It shouldn't take more than thirty minutes or so. Should you require anything, please contact a member of our cabin crew who will be more than happy to help you."

When I looked over at Mercy, her smile was as wide as the Brooklyn Bridge.

I was going to America. To New York City.

15

Wonderful Town

When Mercy woke up, just a few short hours from New York City, I was still looking down on the dark blue water of a sparkling Atlantic Ocean, miles below.

"Hi, hon, everything OK?" she enquired quite casually.

"You're going to get me into heaps of trouble," I said.

"I do hope so," she replied, stopping the stewardess to order a vodka tonic.

For the next hour or so, she talked about her life in New York, her friends, charming stories of her childhood, all involving May who she was so excited to see again. She only briefly mentioned her parents.

After lunch, as Mercy slept, I thought of New York City, thinking I didn't really know much about that grand metropolis. However, that summer, the city was experiencing a global promotion in the shape of the last film I'd seen, *Saturday Night Fever*. Fresh in my mind, providing more or less everything I knew of the city, was a young John Travolta, shimmying his way through the dance halls of the city, doing his thing to win his girl.

Somewhat surprisingly, perhaps, my other font of information about the city was Mum. Her sources were the Sunday newspapers which, in the 1970s, were keenly monitoring what

Mum called the 'carry on' of fledgling British pop stars such as John Lennon and Elton John who had abandoned their country for the bright lights of America. Each Sunday morning after breakfast, as we sat in the living room, she would update Dad on the moral decline of famous Brits who had made New York City their home. One morning she became particularly animated over an article involving the daughter of one of her favourite singers who herself had perished from a drug overdose.

"Dad, listen to this. Judy will be turning in her grave. Apparently, Liza Minnelli was photographed in this club in America, in New York," she said, pausing briefly to see if I was listening. "Well, let's just say, they were… they were," she paused again, and then, in a barely audible voice, fixed Dad with a serious gaze and finished her sentence, "doing it."

"Doing what, love?" said Dad, innocuously, scanning his newspaper for the latest football transfer speculations.

"You know what!" she continued. "They say there's a club there, what's it called, Studio Fifty something. Fifty-Four or Fifty-Five, I don't know. Well, the paper says it's like Sodom and Gomorrah inside. And all of them, killing themselves with those drugs. I honestly don't know what the world's coming to," she said, flicking a page in search of similar stories.

And so, only a few hours from Sodom itself, New York sounded like a lot of fun. But what I most anticipated seeing in the city, among the hundreds of looming skyscrapers, was one in particular, the Empire State Building. I'd seen images of it hundreds if not thousands of times in films, magazines, and on posters at Camden Market.

One poster in particular, still very common today and which I had on my wall at university, is of construction workers perched on a solitary girder, sixty or so stories up, eating lunch. But for me, the building's enduring appeal is because of an early childhood memory. I was about four or five, and one afternoon after dinner, stretched out in front of the fire, I was captivated by the Sunday afternoon film, the 1933 Beauty and the Beast classic, King Kong. Even now I can replay in my mind the moment Kong is trapped, taken from his natural habitat and subjected to such wicked brutality. I genuinely expected a happy ending, especially after he fell in love with the beautiful Ann. I certainly didn't expect the film to end so tragically, with Kong tenuously holding the antenna on top of the Empire State Building, lashing out at the small planes swooping all around him as they riddled his big body with bullets. And when he fell into the avenue below and died, I cried for the rest of the afternoon, and, despite Mum and Dad's tender efforts to convince me it was only "make believe," I was having none of it, my tears letting up only when I fell asleep that evening.

Thinking I might try and take a short nap, I wrapped myself in a blanket, lowered the shutter on the window and closed my eyes and thought of Kong and of those fearless hungry workmen. As I slept, I had a strange dream. I was sitting on a soft velvet couch in a New York nightclub, spotlights whirling and twirling, illuminating a dance floor full of bodies, and given it was a dream, I was only mildly surprised when I saw Mum at one end of the bar holding a large bottle of champagne, waving it at Dad standing at the other end, dressed in a sparkling white tuxedo, just like the one John Travolta wore on posters plastered all over London. He skipped past me, and joining Mum, they looked over at me and smiled, as if I'd done something to please them.

Next to me I noticed a man of almost matchstick proportions kissing a woman. As he got up, he looked at me briefly before disappearing onto the crowded dance floor. It was Mick Jagger. As I waited for him to return, to say hello, I was unexpectedly ambushed by the woman he'd been kissing who spoke in a voice so hoarse I could barely understand her.

"Bethnal, where ya been, hon?" she said. "The party's just startin'," she continued, her long fingers squeezing the inside of my thigh.

"Bethnal. Sugar. Wake up. Sweetheart, we land in half an hour."

I woke to see Mercy standing over me, smiling.

"That was some dream you were having" she said, her eyes nodding towards the protruding lump in my crotch.

A passing stewardess politely informed me the toilets at the rear of the plane were free. As I squeezed passed her, Mercy slapped me on the arse and added, "I hope you were dreaming of me."

I returned to my seat just as the captain announced we had ten minutes to landing. Mercy wrapped her hand in mine, and as we descended into cloud, I steeled myself for my first glimpse of the New World, thinking that in just one day, I'd been in two of the most famous cities in the world and was now slowly descending into my third.

"Ladies and gentleman, we'll be landing in approximately six to seven minutes. If you look out to the right of the plane in a minute or so, you should get a beautiful view of Manhattan. For those of you on the left hand side, I'll lean in a little on our descent so you'll get a good look too. The weather? Well, it's twenty-eight degrees centigrade, that's eighty-two Fahrenheit, and,

I've been reliably informed the weekend is going to be much the same," the captain announced.

As I waited for America to appear, Mercy hopped into the middle seat and rested her chin on my shoulder. I felt her soft breaths on the side of my face, a truly wonderful moment, the two of us, together, hanging in the sky, waiting for America to appear. And then, just as the captain had promised, Manhattan came rushing up towards us, and quite incredibly, the first building I saw was the spectacular Empire State Building, dwarfing all buildings around it, its antenna pointing majestically into the sky. I felt so overwhelmed, and had it not been for Mercy pointing to the various bridges connecting Manhattan to surrounding boroughs, telling me their names, I might have cried. And then sweeping in and out of view, the green oasis in the heart of Manhattan I'd seen in so many films, Central Park. Here it was, New York City, and as we sailed in, I heard her whisper the word 'home'.

But when I turned to look at her, I couldn't decide if she looked happy or sad.

16

In-Laws

In baggage claim, we joined the crush of people pushing and shoving, hovering over carousels waiting for their cases. When our bags arrived, Mercy summoned one of the many smiling porters all dressed in identical dark blue uniforms with a large American flag embroidered into their shirt pockets. He loaded our cases onto his trolley and we followed after him as he skilfully swerved his way out through the exit doors of the terminal where I sucked in my first breath of American air, unexpectedly peppered with the acrid exhaust fumes spewing from hundreds of bright yellow taxis, all honking and spluttering, trapped in a chaotic mess on the ramp that normally took traffic out of the airport.

Filing out of the terminal building into the searing heat, passengers swore loudly when they saw the gridlock, their hopes for swift passage into the city dashed. Responsible for clearing up the mess, a solitary cop, his cheeks aflame as he blew furiously into a silver whistle, his chunky little arms wildly waving, making his silver badge, hanging askew on his sweat-soaked breast pocket, dazzle in the afternoon sun.

A sudden blinding terror flashed through me when I turned to find Mercy gone. But my alarm was short-lived when I spotted her between the cars in the middle of the ramp holding open the rear door of a cab, waving at me to join her. I squeezed between the sweltering chrome bumpers, dragging my case behind me, and handed it to the driver.

"Hey kid, whadja gad in heeya, ya mudder?" he mumbled, as he heaved it into his boot onto a pile of oily rags.

He slammed the boot and hopped into his cab to join the cacophony of other drivers thumping their horns. I slid in across the hot leather seats beside Mercy, and such was the temperature inside the cab, it reminded me of a near-death experience I'd had when I was six, on my first and only trip up north to see some of Dad's family.

The summer was certainly unusual that year with England baking for weeks under an unforgiving sun. Even northern parts of the country received little if any rain, and so when I met my cousin, who was three years older than me, he was thrilled to have a new playmate. Inviting me out to play, he led me to a disused water tower at the end of the street. Once we'd scaled the sturdy metal ladder connected to the outside of the tower, we sat on top for a while, catching our breath and taking in the wilting but wonderful views of the surrounding countryside. He then pointed to the small square hole that provided access to the tower's interior. I shouted into the dark chasm, listening as the echo bounced from wall to wall. To check it was empty I dropped a small branch inside and listened as it landed with a dull clump on the bottom. Just inside the hole a ladder descended to the bottom of the tank, my cousin insisting that I go in first, that he was "right behind me." Though instinct urged me not to trust him, I didn't want him to think I was scared, and so I did as he asked. Which of course proved to be my undoing. The moment my head had entered the darkness of the cavernous vacuum, the light suddenly disappeared, the latch snapped the lid closed, and after thumping across the roof, he clumped back down the ladder to *terra firma* of the street below. I held onto the ladder until the heat made me feel weak and dizzy, draining the strength from me, forcing me to climb down to the bottom of the tank where the heat from the metal quickly penetrated the soles of my shoes as if melting them. As I gasped in mouthfuls of the thin, stale, hot air, I convinced myself death was at hand. But somehow, I managed to survive the twenty minutes until he returned and set me free, and standing at the bottom of the tower shortly afterwards, he casually offered me a cigarette, assuring me I'd only been in the tank five minutes, that I'd "passed the test" and that his dad may have erred to some degree by describing our family as a bunch of "southern softies." Fortunately, I never saw my cousin again, his name cropping up only once when Aunt Ivy made a rare visit some years later, and I overheard Mum telling her that my cousin was safely under lock and key in a facility just outside Manchester.

A light breeze stole in through the window of the taxi and we were suddenly on the move. The traffic moved slowly at first, nudging its way out of the airport, until we were speeding along a busy motorway. Just as I caught my first glimpse of the city, the driver left the motorway and took us through a residential neighbourhood with big solid houses built of chunky brownstone bricks with attractive but crumbling ornate facades. Many of the houses were boarded up, others completely ransacked, their doors and windows gone, leaving big gawking holes, a depressing state of deprivation deeply anchored in neighbourhoods such as these all across America. The conditions, however, mattered little to the hordes of smiling black kids playing happily together on broad steps running up to the door of each house.

But then, suddenly, we were out of that neighbourhood and bumping onto a magnificent suspension bridge spanning a wide stretch of water, and we were back in an America I recognised, an America I expected. I thrust my head out the window to see in the water below boats similar to those I'd seen from the plane. On the other side of the bridge, was the America I imagined, the one with those wonderful testimonies to the genius of human endeavour, a forest of gleaming skyscrapers rising up into the sky, inspiring anyone who saw them to truly believe that this city, this shining beacon of humanity, where anything was possible if you wanted it, really was as good as it looked.

As we entered the city, the driver began punching his horn continuously, weaving and speeding haphazardly up the narrow avenues, almost scraping other cars. We swayed and bounced on the back seat, and giddy with excitement, I wanted to shout and point at things I saw, to show Mercy just how thrilled I was to be in her city. But I noted in her a preoccupation. Seemingly immune to the delights I was experiencing, she stared blankly through the window into the busy streets of a city whose sparkle for her had long since faded.

And so, for the next twenty minutes or so, I contained my excitement, calmly holding her hand, quietly taking in the wonders of being in New York City, until the cab slowed to a stop. Moments later, I was standing on the pavement looking skyward at easily the biggest building I'd ever seen up close. And it was where she lived.

Entry to the building was through two large glass doors. Above them, fluttering in a light breeze, was the biggest flag I'd ever seen, the star spangled banner, immediately mesmerising me, making me feel so honoured to be standing before it, in this, the greatest city, the greatest country in the world. The doors shone like mirrors, and as we approached them, Mercy paused. Again I noted that blank look of apprehension in her face. Then I thought I saw a shadowy movement, just behind the glass, a shapeless silhouette of an indistinguishable shifty figure staring at us.

"OK, let's do it," she said, and as she stepped forward the doors swung open and a little man, no bigger than me in a shiny suit a size too large for him, came out to greet us.

In a perfectly round and happy face, his bright blue eyes narrowed and smiled when he saw Mercy.

"Well, I'll be. Mercy Waters. Welcome home. Boy, I've missed you," he said, embracing her.

"Thanks, Joe, missed you too," Mercy replied, then turning to me she continued, "Joe, this is Bethnal Green, he's from England."

"Well, I'll be. All the way from England. Well, Bethnal, welcome to New York. Welcome to America. You been here before, young man?" he said, flashing another smile then taking my hand and shaking it enthusiastically.

I shook my head.

"Well, you're very welcome, sir. Mercy, so that's where you been, in England. May told me you were somewhere, but I clear forgot where. Here, let me get those bags, you must be pooped coming *all* the way from England," he said, then walked with us to the lifts where he tapped a shiny brass button within a shiny brass plate to summon the lift.

As Joe briefed Mercy on events during her absence, I took in the sumptuous surroundings in the lobby where everything glistened, including our squat and contorted bodies in the polished brass doors of the lift. I watched the numbers flash in quick succession above the doors, counting down as the lift plummeted through the floors of the building until the bell pinged and a rush of air squeezed between the cracks before the doors slid open. The prospect of shooting up through the centre of the building thrilled me, and as we entered the lift, my eyes followed Joe's index finger as he felt for a button. Of course I hoped he'd feel all the way up to button eighty, but when it landed on number fifty-one, I thought it more than adequate. Then, just before the doors closed, he skipped back into the lobby, telling us he'd see us later.

Soaring up through the building, the only indication that we had in fact left the lobby was the gentle quivering of the brass handrail running around the middle of the lift which I gripped with both hands. As the pressure gradually built in my ears, Mercy casually attended to her hair in the dull reflection of the doors. When they pinged open we saw ourselves in a large mirror hanging within an ornate golden frame on the wall opposite the lift. Mercy dabbed on another layer of lipstick and flicked at her hair. She took a deep breath, and I followed her slowly along the soft burgundy carpet running the length of the corridor. Though she'd never given me any personal indication as to just how wealthy her family was, as we walked past the heavy, individually-designed doors of each apartment, it was clear that, wealth-wise, we were from different ends of the spectrum.

When she stopped outside a door and fumbled for keys in her bag, a sudden shiver of inadequacy took hold of me. As if sensing my anxiety, she put her arm around me, smiled, and told me to just be *myself*. I tried to smile, nodding gently, thinking of what, exactly, being *myself* required. She took another deep breath and quietly inserted the key into the lock. The door clunked open and we stepped in to a small reception room.

On a small side-table next to a framed photo of a girl with long hair sitting happily in the lap of a young, attractive black woman, a small lamp scattered light around our feet. To the right and left, corridors disappeared into darkness, and standing silently in the half light, we listened for any sign of life. When it appeared no-one was home, Mercy threw her arms around me, kissing my forehead and whispering "Welcome." But then, quite suddenly, the ceiling light flickered on, and from behind a set of doors to the left of the reception room, a man and woman appeared.

Even today, as I recall the uncomfortable silence that followed that first glimpse of Mercy's mother, a shiver runs through me. She looked first at Mercy, then, twitching momentarily, she looked at me, then back to Mercy, silently observing us, saying nothing, just long enough for me to think that perhaps we were in the wrong apartment. A dress designed for the natural shape of a younger woman, barely able to contain her bulging hips, did little to compliment her. A polite descriptor of her dimensions might be voluptuous, and indeed, in the harsh overhead light she reminded me of those full-figured women in paintings at the National Gallery. Wispy blondish hair fell loosely down onto large, ample breasts that forced her cleavage up into her neck. Her hands, one on top of the other, rested on the upper part of her stomach, just below her breasts. Stood next to her, Mercy's father seemed small in the simmering presence of his wife. He coughed gently and Mercy's mother stepped forward.

"Welcome sweetie, we've been so excited at your coming home," she said.

Mercy stepped towards her, kissed her on the cheek, and then tentatively embraced her father. In the glare of that awful light, I waited for them to turn and examine the stranger among them.

"So, now, tell me. Who is this guest you've brought from merry old England?" her father said, almost jovially.

"This is Bethnal. Bethnal Green," Mercy said, hesitantly.

"Bethnal Green, you're very welcome, I'm David, David Waters, Mercy's father," he replied, stepping towards me and offering me his hand, which I shook.

He took a step back, and I saw Mercy's mother, her hand regally stretched towards me. I thought she held my hand longer than necessary, and when she finally released me, she took a step back, all the while gazing at me, making me feel like a naughty child standing before the headmistress on the brink of a painful punishment.

Thankfully this awkward moment was shattered when a little woman with a broad smile and dancing eyes tumbled into the room. Barging Mercy's parents aside, she swung her fleshy arms in a delightful embrace around Mercy and they stood locked together, clutching each other for quite some time, before Mercy released her and turned to me.

"May, this is Bethnal Green. He'll be staying with us," she said, a healthy rush of colour rising in her cheeks as May turned to look at me.

Eyes that flickered with a sense of mischief examined me. Her smooth round cheeks, tinged with a hint of red, had dark brown freckles sprinkled across them.

"Bethnal Green. Child, you welcome," she said, then taking Mercy's hand in hers, she turned back to her, tenderly looking into her face.

Mercy's eyes began to well, at which point her parents informed us they'd see us for dinner and swiftly disappeared through one of the many doors leading out of the dining room.

As they stood looking at each other, I glanced at the photo on the side-table to confirm it was May and Mercy in the photo.

"Oh honey, I's so glad you home, you just don't know what it's been like without you round here, child, it's like…" she said before pausing. "Well, it just ain't the same," she continued, taking a step back, looking Mercy up and down once more and shaking her head. "My child, you lost weight too. 'fore you leave, and Lord I know that won't be long, I'm fixin' to get some meat on those skinny bones o' yours. Y'all came jus' in time, I'm fixin' dinner right now, an' now you here, I'm gonna rush down and get y'all some okra. I know you like it honey, so you gonna get it, just the way you like it, fried and crispy. Yo' mama's always complainin' when I fix it when you ain't here, but, now you back, I'm gonna buy me a cartload and make it nice an' crispy, jus' the way you like it hon," she said, leaving as quickly as she arrived, flying back through a door into the kitchen where, amid the clatter of pots and pans, she began to sing.

Mercy showed me to my room where I was to rest until dinner. I sat on the bed and thought about Joe and May, about how they possessed an easy air of confidence in the way they greeted me, speaking to me as if they'd known me for some time.

I opened the window, and as the sound of the city came rushing in over me, I looked down into the steamy narrow canyon below, listening to the muted honks of trumpet horns rippling up the sides of the buildings. For the next fifteen minutes or so, I sat in the small armchair by the window with my eyes closed, letting the sound of the city wash over me, thinking, trying to take in this absurd new world I'd suddenly landed in.

I heard the sudden creak of a loose floorboard outside the door. Hoping it was Mercy coming to my room with lusty pre-dinner plans, I hopped up from the chair, and listening at the door, heard May and Mercy whispering in the corridor. When Mercy's door closed and I heard May pass my door on her way back to the kitchen, I turned to survey the room.

Everything was neatly ordered, the bed as flat as a snooker table, the sheets tucked precisely in neat folds under the mattress. When I dived onto it, my head hit the pillow and the fresh scent of recently-laundered linen hissed out. I considered taking a quick nap, but was too excited, and jumping off the bed, I knocked from a chair next to the bathroom, a pile of towels onto the floor. After carefully rearranging them, I flicked the switch in the bathroom and a bright fluorescent light crackled on around the mirror above the washbasin. Twisting one of the gilded taps, water suddenly shot out splashing over the gleaming wall tiles, landing with loud slaps across the polished tiles of the floor. I quickly rubbed the floor dry with a towel, then explored behind the sliding, smoky-grey glass doors of the bath, to find a deep creamy-coloured tub, its polished enamel like a lake of warm milk, and above it, jutting out of the wall, a shower head the size of a small umbrella.

I returned to the bedroom and smoothed out the neat folds of the blankets on the bed and fluffed out the dent my head had made in the pillow. On account of my constant tossing and turning when I sleep, I ran my hand under the cotton sheet, tugging and releasing the sheet and blankets at the bottom of the bed until they were hanging loose, something Mum always did for me.

After a long shower, I felt refreshed, ready for whatever an evening in the most exciting city on earth might bring. Hoping Mercy would notice, I thought I'd wear the shirt I'd worn on our first date, but when I pulled it from the bottom of my case, even after shaking it out, it remained scarred with deep creases, clearly unsuitable for dinner with her parents. Then, one by one, I pulled every shirt from the case to find them all in a similar state.

Initially, I didn't panic, I thought of Mum, who often hung shirts in the steam of the bathroom before ironing them, and so I filled the bath with boiling water, until the bathroom was thick with foggy steam, then hung my shirt over the towel rail and closed the door, hoping the creases would simply dissolve. Using a technique Dad had taught me, to be used only when Mum wasn't around, I removed the scuff marks from my shoes with my sock and some spit, rubbing away until they shone like new.

As I sat naked on the bed admiring my handiwork, May knocked at the door and informed me that dinner would be ready in ten minutes. I checked on my shirt in the bathroom to find it still creased. I assessed each shirt again, selected the least creased, and thinking I might be able to stretch the worst of the creases out, pulled it down as hard as I could, tucking it deep into my underwear, then tightened my belt. After carefully doing up each button, I looked into the mirror, to see my trousers riding up into my crotch, I looked a ridiculous spectacle, like a young Norman Wisdom. Then, after a quick knock, the door slowly opened.

Wearing a white cotton dress with not a crease in sight, Mercy looked simply stunning. Her face was freshly made up, and when she kissed me, I tasted fresh minty mouthwash. She commented on how nice I looked. May then knocked and announced dinner was ready, and as we walked along the corridor towards the dining room Mercy whispered again, to just be *myself*.

As we approached the dining room, I heard the nasal drone of her parents discussing strategies to uncover the truth regarding my illicit involvement with their beautiful firstborn. When we entered the room, they were drinking aperitifs at a small bar near the kitchen door. Mercy's mother held a small sherry glass and her father swirled ice cubes in a small crystal tumbler. As they had on our initial encounter, when they turned towards us they retained a similar sense of detachment. Mercy's mother cut me a frigid stare, I felt on display, out of my depth.

"Oh, sweetheart, how wonderful you look this evening," said Mercy's mother, stepping forward to kiss her on the cheek.

"Thank you, Mother. Is May joining us tonight?" Mercy asked, looking at the table.

Her mother looked to her father who juggled the ice in his glass.

"I did ask her," she replied, "but she says she has so much to do with your being home. She hasn't left the kitchen since you arrived. I told her you were only here for the weekend, but she insisted that while you're here, you'll eat well. She says you've lost weight, but I'm not sure you have, honey. I hope she doesn't make that awful okra she used to spoon-feed you with when you were young. That's perhaps why..."

But she was interrupted by May, bundling through the kitchen door carrying silver trays of various cold cuts which she placed on a small table by the bar before bouncing back to the kitchen. I'd barely eaten on the plane, but etiquette required restraint, polite conversation, trying to smile convincingly and accepting a glass of soda water from Mr Waters.

"Well, Be-than, that's an interesting name. Is it English?" he said.

"Daddy! It's not Bethan, it's Bethnal. Bethnal Green. And it's a very English name," Mercy said, almost with a sense of pride.

"I'm named after my grandfather, I don't really know how he got the name," I said, which, of course, was absolute nonsense.

"It's just, it just doesn't sound like your average English first name. Now, if you'd been a Nigel or a Malcolm, well, that would have put you very much in the category of some fine compatriots of yours who, throughout history, have done your country proud," he countered.

Though unable to recall Nigels or Malcolms saving Britain from barbarian invaders, his pleasant tone gave me the impression his efforts to be nice were genuine. I'd arrived with their daughter unannounced, and so my presence in their dining room that evening must have been as much a surprise for them as it was for me. But while Mercy's chatty father smiled, probing me for clarification of the origins of my surname and enlightening me on particular events from English history, I could feel her mother's eyes fixed on me. On the few occasions I allowed my eyes to sweep in her general direction, I avoided her stare, my eyes seeing only her heavy breasts, swelling like porcelain soup bowls over the cut of her dress.

"Was your grandfather English then? I mean…" he continued, but before he could finish, both Mercy and her mother protested at the tiresome nature of his questions.

"No, no," I assured them, "it's OK. I don't mind. My grandfather, and as far as I know, all my family on Dad's side are from Widnes," I lied, my response met with awkward blank stares, interrupted once more by the ever-industrious May storming in, this time carrying two crystal jugs of ice water which she placed in the centre of the dining table.

"Mercy Waters," she declared, "I don't see yo' eatin' this food I've been slavin' over for the best part of the afternoon. You too

Bethnal, you look like you could do with some feedin' too," she said as she paused at the table to smooth out the creases in a napkin, her eyes widening as they met my shirt.

As Mr Waters told me of his family's arrival in America, elaborating in great detail of his grandfather's escape from a prison in Czechoslovakia, and of his vague Irish roots, May shuttled in and out carrying dishes, until the large dining table in the middle of the room was a resplendent, glorious feast, and she announced dinner was ready.

A new addition at dinner was Jake, Mercy's moody little brother, a boy with sandy-blond hair flopping down over his forehead making it hard to see his face. As he drank his lemonade, he occasionally flicked his hair to the side, revealing a boy bearing little resemblance to other members of his family, with skin so fair and his broad face so pale and freckled, I thought that perhaps he was adopted. His father's attempts to engage him in conversation were met with scowling monosyllabic grunts, the little scoundrel clearly upset at his obligation to be at the table. But I was thrilled with his tantrums. The more he whined, the less attention on me, and so when Mr Waters insisted he dispense with his baseball mitt at the table and he point-blank refused, I was growing really quite fond of him, hoping he'd keep it up until after dinner.

With his head almost in his lap, the tension simmered as he bluntly refused to follow any further requests from his father. Clearly attached to his mitt, he squirmed in his seat, huffing and puffing his refusals, the standoff remedied when May crept into the room and tickled his sides with one hand, while plucking the mitt from him with the other. As he held his hands aloft pleading for the mitt, she reasoned with him, sprinkling rationale into her trickery by explaining the importance of correct nutrition, asking him how he was going to play for the Yankees when he was so small. Then, she sweetened his appetite by suggesting that if he managed just one plate, then she might just be persuaded to let him have one of the tickets she had in her room for the next Yankees' home game, and Jake, suddenly upright in his chair, started to bolt down his mashed potato.

Despite Mercy's pleas for May to join us, she never did make it to the table that evening, claiming she had too much to do. She did linger at the table on one occasion however, coming in and standing behind Mercy, May's hands resting gently on her shoulders. As Mercy reached up for her hand, I noticed she looked more relaxed, the wine bringing a gentle flush to her cheeks. When her father insisted I try the wine, it warmed my insides, reminding me of the French wine we had in the cemetery on the day of that most extraordinary picnic. Clearly happy at how we'd almost cleared the table of what she'd prepared, May was all smiles. Until that is, her eyes fell on my shirt and she rushed off to fetch desserts.

With dessert over, May circled the table pouring coffee for everyone except Jake. Much to my delight, he had kept up his low-level moodiness throughout dinner, his parents' attention on me limited to discussion of London, Oxford and other parts of Britain of which I had no idea. But then, just as I was thinking of escaping with Mercy into the city, like much in this account, it feels as if that perhaps, what followed, didn't really happen, and unknown even to me, I was about to make an impression on the Waters family that not one of them was likely to forget.

In protest at having to remain in his chair, restless Jake had begun kicking the leg of the table. Mr Waters, ignoring him, hummed softly, and Mercy thumbed her napkin as we sat in an awkward silence, listening to Jake shake the table.

Mrs Waters finally broke the silence, enthusiastically declaring just how wonderful dinner had been, but then dropped a bomb when she announced that she, her husband and Jake were leaving for Amelia Island, Florida early the following morning.

Mercy stared blankly at the edge of her plate. A part of me wanted to protest at their impending departure, especially after their daughter had just crossed an ocean to see them. But sitting rigid in her chair, dabbing her lips with her napkin, Mrs Waters appeared completely unmoved by her announcement. Mr Waters cleared his throat, leant forward, and putting his elbows on the table, looked at me.

"Well, Bethan... uh, Bethnal, what do you do?" he said, then leant back in his chair and waited for my answer.

From my frequent visits to the States over the years, I've learned that the *what-do-you-do* question is *the* ice-breaker for Americans when they first meet. However, to a young boy unschooled in social etiquette of any description, this was an incredibly perplexing question. Somewhat bewildered, the responses that flew through my mind seemed either inappropriate or dull. But all eyes were back on me, including Jake's, who had stopped kicking the table and sitting upright in his chair, curious to see if there was anything remotely interesting about me. What did I do? I did nothing, well, not until I met Mercy, but a step by step account of my *doing* his daughter was hardly what they expected to hear.

"Music!" I blurted out.

Staring across the table at Mercy I saw a worried look appear in her eyes.

"Music?" responded Mr and Mrs Waters in unison, both shifting in their seats, their faces adopting an air of intrigue.

Mercy had told me on the plane that if they ask, I was to say I was "in college," and though lying to potential in-laws was not a good start to a possible life-long relationship, under the circumstances, it was all I had.

"I'm in college," I lied.

"You're in college? Studying music?" Mr Waters replied, tapping his fingers on the table as a mysterious and exotic *me* began to unfold.

Mercy, as if defeated, tossed her napkin onto the table, sat back in her chair and crossed her arms.

"Yes. I'm in college. Music. It's…nice," I said looking towards the kitchen door hoping for May to waltz back in. "Yes, I play violin. Classical. Some pop too, sometimes. Yes, violin," I continued, looking at Mercy who appeared increasingly distressed, as if I'd somehow betrayed her.

I suddenly realized I'd never actually mentioned to her that I played violin.

Mr Waters, still tapping his fingers on the table, hummed for a moment then turned to his son.

"Jake," he ordered, "that expensive violin you wanted so much in grade 4 and hated so much in grade 5. Go fetch it."

"Do I have to? Can I be excused?" he said, twisting in his seat.

"Bring the violin and then you may leave the table," interrupted Mercy's mother, intuitively picking up on her husband's intentions.

I was to perform.

"Mom, Dad, come on," protested Mercy, "he's our guest, he's not here to perform for us. Anyway, it's time we were on our way, I want to show him the city tonight."

"But honey," responded her mother, "just a short recital. I'm sure Bethnal wouldn't mind playing us something. Would you Bethnal?" she said, as Jake ran back into the room holding a black violin case which he pushed onto his father's lap. He grabbed his mitt, then shooting me a grin, disappeared from the room.

Mr Waters briefly inspected the case, then held it aloft over the table towards me.

"Bethnal?" he said.

I rose from my chair, accepted the case, then walked to the small side table by the window. Jake's smudged fingerprints ran like scars through the dust across the top of the case. If the violin hadn't been used for some time, I worried (and hoped) the strings would be warped beyond repair, saving me the humiliation about to unfold. However, when I opened the case and lifted the silk cloth covering the instrument, I saw the most beautiful violin. As expected, the strings lay limp but intact on the bow. I worried that without a tuning fork, pitch pipe or piano, which I used in the music room at school to tune my violin, I wouldn't be able to tune it.

I lifted the violin gently from the case; it was a good deal lighter than mine and clearly a violin of excellent quality. I felt Mercy watching me as I placed it back into the case and picked up the bow to make small adjustments to the tension screw. As I continued my preparations, her parents got up, and together, stood in front of me, watching my every movement.

Once I was satisfied with the tension in the bow, I lifted the violin from the case and began tightening the pegs, twisting them slowly, the creaking squeaks leaving Mercy's parents spellbound by the discordant sounds echoing from the hollow of the violin. In my first violin lesson, my teacher assured me that if I didn't practise regularly, the strings would lose their elasticity, become brittle, and break.

But the strings didn't break, in fact, as I ran the bow over them, they sounded fine, splendid even, and when I swung the violin up and under my chin in one rapid and rather dramatic movement, Mr and Mrs Waters stepped back, glancing at each other in muted wonderment.

When Mercy stood up, a worried look still simmering in her eyes, only then did I think of what I might play. It needed to be short, something obscure enough for them not to recognise when I missed chords. I thought back to that midweek meeting with Mercy, listening to Vivaldi's *Four Seasons* in her flat, and then, of course, it seemed obvious I should play *Summer*, the concerto I'd been working on in recent weeks for my final exam.

With the violin under my chin, I felt a slight trembling in my hand. My throat was dry and so I gently coughed. I released the violin from under my chin to feign more inspections, running the bow along a string one more time, frowning at its pitch, and then plucking and tuning random strings, drawing small comfort when I saw her parents nodding. I prolonged these preparations by making further needless checks of the pegs, tapping the end button, even sniffing at my chin rest and blowing imaginary specks of dust from the fine tuners, all simple unnecessary acts conducted solely to stall proceedings.

When I heard her mother sigh impatiently, with no eleventh-hour interventions from May busy in the kitchen, no alarm bells sounding for us to make a rapid exit, it was finally time to play. I cleared my throat and lifted the violin towards my chin. Taking a deep breath, I glanced up at them and lowered my chin onto the rest, her parents' eyes following my bow as I lifted it into the air. Then, I took another breath, held the bow just above the strings, and closed my eyes.

I'll never forget for as long as I live that first note rising into the silence of the room that evening. More equally beautiful notes followed, and though I'd played this concerto along to the recording many times in the Music room, it had never sounded as good as it did that evening. With my eyes closed, I imagined being in the rehearsal room at school, playing for myself, not to the woman I loved and her parents, fifty floors up in a New York skyscraper. I concentrated on each chord, my fingers smoothly sliding along the bow as I approached the middle section of the piece. Only with the final chords approaching, did I allow myself to open my eyes to see May at the kitchen door holding her apron in both hands looking at me. My eyes returned briefly to my bow, and when I looked up again, she had moved into the room where, for the briefest moment, she appeared to be resting on Mercy's shoulder. Then, on the last stroke, I closed my eyes, running the bow slowly across the string and holding it, until the final chord faded and silence took hold of the room once more.

When I opened my eyes, May and Mercy were standing together holding hands, their eyes shining with pure joy. May inched closer to her and pulled a tissue from her sleeve, passing it to Mercy. For a few seconds, I held Mercy's tearful gaze, her eyes speaking to me of things for which there are no words, a thousand messages still buried in me, and though she told me afterwards how wonderful she thought I played, it was only many years later that I learned the real significance of my performance that evening.

The room came back to life when May declared she had work to do and returned to the kitchen. Mercy's parents stood perfectly still, regarding me as if I'd just insulted them, her mother's cheeks a little flushed. Offering weak smiles, they thanked me for my efforts and hurried from the room declaring how they both adored Mozart. Mercy rushed forward and hugged me, whispering it was the most beautiful music she'd ever heard. Finally, it appeared I'd done something to impress her.

Back in my room, I lay on the bed thinking back on the events at dinner, of how Mercy's parents could be so distant. I thought of Mum and Dad, perfect parents who gave me everything, especially love. Suddenly being thousands of miles away from them felt like such an unnatural separation and I was gripped by a deep longing to see them, to be with them, and as I felt a tear welling, someone knocked at the door.

I took a couple of deep breaths to compose myself, then opened the door expecting to see Mercy. But it was May who stood before me, looking at me through sleepy brown eyes, her fragrant scent, like a dusting of talc, sailing into the room. Then, stretching her arm towards me, she said, rather demandingly, "Shirt!"

Five minutes later she returned, and still warm with razor sharp creases in all the right places, she handed me my shirt. I was embarrassed by her kindness and humbly thanked her. Then a strange moment followed. As we remained looking at each other, I had the impression she was examining me. Checking for further dishevelment in my attire, I glanced down at my trousers. She slowly turned to leave, but turned back. I sensed she wanted to say something. And then, from the left-hand pocket of her cardigan, she pulled a $100 bill, and lifting my hand, curled my fingers around it.

"Here," she said, in a tone so tender in its sincerity. "Take this. You, I can tell, are a good boy, and I know you gon' look after my Mercy, 'cos I can see what she means to you. Jus' you promise me you won't let no harm come her way. Ya hear?" she concluded.

"I hear," I responded, this unexpected act of such noble human kindness touching me to my core.

And then from within the darkness of the corridor, she called my name.

"Bethnal, you continue playin' that violin, ya hear? Vivaldi was a Master, and you being so young an' all, well, you did him proud."

"I hear," I said, and closed the door, feeling both flattered and humbled in equal measure.

17

New Friends

In just a few short weeks since meeting Mercy a new world had opened up to me. I'd accomplished more in that brief period than I'd managed to achieve in the preceding fifteen years. In no particular order of priority, I can list these accomplishments: I was no longer a virgin, I'd wowed future parents-in-law with an impressive Vivaldi concerto, I was most definitely in love, and, quite extraordinarily, I had become an international jet-setter. And, for reasons of which you will shortly learn, the events of that whirlwind weekend in New York are a little hazy now, but the strange events at dinner were, in fact, just a warm-up for what was coming later that evening.

In the taxi on our way downtown, Mercy confessed that she suspected her parents might 'try something', then quickly added how 'special' my performance had been.

"So, where are we going?" I asked.

"You'll see when we get there," she said playfully, her eyes smiling once more as she pulled me to her, kissing my cheek and slipping her hand along the inside of my thigh until her little finger was buried in my crotch.

Memories of that taxi ride remain with me, I was intrigued by every small detail of the city, things that most New Yorkers find commonplace. Like the small puffs of steam rising from grates in

215

the middle of avenues then quickly dissolving. And the fading sunlight catching the tops of buildings as it begins to drift westwards, and neon lights popping on, flickering life into bars and restaurants. Even today when I go to New York for work, I'm conscious of its sounds, its aromas, everything that gives the city its charge. I always take a taxi into the city, just as we did, and I stare through the window, waiting, anticipating Manhattan's appearance, its glorious towers rising again, to give me once more that sense of exhilaration, just as it did on my first visit. And when I feel it, I sometimes think that Mercy is near.

The taxi dropped us on a busy street where people were dining by candlelight on loading bays of old warehouses splendidly transformed into busy restaurants. Mercy tugged me to the far end of the street, to where a long queue running the length of a block led to a small door at the back of a warehouse. Just above the door, on the roof, a huge rotating spotlight shot a thick silver beam high into the night sky.

I was excited about meeting her friends in the more informal surroundings of a nightclub, especially as I'd never actually been to one. I thought we'd take our place at the end of the queue, but she grabbed my hand, again pulling me forward, sweeping past people patiently waiting.

About half way up the queue, just as she'd hit her stride, a piercing shriek calling her name came from somewhere in the queue bringing us to an abrupt stop. Mercy's eyes darted in and out of the sea of faces. Suddenly, she dropped my hand and disappeared into the queue, resurfacing moments later, followed by two strikingly large and quivering pale breasts, as white as milk, attached to a woman clearly thrilled to see Mercy again. Proud of her dimensions, the woman wore a strapless red sequin dress, shimmering and sparkling under the lights, held up solely by her enormous breasts. After hoisting Mercy into the air and hugging her, she finally released her and the two of them stood holding hands, looking each other up and down.

"Oh, honey. Where you been? This city ain't the same when you ain't heeya. God I missed you so much. Where you been?" screamed the woman before lunging in for another embrace.

"I've been in London, hon," replied Mercy, "don't you remember my party?"

"Honey," she replied, "you know I don't remember this morning. Lord, how'm I gonna remember way back whenever?"

Her accent was different to Mercy's, more like one of the characters in a show I liked, *The Beverly Hillbillies*, so I assumed she was from the south. Then Mercy went up on tip toes, whispered something, at which point the woman released a squeal her folks down south must have heard.

"You got you a boyfriend? A *real* English boyfriend? Where is he?" she panted, searching up and down the line for me.

Mercy waved me over to join them.

"Well, good Lord," screamed the smiling woman, eyeing me up and down as I slowly approached them.

"Well, girl, ain't he just the cutest little thing," she bellowed.

Stepping forward, she grabbed me and smothered me between her breasts, and though I could barely hear her, she declared that she wanted one.

"Hi. Very nice to meet you, hon. I'm Julieta," she said as she put me down, her breasts still inches from my nose, her hand stretching towards me.

Still dizzy from her initial greeting, I looked nervously up into her happy blue eyes, warily taking her hand.

"This is Bethnal. He's visiting from London," said Mercy.

"Well, welcome to America, honey, and to the greatest city on earth," boomed Julieta.

Then catching me off guard, she took hold of me again, and like America itself, so warm, plentiful, and generous, she celebrated my arrival in her country with another couple of sudden slaps of her breasts.

"Is DeeDee working tonight?" Mercy enquired.

"I'm sure she is. Honey, I reckon she's got a mattress tucked away back in there somewhere, she's always here," replied Julieta.

"Well, we'll see you in there," said Mercy, tugging me forward towards the front of the queue.

A heavy bass sound from inside the club shook the door, and above it, the giant spinning spotlight purred as it swivelled, sending a thick silver column up into the black night sky. On the wall next to the door a whirling blue light, like the light on the top a police car, threw light on those at the front of the queue.

Though fifteen, I probably looked thirteen, so if Mercy had plans of getting me into this club, then we had a problem. Perhaps she was thinking of slinking me in undetected, but the door leading into the club was so small, it would be impossible.

As we hovered near to the entrance, I looked back down the long line of people to see Julieta wasn't the only person out to impress that night. Where she opted to dazzle, others were more spartan in use of colour, one boy in particular catching my eye, his skinny white arms poking out of a black cape held together with safety pins, his dyed hair a shock of yellow, and under the lights, his face, dusted in heavy make-up, made him look ill. Standing beside him was a healthy, muscular young man, of perhaps twenty or so, dressed more traditionally in Levi's and a white T-shirt. He appeared intrigued by the adjustments his skinny counterpart was making to his cape, and shortly after striking up a conversation, he was soon helping his new friend rearrange pins in various parts of his cloak.

With the success of *Saturday Night Fever*, Disco music was still what everyone wanted in New York clubs in 1977. The emerging punk movement in mid-1970's London had yet to have an impact in America. I suppose what I witnessed that night was punk's nervous arrival into America, symbolised by the safety pin, already a notorious must-have fashion accessory in punk Britannia.

I first heard the word 'punk' one Sunday morning a month or so before that New York trip, when Mum declared the end of the world was with us. Holding up and shaking at me and Dad the middle pages of the *News of the World*, we saw pictures of kids in Chelsea, on the King's Road, with different parts of their anatomy pierced with safety pins. A few evenings later, as we ate dinner, I saw the Sex Pistols for the first time. This group were *the* poster boys of rebellion for my generation, and appearing on the early evening news, they famously snarled their way through an interview with Mum's favourite TV presenter, Bill Grundy, an experienced reporter who, seeking the cause of this new generation's dissatisfaction, openly mocked them, somewhat foolishly offering them the opportunity, on live television, to vent their discontent to the nation. Mr Grundy then sat back, smiling, occasionally cajoling his young guests to elaborate on their woes, and then what followed ranks as one of the most memorable moments of television from my youth.

For thirty thrilling seconds or so, producers scrambled to halt transmission as these youths unleashed a string of obscenities, many directed at Grundy himself. For the first time on live British television, the word "fuck" swept into living rooms up and down the country as people had their tea. It was a truly wonderful moment, those thirty seconds launching the Sex Pistols as global icons, instantly making their torn clothing, held together by safety pins, appear irresistibly charismatic. Dressed in designs by the savvy, new style guru, Vivienne Westwood, and under the pragmatic guidance of her sidekick, Malcolm McClaren, images of the band flaunting colourful spiked Mohawks flashed around the world. Their debut album, *Never Mind the Bollocks*, charted at number one overnight, and within a year the Sex Pistols were immortalised in the archives of pop history, elevating punk rock to levels of fame it probably didn't deserve. One evening shortly thereafter, as we watched a documentary charting the rise of this dynamic new youth movement, Mum reiterated something about the end of the world, Dad suggesting we bring back national service.

And so, as I observed this all-American boy, his golden skin and striking smile radiating below a lamppost which spilled a soft yellow light over him making his skinny new friend look undernourished, I was witnessing the first ripple of punk onto the shores of America. But then, just as I was about to join Mercy near the door, something quite unexpected happened. From deep within his pocket, the muscular boy pulled a safety pin of his own, one clearly much larger and thicker than the smaller ones attached to his friend's cape. For a moment he held it aloft, like a trophy twinkling under the light, and he was soon surrounded by a small curious group. But their intrigue suddenly turned to horror when in one swift movement, as if hooking a piece of meat, the boy thrust the pin through his ear lobe, and then smiling, he looked up hoping that those around him, already squirming in disbelief, might be proud of his new punk credentials. The smile rapidly slid from his face, however, when he felt heavy drops of blood running quickly from the punctured lobe down his neck into the fabric of his T-shirt, and people in the queue rushed towards him, surrounding him, calling for help. I moved a little closer to see people pressing handkerchiefs to his ear, trying to stem the flow of blood.

Then, from the front of the queue, there appeared to be another disturbance. When Mercy called, I joined her to see standing in the doorway to the club, a very tall, beautiful woman who, from the reaction of those shuffling forward calling her name, I assumed was a famous American celebrity. However, when she released the crimson rope hanging between two brass stands outside the door, and began checking IDs as people filed past her into the club, it appeared she was the doorwoman.

A sudden wail of wild sirens screamed into the street and the hectic blue flash of ambulance lights thundered towards us, skidding to a halt at the kerbside where the muscle boy sat shivering, holding his ear, his T-shirt saturated in blood. Two paramedics rushed from the ambulance, and after a brief conversation with the boy in the black cape, broad smiles appeared on their faces. They then hoisted the boy into the back of the ambulance and drove off.

When I turned back towards Mercy, I was startled to see the doorwoman towering over us, her face hidden in the glare of the giant gyrating spotlight behind her, the ringed glow of a silver corona shimmering like a halo around the edge of her afro. I thought our plans for the evening were scuppered, but then the woman stepped towards Mercy, a broad smile sweeping across her face.

"Mercy? Mercy Waters? Is that you, hon? Oh, my God," she screamed, then lifted her up, holding her in a tight embrace as she pulled her towards the doorway into the light.

This woman belonged on the covers of glossy magazines, her magnificent body, slender and toned like that of an athlete, made Mercy look like a child next to her. As they talked, the woman stepped in rhythm with the thumping bass coming from inside the club, her platinum blond afro shivering from side to side. Her beautiful eyes, stunning windows to her world, shone like black diamonds, her skin the colour of warm honey glistening like freshly-polished marble. And there was a lot of skin on show, four skimpy articles of clothing covering little, but making her look fabulously glamorous, each piece selected specifically to glimmer in the lights. Adding perhaps eight or nine inches to her height, golden boots with heels like fierce-looking spikes stretched up to the middle of her thighs, to just below a perfectly pert arse, barely covered by electric blue hot pants which matched the colour of her long painted finger nails. Though her breasts were small, teasing cleavage flashed out from within a little red crop-top no bigger than a headband, and when she turned towards me, a nervous tremble rumbled through me.

"Bethnal," Mercy said, a broad smile beaming across her face, "allow me to introduce Yena de Desea."

She extended her long caramel arm towards me, and looking up into her beautiful eyes I raised my hand to meet hers. As her warm, gentle eyes held mine, she took my hand, and the moment she touched me, a strange and sudden sensation jolted me, something about her instantly captivating me.

"Hello Bethnal, it really is a pleasure to meet you. You can call me DeeDee, all my friends do," she said, her wondrous eyes enthralling me.

"Pleased to meet you, too, DeeDee," I said, my voice breaking slightly on the second Dee.

She looked at Mercy and, as if I weren't present, described me as 'adorable', then turned to those at the front of the queue stamping their wrists as they filed past her into the club. We followed DeeDee inside where a long thin strip of ultraviolet light running along the ceiling inside immediately lit up the stamps she thumped onto our wrists. She gave Mercy a quick kiss on the cheek, and as she made her way back outside, called back to her.

"Honey, you make sure you come find me in there, I've got you a home-coming present," she said, winking at her. And then, raising her perfectly-plucked eyebrows and nodding in my direction, she added, "there are laws about that honey, if we get raided, leave through the office," then laughing, she disappeared outside.

Walking hand in hand together along the narrow tunnel leading into the club, the thumping bass grew louder. As we approached the doors, terror and exhilaration gripped me in equal measure, and when they flew open, a heaving rush of sweaty air and pumping high-energy music suddenly rushed over us. As Mercy pulled me through the crowd, lights flashed and swirled between the hectic sea of smiling faces. She seemed to know where she was going, but when she stopped next to a doorway leading to another part of the club, where, dressed in a smart black suit, his white shirt open at the neck, the largest black man I'd ever seen stood guard, I thought she was lost. He looked so serious, until he looked down and saw Mercy, and he smiled, stooping down to kiss her gently on the cheek before his big arm threw open the curtain behind him and we passed through into another part of the club.

Dimly-lit, a few small tables with unlit candles in wine bottles were scattered around the room. We sat on stools at the bar and watched four sweaty barmen in the other part of the club darting back and forth, expertly juggling bottles of liquor as they saw to the needs of the multitude in the other part of the club. Resting one arm on my shoulder, Mercy stretched her other arm out over the bar hoping to catch the attention of one of the barmen. After some moments, without success, she slumped back down onto her seat, pulled me to her, and kissed me.

"Two vodka-tonics. Finish 'em up, then get a room!" came a sudden voice from behind the bar.

Looking up, a barman was holding two drinks, gazing at Mercy with an unusually cold glare.

"You know, you should treat your customers with a little more respect, especially those that make it into this room," Mercy responded in a similarly dismissive tone.

"Oh please," he continued, "the trash I serve this end of the bar ain't worth a shit."

This acidic tête-à-tête grew even tenser when she stood on the rung of the stool, arching her body across the bar towards him until their faces were almost touching. Holding each other's frosty gaze, neither flinched, neither ready to back down. Then, when his face moved closer to hers and she uttered, quite bluntly, a solitary word, "fucker," I considered calling the giant bouncer just behind the curtain. But then the barman's face suddenly softened, a smile appeared, and he kissed her gently on each cheek.

"Welcome back, honey," he said, "I heard you been travelling. London? You back for good?" he said, his eyes then shifting to me.

"This is Bethnal, he's visiting for the weekend," Mercy said, smiling.

"Hi Bethnal, I'm Randy," he said, then looking at her, "and you brought him to this dive. You shoulda taken him uptown to 54, show him some movie stars."

I shook his hand, somewhat relieved that they knew each other. Despite this dramatic introduction to the nature of their relationship, from the warm way they continued talking to each other, they were clearly very close. With a long slug of my vodka-tonic, I finished my drink and crunched into an ice cube. As he continued talking to Mercy, Randy pulled a vodka bottle from a rack below the bar and I watched as he poured, splashing vodka over ice into a plastic glass then squeezing in some lime before running the peel around the rim and dropping it into the drink. He added a splash of tonic, stirred it, and pushed it in front of me.

We were joined in this part of the club by two very tall women, high beehive hairstyles forcing them to stoop as they entered, one tripping, the other laughing then slapping her with a small handbag as they made their way to the other end of the bar where they continued laughing loudly, giving me the impression they were already drunk. Once comfortable on their stools, they lit cigarettes, and Randy, looking at them, in a raised voice commented on "the amount of trash in the club tonight." He then fixed us a couple more drinks and scuttled off to serve them, returning moments later with a small paper napkin folded into a ball which he gave to Mercy.

Mercy went to the bathroom, and with the vodka-tonics creeping through me, I sat listening to the hypnotic thumping of the music, swaying slightly on the stool. I thought back to my performance at dinner, thinking that at last I'd done something to impress her. I felt so happy. The chat from the two women at the end of the bar suddenly softened, and I looked up to see them through a cloud of hazy blue smoke looking over at me, smiling. One of them waved at me, so I waved back, nervously.

"Another vodka-tonic?" Randy enquired, appearing in front of me, the bottle already in his hand. "Don't worry about those two ol' witches," he said glancing back at them, "they just ain't got no homes to go to," he continued, before plopping another drink on the bar in front of me and returning to chat with them.

Randy must have been in his late twenties, clearly a charmer, and though initially I thought his face rather plain, it grew more handsome with each drink.

"How you doing hon? You OK?" Mercy whispered, skipping up onto her stool.

"I'm feeling really good," I replied, my first experience of drunkenness whirling and whistling inside of me. "Really good. No, really, really good. In fact, I'm magic. I feel fucking magic," I continued, and she started laughing, blowing Randy a kiss and waving for a couple more drinks.

And then, the moment I asked how she'd met him, she stopped smiling, paused just long enough to make me think I said something I shouldn't, then described how the man lacing us with liquor had taken her virginity two summers before.

Her goal that summer was, indeed, to lose her virginity. She had left the city to work in a swanky hotel on Long Island, and with so many college students working there, most with similar ambitions, she figured that meeting her objective would be a relatively simple exercise. However, she soon found that pickings were slim, and though she didn't really fancy him, Brad from Boston, whose uncle owned the hotel, was the one she felt came closest to her specifications. On the beach with him on her second night, as she listened to other couples groaning as they fondled and fucked, she let Brad slide his finger inside her. Though very tempted, she resisted his advances for full penetration, confessing her status as a virgin, explaining that she wanted her first time to be more intimate, and promised herself to him the following night in a part of the beach which offered a reasonable degree of privacy.

The following night she arrived thirty minutes early with a blanket and bottle of Jack Daniels. As she waited, she cracked it open and took a couple of sips. An hour later however, she was still waiting, sat on the blanket with the bottle half-empty in her lap, accepting that Brad wasn't coming. Later that night, as she lay frustrated in bed yearning for relief, after taking temporary measures to satisfy her desire, she decided to quit her job and head back to the city to achieve there what she hadn't at the beach.

The following evening, with students still on summer vacation, the two or three college bars where she went looking for guys were almost empty. At last call, she reluctantly finished her drink, and minutes later, stood on the kerb trying to hail a taxi, she felt drunk, deflated, and most depressing of all, still very much a virgin.

When a taxi pulled up, the door flew open and a woman, dressed in an outfit of brightly-coloured feathers attached to a long red cape, not unlike the one Superman wears, stepped out.

Immediately drawn to this peacock's extravagant glamour, Mercy, still very keen to meet a man, followed the woman the short walk to the club, and once inside, introduced herself, the woman instantly thrilled to hear that Mercy had followed her there. The woman was DeeDee, and moments later they were chatting like old friends, sitting at the bar together drinking liquor served by the dashing barman, Randy. He plied them with drinks, large vodka tonics, which in no small way, along with his charming demeanour, resulted in Mercy convincing herself that Randy possessed all the qualities she was looking for in a man that night.

An hour or so later, the club was thinning out. DeeDee was dancing and Randy, who had been dazzling Mercy for an hour or so, invited her outside into the alley at the back of the club for a line of cocaine. She knew this was her moment, and ten minutes later, with the cocaine shooting through her, despite Randy's initial resistance to take her, she re-entered the club having accomplished with Randy in an alley what she'd failed to manage with Brad on a beach.

The next part of her account I found especially intriguing, and was, in fact, quite relieved to hear. On her way home in a taxi, still high on alcohol and cocaine, she felt an overwhelming desire to see Randy again, and so instructed the driver to return to the club where she found Randy straddled between the legs of another barman, both shirtless, and locked in a sensuous kiss.

She stayed in the club until dawn, drinking and talking to DeeDee who filled her in on the charming, but ever-so-versatile Randy. She didn't return to the club for some months, but when she did, in a gesture of no hard feelings, Randy welcomed her back with free and frequent drinks, and by the end of the night they were both laughing about their unusual experience in the alley. Before she left that night, Randy added her name to the VIP list, giving her access to the bar at which we were sat.

"Honey," Mercy said, "enough history lessons for one night. We're going dancing. Come on, finish your drink and let's go. What d'ya say?"

"Sure," I said eagerly, and though I'd never danced before, with warm alcohol flowing through me, I felt invincible.

I was ready to give anything a go that night which, quite unwittingly, proved to be the case.

As I jumped down off the stool, she took my hand and dropped in it a small white tablet.

"Take that," she said.

"What is it?" I replied, thinking it perhaps an aspirin.

"A little something to keep you up, it's going to be a long night by the looks of it," she said, popping one into her mouth.

She threw a twenty dollar bill on the bar, and after shouting our goodbyes to Randy, I swallowed the pill, and we shuffled off towards the dance floor.

18

Double Whammy

Sweat was pouring out of me, flush after flush of extreme happiness, a euphoric soaring exhilaration, made sweeter by the wild and spinning beams, blinding me, zapping me, shooting in, out and across the drenched cavorting bodies thrusting me up closer to Mercy who was running her hands up and down my back below my saturated shirt. I'd never been happier in life, I wanted the night to last forever, to let these feelings of rushing splendour carry me through life. So when the music slowed, the lights dimmed, and we were all plunged into a sudden darkness, total blackout, I shouted to keep the music pumping.

From somewhere deep within the recesses of the club, a powerful blast of trumpet fanfare ripped across the floor, something special was about to happen. Amid the frenzied whistling and shouting I held Mercy's hand, waiting, until suddenly, as the echoing fanfare grew louder, a spotlight lit up a small stage to the side of the dance floor. We pushed our way through until we were stood below it and the fanfare abruptly stopped. A tense and whispered hush ran across the floor before a high-energy beat exploded among us, thundering, thumping through the club, the dance floor erupting once again into that wonderful hysteria. Then, from behind a small makeshift curtain, a dreamy vision appeared before us. DeeDee, a glittering superstar, sparkling below the lights, smiling and blowing kisses, stepped into the spotlight. On legs like well-oiled pistons, she strutted back and forth across the platform before launching into song, and the dancefloor exploded back to life, a frenzy of screaming, waving and yelling made all the more frantic by manic strobe lights crashing across our heads.

I only vaguely remember Mercy shouting to me something I was unable to hear. Then, showing me her tongue and pointing to mine, I dangled the tip of my tongue over my lip which she swiftly stroked with her index finger. Though unknown to me then, joining the little white pill and vodka rushing through my system, was my first hit of acid.

What happened shortly after remains a blur. I can remember looking up at DeeDee and feeling my body, so light and loose, floating before this glorious spectacle, an unstoppable rolling swell of emotion gathering pace within me. I wanted to let her know how happy I was, I wanted her to see this joy on my face, on Mercy's face, on everyone's faces, so she might understand how I loved her for loving Mercy, for loving me, for loving everyone. And then, when she saw me and stooped to touch my hand, a powerful jolt flashed through me again, and when I turned to Mercy, to show her my joy, everything suddenly stopped.

Standing alone, in total darkness, my heart thumped loudly in my ears, my nostrils flaring as I breathed. I called Mercy's name but she didn't respond. When I called a second time, a solitary red light lit up the stage. DeeDee had gone, and in her place, standing in front of a microphone gazing down on me, was a woman with a white cape loosely pinned about her neck, her small penetrating eyes holding me fixed to the spot. I turned, looking for Mercy, only to see I was alone on an empty dance floor. I looked up again at the woman, then heard a noise behind me. I turned to see a line of shadowy figures stretched across the floor. My eyes, slowly adjusting to the half-light, was shocked to see DeeDee standing in the middle of the line staring at me, her outline tall, slender, towering over those next to her. But she looked different. Her smile and the sparkle in her eyes gone, replaced by a blank, ominous aspect made all the worse when I saw Mercy standing to her right. I searched for an explanation in her eyes, but like DeeDee's, they too were peculiarly vacant. And then, looking along the line, I saw the people I'd met that night, Julieta, Randy, the two laughing women from the bar, and, most bizarrely, at the end of the line, his shirt still stained in blood, the boy taken away in an ambulance earlier.

In a mad panic I tried to rush over to them. But I couldn't move. When an electric beat broke the silence, I turned to see the woman on stage glowing ruby under the harsh red spotlight, pointing at DeeDee and the others. In one smooth movement she ripped off her cape to reveal a tight leather bra lined with small silver studs that twinkled in the lights. She shouted, in Spanish, *Vamos*, and all of a sudden, I felt the sweaty heat and energy return to the floor. Marching across the stage in her long leather boots stretching up to the middle of sturdy thighs, the woman performed a series of twists and turns she made look exceptionally easy. I looked behind me to see the line snaking across the floor, stomping towards me in perfectly-choreographed moves, each movement mirrored by that of those next to them, and as they approached me, in the lights splashing over them, I was so happy to see DeeDee and Mercy smiling once more.

But then, a most strange and overpowering sensation took hold of me, as if adrenalin were shooting through me, my arms and legs, my entire body began to quiver, and as a bizarre tingling sensation rushed through me, I felt myself lurching towards them. Though I resisted at first, I suddenly wanted to be with them, and, quite miraculously, my feet began to slide across the floor, as if on ice, gliding towards Mercy and DeeDee, into an opening between them, and taking their hands, my body fell into perfect and spectacular step with everyone else, DeeDee and Mercy smiling, everyone smiling again, and I felt like a child once more, like Peter Pan flying across a starlit sky, and when the floor lit up into a patchwork kaleidoscope, a thousand different colours flowing up and sweeping through me, a feeling of intense love rushed through every part of me, a feeling I hoped would surely last forever.

"Bethnal? Bethnal, hon? Bethnal! Can you hear me? Bethnal, come on, you have to wake up," I heard Mercy saying, as if she were calling me from far away.

"You think he's gonna be OK? I'll come with you if you want hun," said DeeDee.

"DeeDee," I said looking up, straining to see her under the bright light behind her. "I love you. Where are the lights? I want to see the lights again. I want to dance. Where's the music?"

"He's OK," Mercy said, laughing, "I'll give him a couple of aspirin, he'll be fine. Just a bad trip. His first, I think."

"No, no. It was great. I wanna dance. C'mon, let's go dance," I protested as they helped me to my feet and out into the street.

As a taxi pulled up, I heard laughing as they hugged, then DeeDee appeared before my face, taking it in her hands telling me she enjoyed meeting me and that she hoped to see me again sometime before disappearing back into the club. I called after her, telling her that I loved her.

I woke up in a taxi with my head in Mercy's lap, a cool breeze blowing in through the window. As she ran her fingers softly through my hair I recognised her scent, and sat up for a moment to look out into the unfamiliar empty avenues, then slumped back into her lap.

On our way up in the lift, I thought of sneaking into her room, but as we entered the apartment, my body felt so weak, probably why I stumbled over one of the two large suitcases ready for her parents' early-morning departure. Mercy took me to my room, kissed me goodnight then disappeared into the darkness of the corridor.

With the exception of an occasional muted honk from the street below, an unusual hush was running through the city. In the shadowy light coming in through the window I pulled off my clothes, leaving them in a dark pile on the floor. The most adventurous and exciting day of my life was coming to a close and I was ready to sleep. May had been in to remake the bed, tucking the sheets in tightly back under the mattress. I wrenched up the top sheet and slid in, lying flat on my back barely able to move, lacking both strength and desire to loosen them. And, as I lay looking at the dull orange glow falling through the curtains into the room, I tried to drift off, but realised I felt quite awake.

I thought back to the club, trying to piece back together events as they actually happened, but I couldn't remember much. My thoughts then turned to my dinner-time performance, and if it had really happened, but everything seemed so muddled, the frosty dinner, my violin solo, the club, DeeDee, the dancing, it all seemed so impossible, nothing in this city seemed normal.

Just as I felt myself drifting off, I woke with a start, thinking I'd heard a noise outside the room, a creaking sound like the one I'd heard earlier when both May and Mercy had knocked. I sat up and looked towards the door, waiting, listening, watching. Just as I thought I'd imagined it, I heard it again, and watched as the door slowly opened to see Mercy's shadowy figure enter, cross the room and stop at the foot of the bed.

"Mercy? Is that you?" I whispered, my heart pounding, and trapped below the linen sheets, my erection ready for action.

"Shhhh. Yes," she responded.

Resting on my elbows, I strained to see what she was doing. Her frustrated muted gasps ceased once the sheet at the bottom of the bed fell loose, allowing my legs (and erection) to move without restriction. She suddenly disappeared, I thought perhaps below the bed, but then I felt her hands clasp my ankles and slide slowly up my legs towards my knees. I fell back onto my pillow knowing exactly what was to follow, and the moment her mouth surrounded my cock, I came.

As she left, I called to her, telling her that I loved her.

"Me too," she whispered, and slipped out of the room.

The cool air on my feet poking out from the sheets at the bottom of the bed felt good. The most perfect day of my life was finally drawing to a close. "Me too," she had said. She really did love me.

When I awoke, the unusual noise of traffic in the streets below confirmed to me that the previous day (and night) had in fact happened, and that I was in New York.

I made my way to the dining room and listened to subdued chatter inside for some time before finally peeking around the door. Mercy and May were sitting at the table giggling like school children, and only then did I remember that Mr and Mrs Waters had left for Florida.

Over the next two days, we took in the sights. Starting at the Battery after breakfast, we caught the ferry to see the Statue of Liberty before heading back to Manhattan where we spent the remainder of our time taking photos of magnificent buildings including the Twin Towers that stretched into the blue New York sky. At the top of the Empire State Building, I thought of King Kong and his valiant efforts to stay alive. And, in the cold light of day, I told Mercy again that I loved her.

On our final afternoon, we ate Reuben sandwiches in Central Park then fell asleep together below a cherry tree. New York was magical; I didn't want to leave it for the drab familiarity of unambitious London, and sensing my disappointment at our impending departure, Mercy promised we'd return, soon, maybe drive across the country together, to California, stopping off in the deserts of west Texas, New Mexico and Arizona, and trek the Grand Canyon.

May met us at the door when we arrived at the apartment in the late afternoon. In my room she'd left a fresh set of towels on the bed and had washed and ironed my shirts. I finished packing, took a quick shower and then went to Mercy's room to make sure she had my passport. Passing the kitchen on the way to her room, I heard voices. Looking through a gap in the door, I saw Mercy crying, cradled lovingly in May's arms, and seeing this tender embrace made me realise, it was time to go home.

19

Tea

Standing on the platform at Earl's Court station I felt a lump rising in my throat. She kissed my cheek and whispered "I love you." From the tube, I waved at her through the window, and seeing her alone on the platform reminded me of the first day I saw her.

As I headed for the Northern Line platform at Leicester Square, it suddenly occurred to me that my scheming could have all gone wrong, that Mum and Dad were waiting for me at home having discovered my camping trip was a ruse. I imagined them sitting on the sofa comforting each other, Mum crying into her tea towel as they awaited news of my death.

So, as I turned into my street, I approached the house with some trepidation, relieved to step through the door onto a pile of letters. As I gathered them up, the phone rang.

"Hello," I said.

"Bethnal, it's Mum," came her voice, flat, edged with disappointment. "Your uncle passed away on Saturday evening."

"How's Dad?" I asked, softly.

"He's fine, love. We were all prepared for it, and being here, near him, has been the right thing to do. The funeral's today and we'll be home tomorrow. Dad told me to say hello, and Bethnal, we're both so sorry we had to leave you behind. Anyway love, I'm glad you went camping, you would have been miserable up here. How was it, the camping, did you enjoy yourself? Did you get enough to eat? Oh son, there's the pips, must go. Will give you a call tonight if I get a chance. Love you. Make sure you feed yourself."

The following evening I was surprised to see them laughing as they came into the sitting room, the seductive smell of a fish and chip dinner trailing in behind them. Mum hugged me, longer than she might normally, remarking that I looked healthy, that the country air had done me the world of good. As she fetched plates from the kitchen, Dad put his hand on my shoulder and looked at me. Though his eyes looked tired, I could tell he was happy to see me. He shook my hand, which I thought a little strange, then sat in his chair, opened his newspaper and normal family life was back on track.

Over dinner, Mum remarked again how well I looked, repeating that the country air had done me the world of good. I fudged together sufficient detail of a "camping trip" but felt wretched for deceiving them, for keeping them in the dark about having someone other than them in my life now. But they'd just lost Uncle Robert, they weren't ready to lose me. And though unknown to me then, I would need them at my side shortly thereafter, when they would finally learn of Mercy. However, as they expanded on the misfortunes of relatives they'd not seen for years, most of whom I'd never met, I felt so happy to see them free of the strain brought about by death, to see them smiling again.

I spent the evenings of that week in my bedroom sketching and listening to Vivaldi, producing new sets of drawings based on events and people from that marvellous weekend in New York.

By the end of the week, drawings of the city were scattered around my room – the Empire State, the Twin Towers, the Chrysler building, among others. I'd spent a good deal of time working on receding perspective, drawing what I remembered of the long straight avenues disappearing into a single point. Most of my new sketches were of Mercy, and though I tried to draw several of DeeDee, I couldn't capture the magic of her eyes which frustrated me. A sketch I drew of May and Mercy together, holding each other, as they had in the kitchen, was one I thought I might present to her at some point in the future.

Arriving downstairs on Saturday morning, the house was empty. Mum had left early to meet a childhood friend visiting London for the day, and Dad was in the shed banging away at something. I had to meet Mercy at two o' clock outside Green Park station, so I spent the morning on the sofa watching cartoons, keeping an eye on the clock.

When I arrived at the station ten minutes early, Mercy came up from behind and threw her arms around me. As I held her, I ran my chin along the soft skin of her neck, breathing in the scent which reminded me of our taxi ride back from the club in New York.

"What are we up to today? I'm afraid I can't do New York, perhaps we can stay closer to home. Madrid, perhaps?" I said, kissing her on the cheek, my arm draped around her shoulder.

"Honey," she said, "no trains, boats or planes today, we're staying local. And we're almost there," she said.

Then taking my hand, she pulled me off in the direction of Piccadilly Circus, stopping after some thirty seconds outside the Ritz Hotel in Piccadilly.

"Tea?" she said, pulling me up the steps and through the shiny revolving doors into the lobby of the hotel.

Darting in and out of the lobby across soft burgundy carpet in neat hotel attire, hotel employees smiled and nodded at guests. Elegant chandeliers of fine cut glass shimmering majestically overhead made it feel like a palace. It was like I'd stepped back in time, into a scene from one of Mum's favourite programmes she watched on Sunday evenings after tea, *Upstairs, Downstairs*.

As a group of aging Americans ganged up on the small French concierge who smiled patiently as they badgered him for directions to Buckingham Palace, a man no bigger than me, with tassels dangling from the shoulders of a military-looking dark blue jacket, appeared in front of us. He welcomed us to the hotel, bowing his head as he shook Mercy's hand, as if to proudly display the letter R embroidered in gold on the peak of his hat. He summoned another employee, a lower-ranking official who marched towards us carrying a black clipboard, wearing a wide and welcoming smile.

"Ms. Waters. Party of two for afternoon tea. So very nice to see you again, madam," he said, and we followed him along a wide corridor, the walls lined with faded black and white photographs of kings, queens and other people of note, into a small room full of whispering people, the antechamber to the grand tea salon where, inside, amid the delicate clinking of porcelain chinaware, I could hear the low humming of polite chatter.

From behind a podium just outside the tea room, a smiling waitress checked names on a clipboard. She informed us that the next session would be starting in five minutes then gave directions to the nearest powder room. Women scampered off to reassemble minutes later, only marginally prettier, and then another waiter swung open the stately gilded doors and ushered us to our tables in the main tea room.

Mercy's waiter held her chair as she sat, and thinking he might offer me the same courtesy, I paused. But once she was comfortably seated, he smiled, gave a small bow and informed us our waiter would be with us momentarily.

Once seated, I was somewhat disappointed to have my back to the grandeur of our surroundings. This inconvenience, however, was offset by the chance positioning of the biggest mirror I'd ever seen hanging within a solid frame of twisted gilded wood, easily the size of a snooker table, just above Mercy on the wall behind her. In it, I could see, more or less, everyone in the tea room, scores of middle-aged women sitting at tables in twos and threes, hunched over tea cups, laughing, discreetly monitoring women who, just like them, had donned their best hats for a day out in London.

As I sat back, sinking into the plush velvet of my chair, I watched as waiters, snaking between tables, pushed serving trolleys covered in white tablecloths which rattled under the strain of the tiered silver trays loaded with small triangular sandwiches, delightful little cakes filled with creams of various colours and the umpteen accessories required to serve and ingest a cup of tea at the Ritz correctly. As each waiter arrived at his table, he delicately placed the trays before the women, their faces registering genuine surprise as he poured their tea, as if they were witnessing small miracles. Mum often called people like this 'posh', and as I continued to monitor events in the room, I thought of an incident from not so long ago which involved Mum, Dad, and me, one in which this fine establishment was mentioned.

Fresh out of the bath one day, I shouted down the stairs for Mum to bring me up my shirt. Almost immediately, I can't remember his exact wording, but Dad shouted back up the stairs, calling me Prince Charles, Lord Muck, or something similar, informing me that we didn't live at the Ritz, and that I was to come down and get my own bloody shirt. Moments later Mum met me at the foot of the stairs smiling, passing me my warm shirt and asking what I wanted for tea.

As we studied the menus, Mercy took excited intakes of breath and asked me what I was having. I felt slightly embarrassed as, although by no means an extensive menu, I'd neither heard nor recognised the name of a single cake or tea listed.

"Tea and cakes," I responded cheekily, just as the waiter arrived.

"Yes, madam?" he said, flicking open a small pad.

"Tea and cakes," she responded, mimicking me, grinning.

"We have a wide selection of both teas and cakes, madam," responded the pale and lifeless waiter.

"What's good?" Mercy enquired, running her finger up and down the menu, shaking her head from side to side as she tried to decide.

"I can assure you, madam," he continued, his chin held slightly aloft, "that everything is of the highest quality."

"OK then. Bring me a little bit of everything. We'll give it all a try," she promptly replied, thanked him, and passed him the menu.

"You would like a selection of everything madam?" he repeated, scribbling the order in his pad, and once he'd gone, and we'd managed to stop giggling, she told me what had inspired this visit to the Ritz.

One of the requirements of her course was to research the origins of one of London's famous landmarks. And so when her professor handed out the list of buildings from which students had to choose, as a regular at the Ritz nightclub in New York, she thought the possibility of exploring her city's British counterpart very appealing. When she arrived at the address in Piccadilly to find an exclusive hotel, she felt both silly and surprised, but also excited at the prospect of learning more about this swanky London institution. From a phone box outside Green Park station, she called the hotel and was put through to the general manager, a fellow New Yorker, familiar with the demands of the assignment as he had personally authorised the hotel's listing with the university. Minutes later, in the lobby, in his crisp, light grey suit, somewhat younger than his voice had suggested, he greeted Mercy with a warm handshake. Not much older than her, his swarthy good looks and winning smile, probably Italian, were more Hollywood than New York, and as they sat in his office on the first floor talking about their lives back home, his secretary brought tea.

He invited Mercy to see the hotel, and passing from room to room, he provided her with a wealth of historical information, detailing not only facts about the hotel's origins such as dates, architects' names and costs of construction, but also more lurid description of scandalous events that had unfolded within the walls of this fine English establishment. His eyes lit up as he revealed how at one period in its history the hotel had functioned, more or less, as a 'bordello' for mistresses of renowned politicians and select members of the royal household, details he requested Mercy not use in her assignment.

She found it a thoroughly entertaining afternoon which ended with him inviting her for champagne in the bar just off the lobby. It was there he told her of the hordes of suburban English ladies, of a certain age, who packed the tea room to escape the misery of their dull lives on Saturday afternoons. He then insisted she experience it first-hand, and despite a waiting list of months, made an immediate booking for the following Saturday at two o' clock. Though I found her account intriguing, its enthusiastic delivery had me thinking that perhaps it wasn't just the champagne she'd had with him.

"I hope it was only the champagne he had from you," I said, unable to stop such drivel spilling from my lips.

Staring blankly at me, I thought I'd offended her. But her eyes suddenly brightened, and leaning over the table towards me, she continued her account, whispering that the general manager was, in fact, the lover to an MP, a high-ranking member of the Cabinet, married with children, almost the Prime Minister's right-hand man. Knowing nothing of politicians, I was immune to such scandalous intrigue, the type of salacious scoop Mum scoured the *News of the World* for each Sunday. When she finished her account, I sat back looking in the mirror at the industry in the room, thinking of the manager, of his personal connection to the British government, and of the whores who'd made their homes in rooms just above us. And then our tea arrived.

The waiter attended to Mercy's napkin, fluffing it out, handing it to her and then placing the mini-feast of assorted delicacies decorating the multi-tiered sterling silver tray in the middle of the table. He then poured our tea, offered a small nod and left us to study the opulence before us. Shiny cream oozed out from a mountain of colourful pastries, glistening delights we were reluctant to disturb, conjured up by skilful culinary magicians holed up in the bowels of the hotel below.

From the top tier, Mercy carefully dislodged a small cake that resembled a boat. Biting into it, she sighed softly, closed her eyes, and inhaling through her nose, nodded her approval. I tried a pastry neatly glazed in chocolate, whose chilled cream squirmed across my tongue, like nothing I'd ever tasted. And for ten minutes or so, we worked our way through the contents of the tray, communicating recommendations via small nods and sounds to confirm our approval. When our cups ran low, as an Englishman, I insisted I pour, surprised to see tea leaves swirling in the cup, something I'd not seen since childhood, thinking it odd that teabags, such a practical modern invention, had yet to reach the Ritz.

With the tray empty, we sat in silence for some time reflecting on the delights we'd just savoured. I looked up into the mirror, and seeing tables piled high with so many cakes, I was reminded of a robbery in which I was involved when I was nine or ten. A McVities' biscuit factory had recently opened on a nearby industrial estate, not far from my house, and word on the street was that local boys had come away with a rich booty of the factory's creamy contents. When some older boys from the neighbourhood unexpectedly took a shine to little me and another kid my age, and about my size, asking us to go with them to see the factory, we were thrilled at promotion into their gang.

When we arrived at the factory, one of the boys hurled a half-brick through the window, threatening to throw us inside if we didn't do as he demanded. He hoisted me up towards the window, and though I tried to avoid one of the deadly-looking shards of glass still in the frame, one cut me, slicing deeply into my forearm, leaving me with a scar I still bear today. Once inside, we found hundreds of palettes stacked high with boxes of cakes and biscuits. Following orders exactly, we threw them through the window for the boys outside to catch. Afterwards, hidden within the confines of one of the underground camps most kids built at the beginning of each summer holiday, we consumed every single cake, remaining there for some time, slumped like beached whales making plans for a return raid the following night.

Mercy suddenly giggled. She leaned across the table, drawing my attention to two large women sitting at a table not far behind me. I leaned back in my chair and looked up into the mirror, easily finding the two women licking cream from their fingers. Mercy commented that they must be regulars, and to stifle my laughter, I quickly covered my mouth with my napkin. Once I'd stopped laughing, I tossed the napkin towards the table but it fell to the floor. As I stretched down to pick it up, Mercy commented on two other women, not far from our table, who'd been engaged in animated conversation ever since we arrived. One of them was wearing the strangest hat and she insisted I see it. I looked up into the mirror once again, but angled just away from the wall, there was a blind spot and I couldn't see them. Mercy accused me of being 'too British' to quickly turn and glance, and as she continued to provide further humorous description of the woman's hat, it was clearly an object worth seeing.

My plan was to throw my napkin to the floor then stoop down and steal a look at the hat as I picked it up. I gave Mercy a quick wink, tossed the napkin to my right, just behind my chair, and stretched down to retrieve it. However, I couldn't quite reach it. So, to gain a few inches, I leaned back and out towards the napkin, twisting my body slightly, until I had it in my fingertips.

Then, as I pushed back up off the floor, I searched for the woman's hat on my ascent, but unable to see it clearly, I slowed my upward swing, which destabilising my chair causing it first to rock then rise up on one leg, teetering only briefly before keeling over, the toe of my shoe striking the underside of our table, knocking the tray from our table into the air, and just as it landed on the table in front of the woman with the funny hat, I came crashing to the floor.

Initially I heard nothing. But then, slowly, came the sound of chairs shifting in my direction. My face was hot, probably blending quite well with the burgundy carpet on which it rested. I turned my head slightly, and saw the two women's shoes just below the tablecloth. Strangely, despite this absurd and desperate predicament, my only thought was that Mum had a pair of shoes just like those one of the women was wearing. And then, as I lifted my eyes upwards, from the familiar shoes, up over the familiar skirt, to the familiar cashmere cardigan she always wore to Aunt Ivy's, I saw Mum, who got up from the table, pulled me up, and just as she did when I was a child, dusted me down.

"Well fancy seeing you here, son," she said, looking at Mercy, concealing her astonishment with a coolness I'd never seen in her before.

"I'm Mercy. Very nice to meet you, Mrs Green," interjected Mercy, extending her hand towards my mum.

"Mum, this is Mercy Waters. She's American," I said, somewhat lost for words but happy that the chatter in the room had resumed.

Mercy, sensing my awful quandary, piped up again, ingeniously playing the *naive* tourist, delivering a diplomatic version of the truth.

"Mrs Green, Bethnal has told me so much about you and your husband. I'm here from New York City, just for a few days, and your wonderful son offered to show me around London this afternoon, and so I insisted on taking him somewhere nice," she said.

I watched Mum, unconvinced, a suspicious look simmering in her eyes.

"You see, when I arrived in London, it's such a confusing city to get around, I ended up on the wrong subway train going in the wrong direction. The train was full of kids coming home from school and when I saw Bethnal, the only kid on the train acting in a sensible fashion, quietly reading a poem, Andrew Marvell I believe, I approached him and asked where I might find my hotel, this hotel, I'm staying here, my brother is the general manager. Well, Bethnal was kind enough to accompany me here, to my hotel, and as he went to so much trouble, I insisted on taking him to lunch. He refused at first, he has impeccable manners you know, you and your husband have both done a very good job with him, but I can be quite the insistent one. London is such a wonderful city. Oh, and isn't the tea to die for? And so what a wonderful coincidence your being here, it really is a pleasure to meet you," she continued, her improvisation pleasing Mum, now smiling, flattered by Mercy's comments.

"Well, thank you very much, Mercy. It's very kind of you, but you really shouldn't have gone to so much trouble. Well, we were just leaving. Bethnal, we can talk more about this later. And by the way, this is Betty, she's up visiting for the day. And Bethnal, I'll see you at dinner. Thanks again, Miss Waters, very kind of you," she said.

As I watched them leave, the only thing I could think of was that Mercy was right, Betty's hat was, indeed, very strange-looking.

We spent the afternoon burning off our tea-time indulgences by making love and listening to Puccini in Mercy's flat. My pleas to spend the night with her fell on deaf ears; I was expected home for dinner.

Dragging myself from the bed to the shower, I returned to her room and spent the next fifteen minutes or so, sat in the chair in the corner of her room just watching her swaddled deep within the sheets as she slept. As I got dressed I hated that I *had* to be home for dinner, *had* to go to school, *had* to lie to my parents. Even now, so many years later, I clearly recall standing in the doorway reluctant to leave, wrestling with an extraordinary wrench of despair. And my departure that day, even as I write, arouses in me such a stirring sense of loss, probably because those tender moments we shared that afternoon were our last.

On the way home, I dreaded what would no doubt be the most embarrassing and awkward of interrogations and decided to stick with Mercy's version of how we met, exactly as she told Mum in the tea room.

"Bethnal? Is that you?" called Dad from the living room as I closed the front door behind me.

"Yeah, where's Mum?" I said as I entered the room.

"Oh, she called. She's running a bit late, she should have been back by now. Apparently she met Betty, an old school friend of hers in town. You haven't met Betty, well, you wouldn't remember her, she used to look after you when you were a baby. She comes up every couple of months to see your mother and they make a day of it. Moved out of London years ago, Basildon I think, or somewhere like that. Or was it Basingstoke?" he said, turning back to the paper just as the front door clicked open, and Mum announced she was home.

She was breathing heavily as she entered the living room carrying several bags. Dropping them to the floor, she looked first at me then at Dad.

"Bethnal, give me a hand with these into the kitchen love," she said, asking Dad if he'd eaten the lunch she'd left for him in the fridge.

I followed her into the kitchen.

"How was your day love, how's Betty?" Dad shouted.

She turned and glanced at me.

"Oh, we had a wonderful time. You'll never guess what happened," she said.

I closed my eyes.

"What's that love?" replied Dad, flicking a page of the newspaper.

"Betty bought a hat, it was awful, looked like a giant spider on her head, she wore it everywhere, even when we went to tea in this cheap little café. I had the impression we were being stared at all afternoon," she replied, raising her index finger to her lips.

I breathed out a deep sigh of relief, and nodded, understanding that our meeting that afternoon was to be our secret.

"I've got a piece of sirloin. Is that alright, love?" she continued.

"That's lovely, love," Dad replied as he thumped through the buttons on the TV set looking for the football results.

"And what would you like, love?" she asked me, as she emptied the bags into the cupboards.

"I'll, uh, I'll, steak, too," I said.

"Do you want chips with it?" she said, pulling a pan from the cupboard.

Before I had chance to respond, she shouted once more through to Dad.

"Do you want chips with it, Dad?"

"That'll be lovely love, ta," he shouted back.

"Chips, love?" she asked me, once more.

"Yeah," I said.

And then, what she said next reminded me of how May had spoken to me in New York outside my room, which led me to believe that Mum knew more about my first love than she let on.

"Dinner will be a while, love, I have to put some washing in first. Why don't you run on upstairs and work on some of those drawings you've been doing."

And with that, our meeting at the Ritz wasn't mentioned until many years later.

20

Old Friends

I no longer belonged at school. Every minute not in Mercy's presence seemed like a waste of time.

On the Tuesday evening of that week, after an hour and a half calling her without success, I returned home suspecting something was wrong. I was so worried, I barely slept that night, waking a number of times with a start, convinced that she was in danger.

In class the following morning, those teachers trying to engage my dark and moody presence were met with muted shrugs. Only in English did I perk up a little, when Mr Wilson was explaining *courtly love,* a condition common in young men three to four hundred years ago whose distress, both physical and emotional, was a direct result of them dealing with the complexities of first love. Many of these fledgling Romeos sought absolute solitude in nature to contemplate love, but I didn't feel the need to cast myself off into forests to ponder my first love. Like them, however, I too was roaming through a painful emotional maze, constantly thinking about the girl I loved. The general consensus amongst boys in class was that this courtly love business was 'poofy'. But I understood it perfectly. Being apart from Mercy felt unnatural. And having not spoken to her the previous evening, I couldn't shake from myself an enduring state of uneasiness, a strange and terrible yearning for her, a fear constantly summoning dark and gloomy thoughts that my happiness was about to disappear.

When I called on Wednesday evening, as on the previous evening, she failed to answer, and by Thursday, I was a complete wreck. I knew that once I heard her voice, this constant, choking anxiety would disappear.

After dinner that evening, I rushed to the phone box and dialled her number, without success, until darkness crept in, at which point I was certain something was wrong, she was in trouble. I thought of going to her flat but if she wasn't there, what could I do then? A million reasons for her sudden disappearance, all possible, most tragic, raged through my mind. In the most awful state, I spent the remainder of the evening in my bedroom, crying, not knowing what to do, sobbing, until I fell asleep.

At breakfast Mum tried talking to me, commenting that I was "under a cloud." An hour later I was outside Mercy's door knocking impatiently, thumping it loudly until a neighbour threatened to call the police. I left the building and sat on the wall outside, determined to remain there until she appeared. For an hour or so, nothing of note happened, just a few people leaving for work, none of whom I'd seen before. At one point however, the old woman who had shown Mercy to her flat on the day of her arrival opened her door. After putting milk bottles into a small crate on the doorstep, she looked over at me sitting on the wall, staring at me for some time before she disappeared back inside.

The sun gradually climbed into a blue sky warming the day. Rush hour traffic that had been quite busy earlier had dribbled to the odd car speeding by. The tolling bell from a nearby church pealed despairingly every half hour, each clang stirring again dark and weary thoughts about where she might be and what might have happened to her.

Around midday a man turned into the street. I monitored his movements as he walked slowly along the pavement towards the flats. Stopping periodically, he looked at a scrap of paper in his hand. Each time he stopped, I expected him to go into the address he'd been looking for, but soon he was outside the flats, and so consumed in his search for the address, he didn't see me sat on the pavement leaning up against the wall.

Faded blue jeans hung from his waist, and far too heavy for summer, he wore a black leather bomber jacket making the brown skin on his shaven head shine in the noonday sun. Taking a deep breath, he looked up at the flats, and as he slipped the paper into his jacket pocket, he saw me curled up on the pavement and reeled back, a startled look of desperation in a face that had a peculiar familiarity. For a moment we gazed at each other, but then he hurried off up the path, his long strides carrying him quickly to the old woman's door. He rang the bell and waited, shifting uncomfortably on his long legs, his shoulder dipping as if wanting to glance back. When the old woman opened the door, they nodded and smiled at each other and then he stepped in, but before she closed the door, they looked over at me, and I slipped back down behind the wall.

An hour or so later the door opened. The man stepped out, said something to the woman and they looked over at me again. He stepped back inside, picking up what appeared to be a box of some description covered in a black plastic bag. The woman closed the door behind him and he made his way along the path, the box swinging in his hand from a handle poking through a hole torn in the black plastic. His head down, he kept his eyes firmly fixed to the path as he approached me, his pace increasing quickly as he passed, my eyes following him down the street. At one point he stopped suddenly and put the box down. For a minute or so, he remained still, his head moving slightly to the right, just as he had done earlier at the old woman's door, as if he wanted to look back. But then he picked up the case and marched off, gathering pace as he rounded the corner at the bottom of the street.

For some time I thought about the man, his strange behaviour, the way he and the old woman had observed me from the door, and his initial reaction to seeing me. It suddenly seemed so obvious that the old woman knew something, maybe where Mercy was, and cursing myself for wasting valuable time, I charged up the path, skidding to a stop outside her door where I noticed the net curtain inside the window fall to one side. Stamping impatiently, I rang the bell, determined not to leave until the woman, just behind the curtain looking at me, told me where Mercy was. I rang the bell a second time, my finger remaining on the button, a signal of intent, prolonging the annoying shrill of the bell inside. When she didn't answer I stood on the step, trying to look in beyond the gauze netting, slapping the glass with the flat of my hand. I saw a blurred movement inside, the curtain trembled and the woman appeared, cowering behind the thin netted gauze.

"What do you want?" she shouted anxiously through the glass, the net curtain shaking in her hand.

"Where's Mercy?" I shouted back.

"Who?"

"Mercy Waters. The American girl. You know who I mean. Where is she?"

"She's not here. Go away," she said abruptly, dropping the curtain.

My body tightened and I began banging the glass with my fist. She reappeared holding the handset of a telephone in her hand.

"Go away, I'm going to call the police," she said, shaking the phone at me.

"Just tell me where she is, please, I have to know, please?" I begged.

"She's gone," she said, "two days ago. That man came to pick up her stuff. Now go away!" she said before dropping the curtain.

Gone? Gone where? Who with? Where? And that man? Who was he? Picking up her stuff? I had to catch that man, he knew Mercy, had picked up her stuff, her case, wrapped it in black plastic, to hide, from me, but he was gone, long gone, but I had to try and find him. Mercy was in some sort of terrible danger.

I sprinted to the main road where I ran up one side, my eyes sweeping from person to person, glancing at every face, then I skipped through the heavy traffic to the other side, repeating my search there until I could run no further, reluctantly accepting that any chance of finding Mercy had finally slipped away.

As the traffic roared past, sitting slumped on the pavement, I wiped the tears from my face, my mind racing, trying to convince myself I hadn't severed the final fibre in hope's thin thread of finding her. Suddenly I thought that the old woman might just have an address where Mercy had gone, and so on my feet once more, ignoring the angry honks of cars, I cut through the traffic like a gazelle, flying around the corner into the woman's street where I saw her talking to two towering policemen. When she pointed at me, the two officers shouted something before charging towards me, and with a speed and energy I didn't know I had, I was off, weaving in and out of oncoming pedestrians, flying like a young starling, my hands slicing the air in front of me, turning at every corner, running on, and on, and on, until I felt myself fading, the muscles in my legs trembling, my lungs starting to burn, breathless rasping hisses churning in my ears, telling my body to succumb to its limitations, to my inevitable capture, until finally, I fell to my knees, my heart pounding, wiry strings of saliva dangling from my mouth as I drew air deep into my lungs. On all fours, I listened for the clinking sounds of handcuffs, the leaden stomps of my assailants' rapid footfalls, the boys in blue ready to scrape me up off the street. Falling on my side, I looked back down the empty street, it appeared I'd outrun them, and pulling myself up, I sat against the rusting iron gate of a flaking Georgian house.

The depressing reality that Mercy was gone descended once more, *what-might-have-beens* grating repeatedly through me. Why had I wasted such valuable time all morning outside the flats doing nothing? Why hadn't I suspected the man was involved? Perhaps those policemen catching me would have been best, swiftly bringing a definitive close to this humiliating chapter in my life.

High in a clear-blue sky, the sun appeared from behind a large cloud. What was a grey, lifeless side street suddenly shot to life with little pops of colour peeking out from small window boxes on sills and hanging baskets rocking gently in doorways, with cheery, yet cruel exuberance. Far too pretty for my mood, I pulled myself up and trudged off towards the tube station.

Near the top of the street, a large car, its polished black body and hub caps like mirrors glimmering in the sun, slowly turned the corner. Purring as it approached me, I saw perched on the tip of the bonnet of this beautiful black chariot, a small but impressive ornament, strangely familiar, one which suggested elegance, prestige, like the classy Spirit of Ecstasy you see on a Rolls Royce. Momentarily mesmerised by the beauty of this small dazzling ornament, as the car drew level, almost slowing to a stop before suddenly speeding off, I recalled where I'd seen it before. With its little wings curling tightly around its body and its head stretching proudly skyward, it was most definitely a small replica of the tiny bird I'd drawn so many times in Salvatore's café on the day I met Mercy. Suddenly convinced its reappearance was no coincidence, I gave chase, quickly managing to draw level with the car, almost stumbling as I tried to see in the rear window. When it gathered speed, I ran faster, drawing level once more, hoping to see in the window, expecting to see Mercy. I grabbed hold of the door and as the car pulled me along, I managed to look in and saw Mrs Salvatore leaning towards the open window, and just behind her, her husband, holding her back. I called for them to stop but the car increased its speed, and as I sprinted after it I suddenly understood that the Salvatores were responsible for all of this, for my meeting Mercy, for bringing us together, and had returned to reunite us.

The car slipped into a lower gear and sped off around the corner onto the main road. I raced after it to see it pull up about two hundred yards away outside Lancaster Gate underground station. With its hazard lights flashing, Mr and Mrs Salvatore got out and entered the station hand in hand. I called to them again, but they didn't respond. When I reached the station, they were on the other side of a barrier standing at the lift, their backs to me, still holding hands. I shouted to them, but again they didn't respond, and when the lift arrived, they stepped inside. I tried barging past the ticket inspector to get to them before the doors closed, but he grabbed me by the arm.

"You'll need a ticket to get through here, sonny," he informed me.

"I need to see them," I said, pointing desperately towards the lift.

"You'll need a ticket, son," he said, and nodded in the direction of the ticket counter where an old woman had just deposited the contents of her purse, slowly examining each coin as she counted out the exact fare, shoving coins, one by one, through the partition.

Standing impatiently behind the old woman, I glanced back at the Salvatores staring vacantly out of the lift at me. The old woman shoved the last coin across the counter, and as I rushed forward with exact change, I heard the doors of the lift slowly screeching to a close. With ticket in hand, I flashed it at the inspector and sprinted to the lift but the doors had clunked closed. On tip toes, I looked through the small glass panels in the doors to see Mrs Salvatore collapsed in her husband's arms. I thumped the doors and the inspector came towards me yelling, but I slipped past him, and ran down the narrow steps of the spiral staircase leading to the platform below, taking two, sometimes three steps at a time, chasing the lift as it whirred in its descent knowing the Salvatores' reappearance was the key to my finding Mercy. They had the truth, they would bring order back to my shattered existence, they would bring Mercy back to me.

At the bottom of the stairs I sprinted along the tunnel to the point where the platforms split, where I could see almost to the end of both. Everything was unusually still – no soft gushes of air from approaching tubes, no scurrying of small mice into invisible holes below benches, no voices straining in the crackle of loudspeakers. I walked slowly to the middle of one deserted platform, scanning its length before slipping through a small passageway to the other where I heard the clunk of the lift straining in its descent. Thinking that perhaps I'd passed it on my way down, I hurried back to the lift and waited for it to descend. When the doors opened, apart from the crumpled remains of black plastic tossed in a corner, it was empty.

I returned to the platform, again thinking how unnaturally quiet the station seemed for that time of the day. But then I heard a noise. It came from the far end of the platform. A crunching sound, like grit underfoot.

I stepped slowly along the platform to discover it curve near the mouth of the tunnel, a section I'd not seen on my first hasty inspection. The sound came again, it had to be them. I edged my way along the platform, until I saw, just out of sight in the curve at the tail end of the platform, a bench. And sitting on it was the man who had come to collect Mercy's case.

As I approached him I tried to remain calm, holding the gaze of his gentle eyes, soft, apologetic, in a face that was tired and drawn. But who was he? How did he know Mercy? Where was she?

"Where's Mercy?" I said firmly.

He began to say something but stopped. Twisting awkwardly on the bench, his eyes dropped to the platform.

"Bethnal…" he started, but stopped when he saw the shock crashing through me when he said my name.

"How do you know my name? Who are you? Where's Mercy?" I demanded, my anger echoing along the platform, clearly startling him.

He shifted uncomfortably, placing his hands on the bench beside his legs, still looking to the floor, his chin sinking into his chest as he scraped the sole of a shoe on the platform.

"Who are you? How do you know my name?" I repeated, and he sprang up.

"Bethnal," he said, raising his head towards me, looking me firmly in the eyes. "It's me. It's DeeDee," he continued.

Images of DeeDee in New York flashed through me and the most constricting sensation took hold of my throat at the warped and cruel nature of his response. I considered his height, his physique, his skin tone, the peculiar eyes, and suddenly I knew this was DeeDee, and I flew into his arms and held him, sobbing convulsively until he sat me on the bench, and patiently waited for me to say something. Waiting for the questions I was so terrified to ask.

"Tell me," I said at last.

He turned to me, taking my hands in his.

"Bethnal, Mercy's got to go home. She's sick," he said bluntly.

"What do you mean, she's sick?"

"Honey," he said, the tender voice of DeeDee from New York emerging. "She's sick. We don't know what this sickness is. It's a strange sickness, one which seems to be beyond the doctors'…"

But I wouldn't let him finish. Jumping up I walked to the edge of the platform, not wanting to hear these lies when I knew she was so full of life.

"What do you mean beyond the help of doctors? That's a lie, I was with her last Saturday, she was fine, we had a great time. No, DeeDee," I pleaded, returning to the bench, "don't lie to me. Please don't lie to me. I need to see her, take me to her. Please, DeeDee, please take me to her. I must see her. You understand, I know you do," I said, tears welling then spilling from my eyes, and falling into him again, I held him tightly, hoping he'd whisper another version of why he was there, one free of such hurtful blows.

And then, cradling me in his arms, he told me what had happened.

"Bethnal, honey. On Tuesday evening I received a call. It was May. Mercy's...the woman who helps out at Mercy's. She was in a panic. She'd received a call from the friend of Mercy's father who owns the flat. He told her that Mercy was sick, that she had a high fever and was in and out of consciousness. Her parents were in California or Florida, and May called all through the night trying to get hold of them, but she wasn't able to get news of Mercy to them. She thought about flying to London herself, but she was certain the day she flew in a plane would be her last, and she'd be no good to Mercy dead. So she called me and I got on the next flight and went directly to the hospital on landing."

"Hospital?" I shouted.

"The doctors could only tell me that, that the only thing they knew of her condition was that there was *something* wrong with her blood. I tried to get details from them, and they were all so polite, but it seems they have no idea what is wrong with her. I stayed by her bed all day waiting for her to wake but she didn't, not once, just kept on sleeping. She didn't even wake when a group of doctors came in, there must have been six of them, checking various parts of her body. They left with the same puzzled looks on their faces they'd come in with."

He paused, took a deep breath, and resting his chin on my head continued.

"From the hospital I contacted the old woman who takes care of the apartments and made arrangements to come and collect Mercy's things. She said that the owner of the flat, some friend of Mercy's father, had instructed her to gather Mercy's belongings together and put them in her case. She didn't have much stuff and I told the woman I'd be around to pick the case up today."

He took another breath, and wiped the tears streaming down my face.

"As you could tell I was more than shocked to see you outside the apartments. I recognised you immediately and figured you didn't know me looking like this. And, the truth is, I wanted to keep it like that. I didn't want to talk to you; I didn't want you to know me. I didn't want you to have to deal with this. The old woman gave me details of what had happened. On Tuesday evening Mercy stopped in to say hello to her. She did this most evenings which pleased the old woman, she enjoyed the company. That evening, while they were chatting, Mercy, well, she just seemed to drift off, in the middle of a sentence, spilling her tea onto her dress. The old woman knew something was wrong, and unable to bring her around, she called an ambulance which rushed Mercy to hospital. And that's where she is now."

"I want to see her," I demanded.

"The doctors won't allow visitors. They told me that until they know more, apart from me, they won't let people see her."

"They'll let me see her," I said pulling myself from him, "I'll make them. They can't stop me."

He wiped my hot wet face with the side of his hand. He had more to say, words that delivered the most severe and painful blow.

"Bethnal, I'm taking Mercy home. Tomorrow morning. The doctors won't allow you or anyone into the hospital to see her," he said, almost sternly, definitively.

As I considered the enormity of what he was saying, I felt my chest tighten. Finding it difficult to breathe, I stood up and walked to the mouth of the tunnel and unleashed a long and painful cry.

"But DeeDee," I said, turning to him, begging him, "I have to see her again, please. Don't do this to me. Don't," I begged repeatedly, pleading with him to consider what I was asking.

"OK. Listen carefully. We're leaving the hospital at seven in the morning for the airport. You can't meet us or come with us from the hospital, we're going by ambulance. We should arrive at the airport by eight and we're flying BOAC to New York at eleven. If you're in the departure lounge at around eight, and providing she's strong enough, you can see her. But of course, this all depends on whether she has the strength to go. I'm on my way to the hospital to find out now."

We took the lift out of the station into the cool air of the street where Dee Dee hailed a taxi. He gave the driver five pounds and told him to take me home.

"See you tomorrow," he whispered, hugging me again and kissing my forehead.

I arrived home to find Mum and Dad in the hall at the bottom of the stairs as if expecting me. I closed the door, and the three of us stood in silence. I didn't have the strength or desire to keep the truth from them any longer, yet I didn't have it in me to explain either. I rushed past them and up the stairs holding back the tears until I reached the emptiness of my bedroom.

Though I tried, I couldn't soften the sound of my sobbing, anguished howls they heard as they whispered to each other outside my room. The door creaked open and Mum came slowly in. Her eyes were red and swollen. Sitting on my bed, she pulled me gently to her, rocking me, just as May had rocked Mercy in the kitchen on the day we left New York. She knew a sorrowful day like this would come for me, just not so soon. Through incomprehensible fits and starts that followed, she must have thought me delusional as I tried to tell her of Mercy, how I loved her, and how, inexplicably, she was suddenly so sick, she was leaving me, going back to New York, how I'd never see her again.

"Yes, my darling, I know. Shhhhh. Shhhhhh. Sleep my boy, sleep," she whispered, continuing to rock me.

"She's, she's leaving… I don't want… I don't want her to go… I… I can't do anything… DeeDee…" I continued.

And she pulled me even closer and I felt her warmth, her love, her desire to do whatever it took to make me well again.

It was dark outside when I woke. The curtains were drawn and the house was silent.

"Bethnal? Love? Are you awake?" whispered Mum, tapping at my door. "Darling, can I bring you something to eat?"

She came in and sat with me again, Dad joining us shortly after, sitting at the foot of the bed, his hand resting on my leg. I gave them Mercy's departure details, and they suggested I get some sleep, and that they would accompany me to the airport the following morning.

21

Adieu

The thought of Mercy waking up in a strange hospital, in a strange country, surrounded by strange people, haunted me that night. I woke several times crying, pretending to myself that once May had nursed her back to health that *then*...

But there would be no *then*. She was going home, far away, to the other side of the earth, most probably forever.

We arrived at the airport early the following morning, at about seven-thirty. Standing opposite the BOAC check-in counter anxiously waiting, I held a package which contained *moments* of our time together, a selection of sketches to help her remember. Me, London, the park, the little bird I drew the day we met. Us.

After half an hour or so, I wasn't sure I wanted to be there when she arrived, not sure that I could utter words I thought I'd never have to say to her.

At around eight o'clock, an ambulance pulled up outside the terminal. Two paramedics hoisted a wheelchair from inside, placing it gently on the ground. DeeDee thanked them, and as he pushed Mercy into the terminal, I watched as he searched for me in the crowd. I nodded at Mum and Dad that they'd arrived. Seeing Mercy so helpless in a wheelchair scared me, I wasn't sure if I could bear to see her in such a condition, that perhaps it better I should remember her as she was.

As airline personnel came from behind the counter to assist DeeDee with procedures, I felt Dad's hand on my shoulder.

"Son?" he said, nodding towards them.

As final check-in procedures were completed, DeeDee scanned the crowd, and though I desperately wanted to see Mercy, I just didn't have it in me to take another crippling blow.

"Bethnal? Go on, love, say goodbye," Mum said, nudging me gently forward.

Shaking my head, I just couldn't do it, and felt Dad's hand patting my shoulder. I thought that perhaps it was best I didn't see her, that my sudden appearance would prove too stressful for her. And so from afar, the three of us watched DeeDee and Mercy disappear into the crowd, and I bid her a silent, dignified goodbye, the most fitting way of ending this for all of us.

Walking to the car, Mum and Dad agreed that perhaps my decision was for the best. As we waited for the lift, I clumsily dropped the package, and picking it up, a sketch fell out, the one of her sleeping in the boat on the Serpentine. Seeing it again, seeing her again, I suddenly realised it couldn't end like this, I had to say goodbye, and rushing back into the terminal building, I ran towards the departure lounge where staff were counting tickets at the gate. I asked an employee if a tall man with a woman in a wheelchair had passed through, but before he could respond, from behind me, someone called my name and turning, I saw DeeDee standing behind the wheelchair, trying to smile. He withdrew a few steps, and turned his back.

I approached Mercy slowly. Using the arm of the wheelchair to steady myself, I knelt before her. Limp pale hands lay lifeless across a blanket covering her legs. I gently lifted the floppy hat covering her face to see her head resting on a shoulder. DeeDee had applied a thin layer of powder to her face, but it couldn't disguise a pale-grey hue confirming her ailing state. Her beautiful neck, the neck I'd kissed and caressed so many times, was a shade darker, and a small vein, one I'd not seen before, pulsed slowly. Only a few days had passed from when we'd laughed and made love. But here she was, so clearly very weak. Though tempted to kiss her, I didn't want to wake her. I tenderly lifted one of her hands and placed the package below it. Then bidding her a silent goodbye, I kissed her hand.

"Bethnal," she suddenly whispered, somewhat distressed, her beautiful eyes shining as she tried to lean forward. "Bethnal," she said, "I'm sorry, I…"

"Shhhhhhh…" I said to her. "Relax. I'm here," I said, my voice quavering as she lifted her hand onto my head, running her fingers tenderly through my hair, just as she had done so many times before.

Tears welled in our eyes as a million silent messages ran between us as we looked at each other for the last time.

"Bethnal," she said "you really are the best…" before I stopped her.

"I know you have to go," I said. "But I don't want you to go. I'll come and visit you in New York, I promise, when you're well," my voice breaking as her tears spilled onto the package.

"I love you," she said, just as DeeDee put his hands on the chair indicating it was time to leave.

"I'll always love you – always," I said, her fragile hand lingering in mine as I stood.

DeeDee hugged me and I clung to him tightly. Through tears he couldn't contain, he whispered, "she's in good hands."

And then he wheeled her away. She was gone. I suddenly felt so alone, unsure of what to do, and looking all about me, I turned to see Mum and Dad rushing towards me, and I ran to them, falling into their arms, burying myself between them, hoping they'd hold me forever.

22

Flight

May 2014

I neither saw nor heard from Mercy again. When I think back to that summer of 1977 now, I do so with fond memories. Though devastated for some weeks after she left, remaining alone in my room for much of that time, Mum and Dad gently encouraged me to find ways to occupy myself, constantly reminding me that my life had yet to start, that dwelling on such a painful chapter could serve no possible purpose. And so, they were thrilled when I met a local girl at the Silver Jubilee party in our street who entertained me in all manner of ways for the rest of the summer. I can't recall her name.

I gave a stellar performance at the end of term concert, playing again the Vivaldi concerto I'd so successfully pulled off in New York which reduced both Mum and Dad to tears. And then in August, I surprised both myself and my parents receiving impressive O level results which took me into sixth form and then onto university where I studied Art.

Though I'd had a number of girlfriends throughout my twenties and thirties, none lasted more than six months or so. I never really considered myself the marrying type, so at my fortieth birthday party I was very surprised to meet Carla, a beautiful American, who within six months I had married. She's a super wife and a wonderful mother, and I'll be eternally grateful to her for giving me two adorable children.

On the odd occasion when events of that summer in 1977 come to mind, I reflect on them with a mature sense of pleasant detachment. However, one morning, as Carla and I were leaving for the airport to pick up her niece, flying in from New York to take part in a student exchange programme in Spain, Mum rang to say a package had arrived at her house addressed to me. It seemed odd I should receive anything at her address, I hadn't lived there for some twenty-five years. I told her I'd pick it up when we dropped off the kids later that morning. She loved seeing the kids, and ever since Dad died in 1994, I always worried she might be lonely in the house on her own. When we pulled up outside her house that morning, as usual, the kids flew out of the car into her arms.

"Hi, Mum. We're running a little late. I can't stop," I said, kissing her on the cheek and handing her a bag of toys.

"What time will you be back to pick them up, I can have them overnight if you want?" she said, waving to Carla in the car.

"About five. I'll call you from the car," I said, closing the gate.

"OK, love. Drive safely then. See you at five."

Just as I was pulling off, I saw Mum at the gate waving a yellow package.

"This is the package that came this morning. I had to sign for it too. Who's it from?" she said, handing it to me through the window.

The return address had an M. Johnson of Decatur, Georgia, as the sender. I had no clients in Georgia, had never heard of Decatur, so I threw it onto the back seat to look at later.

At Heathrow, Carla went to the gate to wait for her niece while I parked. Whenever one of us returns from a trip, we always meet by a row of seats with quick access to parking. On my way up to the terminal, as the doors of the lift up opened and two Royal Mail employees wheeled out a large crate, I remembered the package and ran back to the car to fetch it.

Inside the terminal, I bought a coffee, read the Sports Section of the Guardian then looked at the package.

I read again the sender's name and address: M Johnson of Decatur, Georgia. Never heard of him. I thought it strange that Mum had to sign for it. Whoever sent it, wanted it landing in the right hands.

I opened the package carefully, trying to remember if, even briefly, I'd met an M. Johnson on my last business trip to the States. Inside I found three medium-size white envelopes numbered one, two and three. I hesitated before opening the first envelope. Such intrigue made me question for a moment what these envelopes might contain.

Inside was a letter, and as I unfolded it and began to read its contents, it soon became clear not only who had sent the package, but of the unimaginable burden the message carried.

Dear Mr Green,

I imagine you will be very surprised to receive this letter. I can't be at all sure that it will ever get to you as it's been so long, but I feel I have an obligation to send you what I enclose herein. I found your address in London on an old envelope which you will see I have enclosed in the envelope with number two written on it. I do apologise for such a system of correspondence, but I thought it necessary you read my letter of introduction before you open the other two envelopes.

Firstly, I think I should reintroduce myself. We met many years ago when you were just a young boy. One weekend in the early summer of 1977 when you came to New York and spent the weekend with Mercy Waters. If I recall correctly, you were an excellent violin player. I sure do hope you still play. My name, if you don't remember, is May Johnson, and I worked for the Waters for many years. I've been gone a long time from there though. I now live with my son and his family in Georgia where I'm from originally. As I look back, the time I spent with the Waters seems a lifetime ago. And in many ways it is.

I don't mind telling you that I have written this letter so many times in the last month, and I imagine it will be as difficult for you to read as it was for me to write. This letter then, is to tell you of Mercy and of events after she returned to New York from that summer in London.

When she arrived back in New York she was so weak. I looked after her for a day or so, but she could barely stay awake, and with her growing so weak, I dared not leave her room. I sat by her, watching over her as she struggled to breathe. But when the sweating began and wouldn't stop no matter what I tried, I realised that she needed to be in a hospital.

DeeDee, who I believe you met, was with me and we took her to the hospital. I was so worried, she looked as if the life was draining from her. I'd got a message to her parents who were on their way back from California. DeeDee sat with me and we watched over Mercy, but despite our enquiries, the doctors kept coming in and out, doing so many tests on her unable or unwilling to provide us with information about her condition. So many times they came back to her room sticking her for more blood. It still upsets me now, so many years later, to even think about it. DeeDee was so nice, sitting with me until the following day when Mercy's parents arrived. They, of course, were so upset, and we all shed rivers of tears seeing Mercy in such a condition.

On occasion, she would seem to come to, and we'd all get excited, thinking she was showing signs of improvement. But, as quickly as she would wake, she'd fall straight back into a sleep that might last for more than a day. The doctors and nurses were all very good and treated Mercy with the utmost of care. But it was so difficult to see her laying there with tubes running in and out of her body.

Initially, Mr and Mrs Waters were surprisingly patient with the length of time they had to wait for a diagnosis, but after the second, or maybe the third day, in consultation with an attending doctor, Mrs Waters, for some reason, began to shout so hysterically at him, that I saw Mercy stir a little in her bed. I just guess she couldn't take the stress and strain of not knowing what was wrong with her daughter.

You see, as I said, the doctors had to carry out so many tests. The problem was that they just didn't know what was wrong with her. So many tests, so much blood, I wondered if it weren't all those tests that was keeping her ill. The only "half" answer I got was when two doctors were standing over her one night, discussing her condition. They must have thought I was asleep but I wasn't, I was listening. They said that cases of a similar nature had recently been registered in other hospitals in the city, but only in young men, young gay men, something about weakened immune systems. I didn't understand what all that meant then, but they were certain the condition had yet to be reported in a woman. As if that mattered I thought, we're all human after all.

It all became too much for Mrs Waters, and Mr Waters had to take her home, she was so upset by Mercy's condition, she was making herself ill, and she'd be no use to Mercy in such a state. I stayed though. I couldn't leave her alone in that hospital. I was determined not to leave her side until she was strong again. She was like my own child, you see, I'd raised her since she was born, I loved her like I loved my own.

On one or two occasions she would say something, but for the most part, it was indistinguishable. I do know however, Bethnal, that she mentioned your name, and that in whatever place she was, I believe that you were there with her.

And then Mercy died. She just fell asleep one night and didn't come back. I don't mind telling you that I prayed that if He wanted to take her, then He would do so in a way where she didn't suffer. And she didn't, and for this I am always so grateful.

Shortly after the funeral I left the Waters and moved to San Francisco where I worked in a care home for the elderly. I couldn't live in that apartment without that child.

Over the years I've kept mementoes, small memories of the people I've known and places I've been. Six months ago, my son helped me look through some of my old trunks in which I've stored things over the years. He was moving house and thought there was no point in taking stuff with us we didn't need anymore. In his basement he had a space set aside just for my things and when he called me down there one day, when sorting through some of my stuff, I was surprised for him to pull out a trunk from my New York days and my time with the Waters. I'd completely forgotten that I shipped it down to him after I left them. Well, seeing it again, I felt once more the pain of losing my Mercy. It was so long ago, and so it was with some reluctance that I decided to open it, and when I did, like I knew they would, the memories came flooding back, and such was my distress at seeing and touching again those objects connected with Mercy, it took me quite some time to send this package and its contents, some of which I've enclosed in the other two envelopes.

Before you open the second envelope I should tell you that it contains a letter to you from Mercy. It's from this envelope that I got your address. I suppose she wrote it the day she arrived back in New York, before she went into the hospital. When I found it in the trunk, I assumed it must have got mixed in with things I put in boxes when I cleaned out her room after she died.

Mr Green, Bethnal, I do hope I have made the right decision in sending you all this. Believe me, I hesitated so much before contacting you, not sure if it was wise for me to reopen a part of your life that was, really, a part of your childhood. But, I'm sure you'll understand when I tell you that I felt I had one last obligation to Mercy, and now it's done I feel as if I can pass the days I have left here, and I believe there's not too many of those, with a clear conscience before I meet her in my final resting place.

Over the years I have kept in touch with DeeDee, and just to give you an update, he too left New York City shortly after Mercy passed. Where he went, I can't remember. But, the last I heard from him, you might be surprised to hear, is that he married a Swiss or French woman and that he had had a family and was living happily somewhere in Europe. He always sounded very happy and he was so good to Mercy.

I'll close here Bethnal. I hope that I've done the right thing in sending you this. I do hope that in whatever direction your life has gone, that you are happy. I know you made Mercy happy.

Regards, May Johnson

Not for one moment had I imagined that Mercy had died, believing that her recovery under May's wing was simply a matter of her getting strong again, and that she'd gone on to live a normal, and hopefully, happy life. I felt so honoured to have known May, and thought back to how humbled I felt when she so generously gave me that $100. Here again, so many years later, she had reduced me to a similar state of humility. That there were still people in the world who understood the importance of such simple human kindness, like May's selfless devotion to Mercy, moved me to the core, and sitting alone on the bench I started to cry.

I paused before opening the second envelope, the one from Mercy. Looking at my name on the envelope, I recognised her handwriting from notes she'd given me all those years ago. I raised the letter to my nose in the foolish hope of catching a lingering scent. My hands shook as I broke its seal and pulled from inside the envelope a fragile sheet of blue loose-leaf paper folded in half. Conscious that the last human touch of this paper was Mercy's, I held it delicately between my fingers before opening it, and started to cry again. When I finally stopped, I dried my eyes and read the letter dated June 1977.

Dear Bethnal, my cute English boy,

Well, I guess I had to leave the party early this year. I'm so glad I got to see you at the airport, I feel like I've abandoned you but I hope you know that was never my intention. The truth is, the day I met you was the most wonderful day of my life. The kindness you showed me touched me so deeply, and the fact that you wanted to see more of me really excited me. I loved being with you in your beautiful city, I wish I could be back there right now, and hold your hand and once again go strolling and running in the park.

But the sad fact is, Bethnal, I'm sick, and I suppose the purpose of this letter, apart from sending my love, is to give you an explanation. About six months ago I went to the doctor as I kept feeling so run down. It was very strange, I couldn't seem to get through the day, and for a young girl barely out of her teens it worried me. I didn't say anything to my parents, or May, I didn't want to worry them, and I was sure that this was something that would just pass. However, the doctors, I went to two, said that there was something "going on" in my blood, that my immune system wasn't working right. Well, I'd never been any good at science and didn't even know what an immune system was. One of the doctors suggested a spell abroad, to get out of the city and to let my body's system work it out! That's modern medicine for you!

Well, I'm glad he suggested this as I came to London and met you. You enriched me so fully in so many ways. You know, when I drift off to sleep, as I seem to do quite a lot, in my mind I hear you playing Vivaldi once more. You just don't know what pleasure you brought me playing so wonderfully that night, and I know you were playing for me. In fact, May's been playing Vivaldi's Four Seasons constantly since my return, even when I'm asleep. Each time I listen to the small part you played, I feel so, so happy.

As I write, I'd like to promise you that the moment I get better, I'll be back in London and we'll be back together again. But the truth is, and I hate to say this as it scares me, I don't think I'm going to get over this. I don't know what it is, but I feel as if the strength, life, is escaping from me. The amount of sleep I need (and want) is increasing, and I think soon, I may, sadly, fall asleep for the last time. I don't like to be so morose, but I wouldn't lie to you as I love you, and that sustains me in my every waking moment.

I'm tired now, my love. I must go, but before I do, I want to thank you so much for the sketches. While I listen to your music, as I sleep, I see that small bird, the one you showed me the day we met, I see it flying high, and free. It makes me happy.

Goodbye, my love.
Mercy

Mercy. Dead. That numbing strain in the pit of my stomach, a feeling I never imagined I'd feel again, had lodged once more like an immovable weight inside me. I worried about Carla arriving to find me in such a state, and I still had the final envelope to open.

I gently opened it and found inside the sketches I'd given to her in the airport the day of her departure. On the top of each sketch remained a faint imprint of her lips where she'd kissed them. I held the sketches in my trembling hands, I felt fifteen again, and people passing by shot concerned glances at the man sitting on the bench sobbing. I pulled the sketches up to cover my face and something fell into my lap. It was a Polaroid picture of a couple. It was me, a boy I barely recognised, a look of complete surprise on my face as Mercy kissed my cheek, taken at the Serpentine in Hyde Park on our first day together.

The airport was hot, I could barely breathe, and after putting the letters and sketches back into the envelopes, I went to the bathroom and splashed water in my face trying to wipe the grief from my eyes.

I returned to my seat hoping it would be some time before Carla arrived, but the moment I sat down, I heard her call. Watching her coming through the crowd, I took deep breaths hoping to regain some degree of composure, but it was all too much, and I ran to her, wrapping my arms around her tightly, and as she held me, she stroked my hair, and whispered, "She's here."